a wasted talent

a
wasted
talent

JAMES I MORROW

The Book Guild Ltd

First published in Great Britain in 2021 by
The Book Guild Ltd
9 Priory Business Park
Wistow Road, Kibworth
Leicestershire, LE8 0RX
Freephone: 0800 999 2982
www.bookguild.co.uk
Email: info@bookguild.co.uk
Twitter: @bookguild

Typeset in 12pt Adobe Jenson Pro

Printed and bound in the UK by TJ Books Limited, Padstow, Cornwall

ISBN 978 1913913 724

British Library Cataloguing in Publication Data.

A catalogue record for this book is available from the British Library.

*It is better to waste one's youth
than do nothing with it at all.*

Georges Courteline

prologue

John McDaid stood looking steadily at his image in the mirror. He was thirty-six years of age; he tried to examine his facial features in more detail. Ruggedly handsome, he liked to conclude, but in truth probably a bit wrinkled and in need of a good ironing. His eyes continued to have a twinkle in them, but whilst their dark brown lustre had sometimes had a 'come to bed' feel about them, they were now more hooded and seemed to say 'I need a nap'.

He brushed back his dark curly hair, still damp from the shower, scratched the stubble on his chin and then rubbed on the shaving foam.

He stopped halfway through the first stroke of the razor, not because he had nicked himself, something he had been prone to do of late, but because he had become consumed in thought.

Despite his relatively young age, he had relatively recently attained the rank of Detective Inspector in the serious crimes squad, of An Garda Siochana based in Dublin. So far, though, his workload had been relatively mundane and he was itching to get his teeth into a more worthwhile investigation.

He started to dress, pulling his trousers up, buttoning his shirt and putting on a tie, one that he felt befitted his new rank. Though he was still in the habit of leaving the knot gaping under an unfastened top shirt button.

He stood on one leg trying to get his foot into his newly polished shoe, when his mobile started to ring...

chapter one

The body was badly decomposed. It had clearly lain undisturbed in the rushes at the edge of the river, where it had been found, for some time.

Detective Inspector John McDaid gazed at the lifeless figure now lying face up on the riverbank where it had been placed after being dragged out of the water. On initial inspection it seemed to be the body of a young man. However, it was hard to be absolutely certain – the flesh was bloated from the length of time it had lain in the water and the exposed areas of its anatomy were badly disfigured. The corpse's clothes were in tatters. The upper half of the torso seemed to be draped in the remnants of what looked like an American flag. His lower half was clothed in more complete but nevertheless waterlogged jeans which now had a greenish hue, covered as they were with algae from the river. The corpse's legs appeared entwined in weeds, presumably from the riverbed. One trainer remained in situ; the other, now swollen foot, was exposed, its shoe lost in the murky water of the river that flowed gently past a few feet from where the small assembly of Gardaí now stood gathered around the body.

The lone angler that had made the grisly discovery now

stood a little way off, his head bowed. John moved across to question him, about the discovery.

'I know this area well,' he reported, his soft Irish brogue just detectable, though his voice was reduced to a tremulous whisper. He was still obviously badly shaken by his grizzly find. 'I fish here quite often. Others rarely come down here – not many people even know that this small area of greenery exists so close to the city and, if I'm honest, there are not many fish either,' he reported. 'I just like to come here for the peace and quiet. Though I've not been down in the last four or five weeks. My wife had been ill, so I didn't like to leave—'

John cut him off, his stronger Belfast intonation betraying his impatience to know more details of the actual discovery of the body, not of the fisherman's spouse's illness. However, he had to admit the angler's timeline was helpful and did tie in with the appearance of the body.

'My line snagged on something and when I waded out to try and dislodge it, there it was, the hook had caught in its clothes. It had been lying face down, hidden from view in the reed bed at the edge of the water, just over there.' He pointed beyond the group of Gardaí gathered around the body.

The riverbank at this point was flat and only slightly above the level of the water itself. The reed bed in which the body had been discovered seemed to stretch the length of the river but was densest at this point. Looking upstream John noticed a small bridge that swaddled the river and some houses that marked the beginning of suburbia further along the road that crossed the bridge. But it was, as the other had suggested, a quiet area: there were not many people about, unlike the rest of the bustling city less than a few miles away.

'Gave me quite a shock, I can tell you.'

John sympathised and thanked the man but, realising he had little else to tell, moved off to re-join his colleagues.

The two Guards who had retrieved the corpse by pulling it out of the water by its arms, were now simply standing by the muddy riverbank looking down at what was left of the former human being. One, the younger of the two, suddenly turned away, retreated a few steps and then bent over and vomited into the rushes at the side of the river.

John didn't blame him: the combination of the smell of decay and the corpse's appearance would be upsetting for even those with the strongest of stomachs. It was obvious that any exposed flesh had been preyed on by local freshwater parasites and, judging by the deeper gauges on the face and arms, probably rats as well. With the back of his hand John swept the wisps of his dark curly hair, which had been blown over his eyes by the soft breeze that now engulfed the scene. Then he simply stood with folded arms looking over towards his uniformed colleagues. As the older of the two officers let go of the corpse's legs, allowing them to fall to the ground, he slowly straightened up and almost mechanically reached for a packet of cigarettes from his breast pocket and then attempted to light one. It was a vain attempt in order to try and shield himself from the now all-encompassing smell which was emanating from the body a few feet away and defying the breeze. He struggled to shield the flame of his lighter from the wind with his hands, swearing quietly to himself.

Having done their best to make the body accessible, it was time for the two constables to withdraw and allow the forensic team to take over.

Three white-suited officers who had been standing just behind John stepped forward.

'Sorry, Inspector.' The lead officer excused himself as he and the other pushed past. John stepped back to allow them through. Then he turned to make his way, if somewhat gingerly, through the sodden mud and back to where his car was parked on the roadside at the edge of the soggy bog that bordered the river. As he walked his boots made sucking noises as he lifted each in turn, pulling it out of the wet ground.

Nearing the car, he reached into the pocket of his overcoat to pull out his mobile phone. He tapped on the address book symbol and then scrolled down until he found the number he was looking for.

The call was answered after just two rings.

'Well?' came the impatient reply voiced in a deep Dublin accent, not waiting for any formalities.

'Well, sir. It appears that the information was indeed correct. We've found a body, a male, at least we think it is a male. Possibly a young male, by the look of the clothes.' Then he quickly added by way of explanation, 'Or at least what's left of them.'

'Is it him?' The voice sounded apprehensive about the reply.

'Too early to be certain. Forensics have just taken over. But chances are, yes, it is.'

'So are we looking at a murder inquiry?'

'Possibly, but he might just have fallen into the water accidentally.'

'Okay, McDaid, get back to the station. There isn't much more you can do there now. We'll know more when the forensic team have finished.'

With that, the call was abruptly ended.

John McDaid breathed a sigh of relief. He hated these sort of cases anyway and by now a cold wind bringing with it spots of early rain. Giving an involuntary shiver he pulled his coat tighter around himself and then, with one last backward glance, he noted the forensic team erecting a small screen around the area. *Probably*, John thought, *in an effort to thwart the small crowd of onlookers that had gathered further down the riverbank and speculating on what the Gardaí were doing there.*

*

By the time he'd reached the Garda station he felt that he had nearly, but by no means completely, thawed out. The heater in his car had taken a while to warm up and the journey itself was relatively short.

On entering the station building itself, he looked about and then made his way through the reception area to key in the code on the door at the far end of the public area. This allowed him access to the main building beyond.

As he made his way through the doorway, another door opened further down the corridor and a short, balding man leaned out. The occupant turned towards John and gestured. 'DI McDaid... A word.' Without waiting for a reply, the speaker retreated back into his office, leaving the door ajar behind him.

'Yes, sir,' John mouthed silently in the once again empty corridor.

Entering his boss's office, he closed the door gently behind him, turned and moved towards the desk in the centre of the room. The man who had summoned him with a small wave of the hand then motioned, almost absentmindedly, it seemed, for John to sit down.

Behind the desk sat his boss, small, bald and bespectacled. Chief Inspector Sean O'Brien rested his forearms on the desktop and leaned forward to fix his junior officer with what he hoped was a strong and formal gaze.

John knew that this was the way his boss worked. Many in the station had speculated that he had 'small man syndrome'. Those that did, postulated that he lacked self-belief and overcompensated by trying to intimidate and belittle others. John himself did not share all of this view but he was not, and never had been, particularly impressed by the chief inspector. Their relationship was also marked by an unspoken degree of animosity between the two. But, then again, O'Brien was officially the boss.

John did as he was bid and sat down. As he did so, he became aware that somebody else was in the room, behind him, standing but leaning back, his shoulders resting against the wall. John hadn't noticed the other man on the way in, mainly because he had fixed his gaze on DCI O'Brien, trying as he was not to allow himself to be intimidated by him.

'DI McDaid, this is DI Alan Marshall.' John swivelled around to face the newcomer. He in turn reached for another chair and seated himself down beside John.

The other man stretched out a hand in greeting.

John shook the hand, if somewhat suspiciously.

The other Guard couldn't have missed the questioning look on John's face. 'DI McDaid, pleased to meet you. I've heard a lot about you.' He spoke with a slow, country drawl.

'From Chief Inspector O'Brien, I presume.' He didn't think that his boss would have given him a glowing report.

'From him… and others.'

John caught the implication and figured that the other was trying to reassure him. *Perhaps*, John thought, or maybe hoped, *the other Garda officer harbours some reservations about O'Brien as well.*

'DI Marshall,' the Inspector interrupted, 'is here on secondment,' then he added, smiling in the direction of the other man, 'from headquarters.'

John continued to look at him quizzically.

Alan Marshall seemed to have picked up on his questioning expression as he turned to face John directly, taking over the explanation of his presence. 'There has been a lot of interest in this case, as you probably know.'

'I know the media are all over it, but that's not unusual when a young person goes missing and then ends up dead.'

'Yes, that's true. But it also in this case, who he is. Or rather, was,' he corrected himself, before continuing. 'Given, of course, that the body you found turns out to be who we think it is. That adds a whole new dimension to things. Don't you think? Headquarters certainly do, and that's why they've sent me down here.'

'To do what exactly?' John queried. As he said it, he noticed Sean O'Brien stiffen at his forthrightness of the question.

But despite his boss's clear displeasure John continued unabated and even more confrontationally. 'To take over my investigation?'

'To work with you, DI McDaid, that's all.' The chief inspector quickly interjected, using the more formal address, probably as he knew it would irritate him. 'Given your relative inexperience in the job.' O'Brien twitched slightly when he spoke. John's keen detective's eye had noticed this habit or tic a number of times previously. *It is*, John had thought, *usually associated with whenever O'Brien is lying, or at least not telling the whole truth.*

chapter two

Six weeks earlier...

'Come on, Dad, keep up!' the small boy shouted over his shoulder.

In truth he was trying to, really trying to, but he was losing ground as the boy raced ahead.

John was struggling to catch him, even though the boy was young and only had a small boy's legs, short legs. Similarly John wasn't that old, only mid-late thirties, and had thought himself reasonably fit.

Niamh, John's new partner, watched the two impassively from the top of a hill not far away. The two were running after an overfed black Labrador which was doing a fairly good job of evading their clutches.

'Alfie, come back. Come here now!' John called.

To those others in the park who had stopped to watch the action they saw a slightly overweight man running across the park but being overtaken by a boy of about eight. It was probably obvious that 'Alfie', which they were unsuccessfully trying to catch, was the two chasers' own pet dog.

Those that had seen the chase begin knew that the dog had stolen a tennis ball, a ball that moments earlier they had all being playing with. The dog had intercepted a throw between the man and the boy and, now gripping it firmly in his jaws, had refused to give it back. The miscreant animal had then headed off down the park and was doing his best to try to evade their clutches.

'Hurry up, Dad!' the boy called again; he, at least, was gaining on the escapee.

John had to admit to himself that he used to be much faster on his feet, but here he was being outdistanced by his own eight-year-old son. Either the boy had got faster or he'd got slower. *Probably a mixture of both*, he thought. A while ago he had simply put it down to age; he wasn't getting any younger, after all. Well, he supposed, he was nearing middle age. The thought horrified him.

But as time had moved on, he began to realise that there was probably more to it than simply the ageing process. His legs actually felt stiff, stiffer than they should be. The left one particularly. Too much time sitting at the computer. Too little exercise. Undoubtedly that was it.

Patrick finally caught up with Alfie and was holding him, one hand by his collar, the other trying to wrestle the ball free from the dog's grip.

'Come on, Alfie, give it up,' he said with all the firmness and command that an eight-year-old could muster.

His father finally puffed up beside the pair. 'Right, you.' He glared down at Alfie with what he hoped was a masterly look. 'Drop,' he commanded.

Eventually and somewhat reluctantly the black Labrador relaxed his bite and the ball fell at Patrick's feet.

John stretched his legs to try to ease the stiffness. More exercise, that's what's needed, he rationalised.

9

After a short rest, the young boy ran off down the long green parkland, his arm outstretched and holding the ball aloft, teasing the dog who was now the one in hot pursuit.

Alfie ran and jumped at intervals, trying to dislodge the ball from Patrick's grasp.

John stood back then leaned forward, hands on knees, breathing heavily. He watched the pair, envious of their stamina. Niamh, who had crept up behind him, laid her hand gently on his shoulder.

After a coffee, and an ice cream in Patrick's case, Niamh headed off to her own apartment, leaving father and son time their together.

As they walked home, Alfie was now firmly held on a lead, pulling Patrick along as he tried to control his pace. As he did so, he suddenly turned and looked up at his father with an inquisitive look on his face.

'What's up?' his father asked, noticing the look on his son's face.

'Uh, nothing really. Is your leg sore, Dad?'

'No. Why do you ask?'

'Well, it's just that you seem to be limping, that's all.'

After his son had said it, he realised that he was actually limping and that Patrick was indeed correct; John himself hadn't initially been aware of it. The more he thought about it, though, the more he was aware that his left leg was indeed lagging behind and that he kept scuffing his toe. It had taken Patrick to point it out for him to start to notice it.

'Must have stubbed my toe or something when we were chasing Alfie,' he lied, not wanting to upset the boy.

When they got home, Patrick disappeared upstairs to play on his computer. Alfie retreated to his basket and went into a well-deserved slumber. John himself simply collapsed onto the sofa and flicked on the television.

Days off, he mused, you so look forward to them, with great plans as to what you will do, and then here he was simply watching a repeat of a programme that he had to admit, he didn't really enjoy first time round.

He massaged his leg.

It still felt a bit stiff.

It wasn't painful, though. Just a bit stiff.

Maybe I should see my GP about it sometime, he thought, knowing that in reality he probably wouldn't. It was in his makeup and probably also down to being a male of the species that he tended to ignore health issues, relying more on nature and time than the medical profession to resolve the problem. As indeed they often did.

He thought that maybe just a bit more time at home resting or with Patrick would cure all ills. In truth he had to admit, if only to himself, that he had found it difficult these last few years after Patrick's mother had left. Now he only saw Patrick sporadically, usually at weekends and even then there were many weekends when he had to work and so disappoint his son.

He thought to himself, *It isn't my fault; I work too hard.* Then again, no, maybe it was his fault. He had said that he just couldn't accept being married to an independent, ambitious, hard-working woman. Of course, it didn't help that both of them were in An Garda Siochana. Though that was how they had met in the first place, fell in love and got married.

How clichéd! he said to no one but himself.

It didn't help, though, that while she was ambitious and rose through the ranks to become a detective chief inspector, he had remained at constable level for much longer and even now was still only an ordinary detective inspector. That actually made it worse because on the albeit rare occasion they worked on the same case it led to friction between them, he not fully accepting her superior rank and responsibility.

Anyway, it had been a couple of years since she had walked out, taking Patrick with her. Patrick missed him; he knew that. He hoped, in a funny sort of way, that maybe his wife missed him too. But things had been a lot calmer, more settled since she had left. He still saw her occasionally, but only occasionally, as by now she had transferred to another station.

'Best for both of us,' she had said. Probably right.

It hadn't been easy for her, balancing being a full-time DCI with being a mother, he did acknowledge that. It was probably a little better in recent times after Patrick had started school and there were good after-school activities to keep him occupied (and away from computer games!). But even before these distractions his mother had limited John's access to Patrick.

He wasn't completely sure why.

He'd met Niamh only about a year ago, about a year after Patrick's mother had left. She had been good for him. A stabilising influence. He hoped Patrick liked her too. Niamh had understood and she always made a point of not intruding on the pair's relationship. Like today, she made no attempt to stay over when Patrick was at home.

The following morning, John drove Patrick back to his mother. She still lived in their marital home and, much to John's chagrin, she had recently moved her new partner in too. He had a brief conversation with both of them before leaving and returning to the small two-bedroomed house that he now called home.

He spent the rest of the day doing a bit of long-overdue gardening and trying to tidy the house before Niamh came round, as he hoped she would. Although it was only a small garden and the house had been pretty tidy anyway, he suddenly felt unusually tired. Probably the unaccustomed exercise in the park the day before. He lay down on the sofa and idly pressed the TV remote and then, almost without realising it, he slowly drifted off into a light sleep.

He hadn't rested long, or at least he didn't think so, when he was awoken by the incessant buzz of his mobile. He sat up and looked around at first, in his still half-asleep and muddled frame of mind. He searched for the phone, forgetting where he'd left it, then he saw it sitting on the coffee table beside him. He rubbed his eyes as he answered the call.

chapter three

If somewhat reluctantly, he had responded to the request and agreed to return to the station despite it officially being his day off.

He had no sooner reached his own office door than his desk phone started to ring. In his haste to get to it some of the bundle of papers he was carrying slipped from his grasp and floated in different directions onto the floor.

John swore under his breath as he tried to re-adjust the pile and deposit it carefully on his desk before reaching for the receiver.

'Yes?' he barked into it, immediately regretting his brusqueness.

'Is that DI McDaid?' the caller asked.

'Speaking,' he answered, still trying to get the final hint of irritation out of his voice.

'DI McDaid, this is Garda constable Walsh.' Then he added unnecessarily, as John thought, 'At the front desk.'

'Yes, Constable Walsh, I know, you rang me at home. You wanted to see me.'

'I just wanted to check you were in, I thought we needed to discuss the matter face to face.'

'Do you know where my office is?' John asked, remembering that the constable was a relative newcomer to the station.

'No problem. I'll find it,' was the answer.

Within a few minutes later, the young constable was hovering outside John's domain, even though the door was widely open.

'Come in, come in.' John ushered him in, trying, but failing, to keep the impatience out of his voice.

'As I said on the phone, I took the call,' said the young man standing to attention across the desk from his superior officer.

'Yes, you said. Apparently something important has come up? Something that needed the attention of a senior officer?'

'The call was from the embassy.'

'The embassy?...Which one?' John felt the hint of irritation evaporating and being replaced by one of inquisitiveness.

'The United States...' then, after a short pause,'of America.'

'Is there another one?' He felt he just had to ask somewhat sarcastically.

'Sorry. Another what? I don't understand.'

'United...' He started but then stopped himself, feeling suddenly a bit guilty at baiting the young constable. It wasn't his fault, after all, that he'd caught John on a particularly bad day.

'Just tell me about the phone call you received,' he added, still somewhat tetchily.

'Uh, okay... The ambassador wants to see somebody, somebody in charge, as soon as possible, apparently. I can't locate Detective Chief Inspector O'Brien, so I thought you would be the next best thing.' He released an audible intake of breath, then: 'Sorry, sorry, I didn't mean it to come out like that.'

'It's okay, happens all the time.' John himself had often found DCI O'Brien difficult to find. He was a man who liked to delegate. Not so much to give his junior colleagues experience in the field, but rather so he didn't have to do the grunt work himself, preferring to follow pursuits more to his liking… mainly golf. John thought through all of this but kept his conclusions to himself. Then, he reasoned, *No. That's a tad unkind… if only a tad.*

'So what does the ambassador want?' he asked.

'The woman on the phone – his PA, I think she said – wouldn't say. All she would say was that it was a matter of extreme importance and that a detective should come down to the embassy as soon as possible.'

'Okay, leave it with me.' Then, as an afterthought: 'Have you got a number for me to contact them to arrange the visit?'

The constable reached into his top pocket, retrieved his notebook and recited the number; in doing so though he stressed that it was, apparently, a direct line, not one that meant having to go through their switchboard.

John let the young constable return to his duties at the station's front desk. While still a bit annoyed at having to give up part of his day off and the absence of his DCI, he couldn't help but admit that he was at least a little intrigued. He decided immediately not to bother or even try to locate the DCI. He need not trouble him with the 'trivia' of a case involving the US ambassador. He smiled… if a little smugly, to himself.

The traffic had been a little lighter than usual as he drove to the United States Embassy in Ireland, to give it its full title. The US embassy was located in the Ballsbridge area of Dublin, a smart, up-and-coming area in the south of the city. As John approached he watched the large and unusually shaped building slowly come into view. As if the structure of the building was not distinctive enough, standing out as it did from the surrounding rows of terrace houses, the prominent perimeter fence and Stars and Stripes flying high above its entrance left no one in any doubt of the provenance of the building. It occupied a prominent position in Elgin Road and, although not far from the centre of Dublin, it was closer to the Garda station. He reasoned that probably was the main reason the call had come through to them first rather than headquarters. So in less than fifteen minutes after talking to the constable, John found himself stopped in the roadway in a small queue of cars just outside the building itself.

Looking up, he had to admit it was indeed an impressive structure, obviously modern in style and relatively new. The building was, for the most part, three storeys high and boasted a plethora of mirrored glazing covering a high percentage of the exterior. *Undoubtedly*, John thought, *allowing for uninterrupted views of the surrounding streets.*

Though, when he examined the building again, the facade, he thought, at least to the uninitiated, could be said to look simply like a giant egg box standing on its end.

Better not make that comment when inside. He smirked.

The building was complemented by a landscaped park with large oak trees. John glanced around him, taking in the immaculate greenery as he drove around the building trying to find somewhere to park.

Reaching the impressive gates that barred the entrance to the compound itself stood two armed guards wearing full military garb. John stopped his car, leaned out of the window and shouted to them, asking if there was anywhere he could park. One of the soldiers approached, if somewhat suspiciously, his weapon readied.

Times we live in, John reflected. A number of US embassies had been targeted recently and there was no reason to think that this one here in Dublin was in any way immune from such attentions.

Following some initial questioning by the guard who had bent down to the level of the car's open window and now seemingly satisfied by John's explanation of his presence, reached for the small microphone that was attached to the upper part of his uniform and put a call through to the ambassador's office.

The gates slid open at the press of a switch by the other guard following a nod of the head by John's interviewer. The second soldier retreated to his small office and then, with a wave of a hand from the first guard, who by now had walked around towards the front of John's car, he was permitted to drive into the compound itself.

The level of security he witnessed as he drove through the compound confirmed John's suspicions that there was undoubtedly a heightened sense of awareness because of recent bombings of similar establishments in other parts of the world, all of which probably only served to increase the Americans' inbred distrust of foreigners.

Nearing the end of the driveway, he was directed to an underground car park by another smartly dressed soldier and then by yet another guard within the car park to an empty space marked in bold white lettering: 'Visitors'.

As he climbed from the car this final soldier turned and silently motioned for John to follow him to the lift.

Once inside, his new companion pressed the button for the ground floor and then stood stiffly and silently by John's side until the lift had stopped and the doors had opened. John was ushered out of the lift as the guard pressed the lift button and returned to his post in the basement.

As the lift doors closed, John stood and surveyed the area around him. It was truly awe-inspiring. The foyer was huge, with marbled flooring and high walls around the expanse of the room itself.

People were milling around. Some were in groups chatting, others huddled in pairs sharing some piece of confidential information, more again scurrying across the hallway to get to some meeting or other.

As he stood watching the activity in front of him John didn't at first notice a small female figure emerge from another lift behind him.

The woman spoke loudly to grab his attention. 'Detective Inspector McDaid?' The accent appeared to be Midwest American.

'The ambassador is waiting for you. He's in his office,' she continued. 'I'm Mandy, his PA – we spoke on the phone.'

John offered his hand.

The PA shook it in a business-like manner while simultaneously asking for his ID card, no matter that the soldiers on the gate had already inspected it.

'Can you tell me what this is about?' John asked.

'I think that it would be better coming from the ambassador,' was the only reply she was prepared to offer. She turned and led him into the smaller lift.

The PA maintained her silence in the lift, or 'elevator', as she called it. John had noticed that Mandy had to swipe an identification card that hung around her neck in order to be granted permission for access for the lift to proceed to the top floor. No doubt this was where the ambassador had his office.

John silently watched the numbers above the lift doors illuminate in turn until finally it reached its destination and the doors opened. Directly ahead was a short hallway and then a large, spacious office opened up beyond. Within the office sat a number of mainly young men and women, all perched behind desks, many with their heads down, engrossed in their computer screens. No one bothered to raise their heads or pay much attention as Mandy and her guest walked the length of the office to reach the large wood-panelled double doors at the far end.

There the PA stopped and then tentatively knocked the door, looking around and smiling at John as she did so.

Almost immediately, the door was opened by a rather large and certainly intimidating man. Although dressed in a smart bespoke suit, tightly knotted tie and immaculate white shirt, there was no mistaking the shorn head and the strong, square jaw: the face of a hardened military man.

He in turn ushered them in, before looking around behind them as if to ensure there was no one following them, something that was probably impossible in any case as they had just emerged from the small, private lift. He strode past them and, just as he made his way around, he dismissed Mandy with a brusque wave of the hand.

'Please, Detective Inspector, won't you have a seat? The ambassador will be here directly.' The large man indicated a chair in front of an impressive dark wooden desk which occupied a space in front of the main window in the room. A stars and stripes flag hung limply from a pole in the corner of the room. Pictures of the current and a number of past presidents adorned the otherwise bare walls.

John took in the views over the River Dodder which bisected the Ballsbridge area of Dublin, the surrounding streets and the RDS stadium beyond.

'Magnificent view, isn't it?' the big man asked, not really expecting an answer. 'One of the perks of being the most powerful nation on Earth, I guess.'

John nodded his agreement, choosing not to rise to the larger man's obvious display of self-importance, if not frank, boasting.

A door opened at the side of the room. John swivelled around to see who had entered. It was, he observed, a tall, strong-boned man, probably, John guessed, in his late fifties but trying to look younger. He had an impressive head of hair, greying only at the edges; his face was perhaps just a little too tanned and his teeth a little too white. Although now showing his age, he had retained his handsome looks. He wore a smart, tight-fitting suit but had discarded the jacket, just now donning the trousers and waistcoat. His tie, though, a little incongruously, hung limply from the collar.

The ambassador approached and extended a hand in greeting. As he did so John noted the stern and worried look on his face.

'Detective Inspector. Ambassador Wilson. Thank you for coming.' He then made his way purposefully around to the far side of the desk. 'Mitchell. That will be all.' He gave a wave of dismissal to the large assistant.

'But, Ambassador—'

'No buts, this is between myself and Detective Inspector McDaid. Now go.' The last words were delivered with authority, clearly from a man used to giving orders.

The subordinate clicked his heels and strode purposefully out of the room. A dark expression appeared on his face which did little to diminish the man's displeasure at being removed.

The ambassador turned to John and spoke softly. 'He's okay... Mitchell, I mean.' He pointed in the direction of the door. 'But this is way above his pay grade.'

John was intrigued.

The ambassador pressed a button on the intercom on his desk. 'Ms Brooks, can you ask Mr Sanders to step in, please?'

'Yes, sir.' John recognised Mandy's voice.

A few minutes of silence between the pair passed before the door opened and a man in his thirties – dark-haired, fair-skinned, slim and toned – entered. He offered his hand to John and then stood stiffly behind him.

'Detective Inspector McDaid, this is one of our legal attachés, Thomas Sanders.'

John turned to look again at the man, John knew that the term 'legal attaché' meant that Sanders was in all probability an FBI agent. The handle of legal attaché was one that was frequently employed by the United States for agents domiciled in a number of other countries.

'I'm not sure I fully understand.' He looked back and forth from one to the other.

'Let me explain.' The ambassador placed his elbows on the desk and leant forward towards John. Then, turning to the FBI man: 'Sit down, Sanders, for goodness' sake, I'm getting a crick in my neck.'

The younger man pulled up a chair beside John. The newcomer, rather than the ambassador, took up the explanation for John's summons to the embassy. 'We have an issue,' he stated bluntly.

'An issue?' queried John.

'A serious issue,' the FBI man confirmed, giving little else away.

John continued to look towards the speaker but noted out of the corner of his eye that the ambassador seemed to slump in his chair and then bury his head in his hands.

John turned back to face him. 'Are you alright, sir?' he asked.

'Sanders will explain,' the older man said, not bothering to lift his head. 'Do get on with it, Sanders,' he barked.

John turned back to the FBI agent.

'The Ambassador's son has gone missing' he informed John.

'Missing?'

'Missing. Yes,' he confirmed.

'What do you mean, missing? Gone off somewhere? With friends, perhaps? Or…' He paused. 'Something more sinister.'

The Ambassador seemed to shrink even further into his desk. 'That's just it, Detective.' He spoke still with his head bowed. 'We don't know. He didn't return from a night out with some friends and I haven't heard from him since.'

'Have you talked to these friends?'

'To be honest, Inspector McDaid,' the FBI man took control once more, 'they are not the most reliable people. But they certainly say that they haven't seen or heard from him since their night out.'

'What do you mean, "not the most reliable"…?'

'Mmm… Well…' The FBI man hesitated, looking towards the ambassador as if for support.

'Just tell the man, Sanders.' The ambassador spoke more firmly, his irritation overcoming his anxiety. 'Now is not the time to spare my blushes.'

The FBI man, still looking at the ambassador, rather than John, continued. 'Following Daniel's… That is the ambassador's son's name,' the FBI man added by way of explanation. 'After Daniel disappeared, we conducted our own inquiry.'

'Oh, yes?' John replied, letting the FBI man know that he was aware of the rules, even if the other wasn't or had ignored them. The rules were that if any criminal activity was suspected then it was the responsibility of the local Gardai and the local Gardai alone, not, as Sanders was clearly saying, their own personal investigation.

Sanders stopped momentarily, perhaps realising his mistake, but then continued anyway. 'We just felt that, in the first instance at least, that Daniel had just gone off with his friends for a bit of – well, you know, *fun*. He is only a teenager, after all.'

'What made you think differently?'

Again it was the ambassador who was first to offer an explanation. 'It was very unlike Daniel to go off like that and certainly not to contact us to let us know where he was. He understood the rules and indeed the dangers posed of being the son of a United States ambassador, even here in Dublin.'

'So you've had no contact with him?'

'Not since a week last Saturday.'

'Ten days ago,' John calculated.

'Yes,' confirmed the FBI man.

'Didn't he have any of your lot keeping tabs on him?' John turned again to confront the FBI agent. 'Isn't that usual, even if it is just for a relative, but particularly given that his father is a high-profile diplomat?'

'Under normal circumstances, yes. But Daniel was...' Again he hesitated, glancing at the ambassador. 'Daniel was... how shall I say it? Difficult.' The FBI man shifted uncomfortably in his seat, aware that his boss might be displeased with this explanation.

But the ambassador simply lifted his head with a look of resignation. 'What Agent Sanders is trying to say,' he butted in, 'is that my son didn't like the attention he was, or rather is,' correcting himself quickly, possibly realising the implication of his words, 'a free spirit. If you understand. He repeatedly refused to countenance any bodyguard or official following him around. And, to be frank, I think he resented my position here. I know that he wasn't really happy for us to leave America and come to live here. Although recently,' he reflected, 'to be honest I thought he had become more settled, more reconciled. In fact, I actually thought he was starting to enjoy being here.'

'Did he have any friends locally?' John asked.

'I think he had made some, yes. I thought that was why he had become more content living in Dublin.'

'Did you meet them? Did he introduce you to any of them?' John asked.

'No, I never did. He tended to keep them at arm's length from me. It was almost as if he was ashamed of me.'

'I'm sure that's not it, sir.' John tried to sympathise; this was a man, after all, who was worried about his son's wellbeing. 'A lot of teenagers are like that in my experience.'

'Daniel wasn't like that before – I know all parents say that, but we had been very close, particularly after we came here to Ireland.'

'If I may, sir.' Sanders had stepped forward.

The ambassador returned to his more introspective demeanour, simply nodding at his subordinate to continue.

'Even before Daniel's disappearance we did harbour some concerns regarding the company he was keeping.'

'I thought Daniel didn't have any protection?' John asked.

'Officially no, but that's not to say we didn't try to keep an eye on him. The ambassador was in agreement with this policy.'

The ambassador nodded.

'So what happened on the day he disappeared?' John asked.

There was another pause. The FBI man and the senior diplomat looked at each other. It was the ambassador who spoke. 'They lost him—'

'Well, sir, in point of fact—'

'In point of fact, nothing. You lost him and now we can't find him.'

Sanders looked down at his immaculately polished shoes and shuffled his feet, clearly embarrassed by the older man's outburst.

'All we know, Detective, is that he had intended to go to some party or other, then he and his brother slipped out of the embassy before Sanders and his crew realised they was gone.'

'His brother?'

'Yes, Daniel's younger brother. He came back early. Says Daniel was meeting some friends and didn't want him tagging along. He's quite a bit younger than Daniel, so probably understandable.'

'And you haven't seen or heard from Daniel since?' John asked, immediately realising that the question was essentially unnecessary given his current presence at the embassy.

Both men nodded.

'Then,' he said, turning again to face the FBI agent, 'you made some enquiries.'

'Yes, we did,' Sanders confirmed, regaining some of his composure.

'And what did you uncover, may I ask?'

It was the ambassador who answered even though the question had been asked of Sanders. 'The so-called friends that Daniel was hanging about with were not the sort of friends that I would have wanted him to socialise with.'

'May I ask why?'

Now Sanders took up the challenge. 'We were actually keeping tabs on Daniel, despite his protestations. We observed him,' then he quickly added, 'from a distance.'

'So what did you learn?'

'He had made some friends and we even think he might have had a girlfriend—'

'That was around the time that he seemed to settle, be more content living here,' the ambassador added quickly.

'But you had some concerns about these "friends", Mr Sanders?' John tried to keep the conversation focussed.

'We did. Yes, I did.'

'And did you raise these concerns with the ambassador? His father?'

Sanders paused then, looking towards the ambassador: 'Yes, sir. I did.'

Now it was the ambassador's turn. 'To be fair, Inspector, Sanders did raise his reservations with me, but to my shame I ignored the warnings. I was just happy to see Daniel coming to terms with living here.'

Turning back to the FBI man once more, John asked, 'Just what was it that worried you about Daniel's friends, Mr Sanders?'

Before the FBI man could answer, Ambassador Wilson rose from behind his desk and, offering his hand to John, said, 'I think I'll leave it to you and Sanders. I don't think I can add anything more, Inspector, but if you think there is anything else you need to know, you'll know where to find me.'

'Just one more thing, Ambassador. Where is Daniel's mother? Here? Or did she stay home in America?'

'She's dead, Inspector. She died a while back. Daniel took it hard. Indeed as I did. It was part of the reason that I accepted this posting. Too many memories back home. I thought the change of scene would help Daniel and Jake get over her loss.' He paused, turning to open the door to the office, then muttered, almost to himself, 'See where that's got me.'

When the door closed, leaving John alone with the FBI man, Tom Sanders slipped around the ambassador's desk and settled into his boss's chair. He raised his hands behind his head and stretched back in a somewhat leisurely fashion.

'Understandable,' John replied, being not a little surprised at the other's seemingly off-hand manner now that his boss was out of earshot. 'You don't seem overly worried about Daniel's disappearance,' he continued.

The FBI man simply shrugged and continued to stare up at the ceiling.

'So, explain,' John said, becoming a bit irritated by the other's sudden change in demeanour now the boy's father was out of earshot.

'Well, as Ambassador Wilson said, initially Daniel wasn't

very happy here, then he got into a crowd. A group of boys I think he had met when he was at school. He went to St Columba's. He's just left, actually, he's taking a gap year before going to university.'

'What age was, sorry, is Daniel?'

'He's nineteen,' Sanders confirmed.

'And the group he was hanging around with?'

'About the same. Though I think that there were only a couple of them actually at school with Daniel.' Then, by way of explanation: 'Daniel was a year older than his school friends – he'd been held back a year because of the interruption to his studies on moving here and, of course, the different courses. The ones he knew, though, I believe hung around with some older boys, some of whom they'd known from school previously but by now had left.'

'So what worried you about this group he was hanging around with?'

'Well, there were reports from my colleagues that they were into petty crime, shoplifting and the like.'

'That's all?' queried John. 'Many young boys, and even girls of Daniel's age, go through a phase of doing things they shouldn't. It's almost a rite of passage.'

'But my agents suspected there were some more serious aspects of behaviour that might reflect very badly on the ambassador if they were to come to light.'

'You mean drugs…?

'I'm afraid so. Yes. But,' he continued, 'we didn't think Daniel was heavily into it. Maybe a bit of marijuana here and there, that's all.'

'Did his father know?'

'We had no option but to tell him. So, yes, he did know.'

'And how did he react to the news that his son was hanging about with drug addicts?'

28

The FBI man now leant forward, resting his hands on his thighs, elbows facing outwards at ninety degrees to his body and his head tipped slightly forwards. 'He blew his top.'

'Again, understandable,' John asserted. 'So what did he do about it?'

'He confronted Daniel,' Sanders confirmed.

'And how did that go?' John asked, sensing he already knew the answer.

'There was an almighty row. The staff could hear the argument from rooms away. At first, Daniel tried to deny it – he finally had to admit that there were some drugs involved but was adamant that he didn't have anything to do with them.'

'Did the ambassador believe him?'

'I don't think so.'

'Why do you say that?'

'Well, his next action was to forbid Daniel from seeing these friends again and he threatened to report them to the Guards.'

'So what happened then?'

'The ambassador ordered Daniel to go to his room and to stay there, while he "sorted things out". It was shortly after this that Daniel slipped out and disappeared. He hasn't been seen since.'

'So,' John concluded, 'that's why you are a bit more relaxed than the ambassador by Daniel's disappearance?'

Sanders nodded in agreement.

'You think he's just run off to warn his friends and will eventually slink back to face down his father's wrath.'

'Precisely.'

'Have you made any efforts to locate him before contacting us?' John asked.

'Few questions here and there, but as you know we are limited in what we can do in a foreign country.'

John didn't really give much credence to that remark; he was quite sure that the FBI man and his colleagues did a lot more here in Ireland than they were prepared to admit.

As the FBI man rose, he admitted, 'We did try and track his phone, Inspector, that's not illegal here, is it?'

John shook his head; he knew there were apps that people had on their phones that, without them realising it, could enable them to be easily traced.

'And…?' he asked, turning to squarely face the American.

'No good. The phone was here in the embassy. His brother had it.'

'Was it usual for Daniel to go out without his phone on him?' John couldn't think of another nineteen-year-old that could bear to be parted from his mobile for more than five minutes.

'No, obviously not.' The FBI man was on John's wavelength. 'But we guessed that he left it behind simply because he knew that we could trace him on it and he wanted to disappear.' After a pause he continued. 'Any help you and your colleagues can offer in the interim will be much appreciated by the ambassador.' Then he added after a short pause, 'And by myself, of course.'

John remained seated. The FBI man clearly thought that the interview was over, but John still harboured doubts. 'I'll need a list of these friends and where I might find them.'

'Of course.'

'And I may want to interview his brother and some of your operatives, the ones involved in the surveillance work.'

'Jake, no problem, he's at school at the moment but we can arrange for you to see him,' then he added, 'with his father – he's only fifteen, you know.'

'Of course,' John confirmed. 'And your colleagues?'

'Mmmm…' Tom Sanders shuffled his feet awkwardly. 'That may be a little more problematic.'

'Why might that be?' asked John, already suspecting what the answer would be.

'Some of our agents – well, they tend not to want to be in limelight, so to speak.'

'You mean they work undercover? Even here in Ireland? One of your country's main allies?' John tried to suppress a smile, sensing the other's discomfiture.

'I'll see what I can do, Inspector McDaid,' came the somewhat curt reply as he ushered the Garda inspector out the door.

*

Down in the car park once more, John paused for thought. He stomped his foot on the ground; his leg was still a bit stiff from yesterday's exercise.

He mulled over the information he had been given. Clearly, the ambassador was worried about his son's disappearance, but it seemed his own security advisor didn't share his concern. John lit a cigarette whilst deciding which side to come down on.

In the end he decided that he couldn't make his mind up, so the only course of action was to follow things up, in the first instance by trying to contact Daniel's friends and then, depending on their response, take it from there.

He stubbed the cigarette out even though he'd only had a couple of puffs; he was supposed to be giving up, after all. Then he turned and headed back – still, he noticed, limping slightly – to the visitor's bay to retrieve his car.

chapter four

It was later that day that the FBI man emailed through the details of Daniel's former friends.

When he went down the list, John thought he knew at least one name on the list.

He checked the name against the Garda database.

'Cathal Murphy' a local teenager with a history of petty crime and more recently a couple of counts of 'procession of an illegal substance'. Not enough for a charge of dealing, just for 'personal use', the defendant had claimed each time. The fact that he had a wad of money, which he couldn't account for, wasn't enough to convince the local magistrate to impose anything more than a fine, one that the bundle of money could have easily covered.

The database also had a list of known associates, a list which roughly coincided with the list Sanders had provided. John was, however, somewhat glad to note that the ambassador's son wasn't on the database's list. Although again, this might just suggest that the database wasn't just as up to date as the Garda would have liked.

John motioned to Detective Constable Jo Roberts, who was seated at her own desk near the back of the open-plan office, to come over and join him at the computer. Roberts was relatively young, inexperienced and only recently promoted to the detective team, but John knew that she was energetic, keen to please and, most importantly from what he'd seen so far, apparently quite reliable – traits that many of his older colleagues had allowed to slip into abeyance, borne most probably out of disillusion in their chosen profession. Disillusion that they hadn't actually been able, or allowed, to put the world to rights as they had initially hoped on joining An Garda Siochana . Now their only ambition appeared to be to bide their time until retirement and a comfortable pension.

Jo Roberts didn't quite fit the usual profile of a woman Garda officer; she was of Afro-Caribbean descent. John had heard that her father had left not long after her birth to return to Jamaica, leaving Jo's mother to bring up their daughter alone. Jo's mother by all accounts was a stoical woman who had taken desertion and being a single mother in her stride – qualities of self-determination that she was to pass on to her daughter.

John admired her character; it was one of determination mixed with humour. His own origins were from Northern Ireland, still part of the United Kingdom, but his name reflected his true Irish ancestry – one which was well buried in the sands of time.

Jo Roberts was tall, probably just under six foot. Certainly she put John in the shade, he being a slightly more modest five foot ten inches. She had a severe yet still attractive face, high cheekbones, dark sultry eyes and well-rounded lips which more often than not were revealed in a smile of brilliant white teeth. Her frame was solid and upright, with broad shoulders for a woman; again, the contrast with John's more relaxed and shambling posture could not be more acute. She invariably, or at least at work, wore her hair braided, pulled back and fastened behind her head. He suspected that the reserved hairstyle coupled with the minimal makeup she wore whilst on duty were precisely designed to deflect from the stereotype often applied to young female Garda officers. Similarly, he had noticed that she tended to dress in a fairly conservative manner, again a concession to the primarily male environment in which she worked. Today she wore a plain blouse, trousers and flat, sensible shoes.

John motioned for her to look at the computer screen with him and the young constable sidled around behind John as bid. Initially, she stood somewhat formally behind her superior officer. Then, intrigued, she bent down to peer over John's shoulder in order to look more closely at the computer screen on the desk in front of him.

With the cursor John pulled up Cathal Murphy's profile on screen and indicated for his colleague to read the details contained therein.

Having scrutinised them the young DC turned to John, asking why he had wanted her to read the on-screen information.

John shared with her the details of his earlier meeting at the embassy and then added, 'So we need to talk to this little toe rag.'

Jo Roberts bristled with delight. It was obvious to John that she had been waiting for an opportunity just like this, one where she felt could do some real detective work – an opportunity that had probably been denied to her by some of John's colleagues, undoubtedly more sceptical than he of the worth of a woman detective, especially one as young as DC Roberts.

'What's first, boss?' Her accent was undoubtedly Irish yet there was just a hint of a Jamaican lilt to it. She smiled from ear to ear.

'We go and see him,' John stated bluntly, pointing at the computer screen and then noting down Cathal's last known address. He lifted his jacket from the back of his chair and pulled it roughly over his shoulders as he rose to leave.

DC Roberts hastily ran over to her desk to retrieve her own outdoor jacket and struggled into it before following John, who was already striding purposefully out of the office, down the stairs and on to the car park.

'You drive,' John commanded, tossing the keys to his younger colleague.

*

After the second knock, the door opened, but only by a few inches. A spotty-faced youth peered through the small aperture between door and frame.

'Cathal Murphy?' John asked, already knowing the answer; he'd seen Cathal's photograph in his Garda file.

The younger man suddenly made an attempt to shut the door but was immediately thwarted by John's boot, which had been previously and unnoticed by the inhabitant, inserted between door and frame almost as soon as the door had crept open.

'Mind if we come in?' John asked, pushing past the reluctant doorkeeper.

'Actually, yes, I do mind,' the younger man protested angrily as Jo followed John into the small mid-terrace house.

The two Garda officers looked inquisitively around as they made their way down the short hallway. Cathal Murphy simply stood by the open front door. He made no attempt to follow them nor indeed did he make any attempt to escape. He knew to do so was probably fruitless, expecting there to be other Gardaí outside waiting to apprehend him if he made any attempt to get away.

In fact John and Jo had come alone, but they reasoned Cathal wouldn't know that. Cathal's residence had been raided before.

There was a small sitting room on the left. The curtains were still drawn even though it was mid-afternoon. The room was untidy: the small table in the centre of the room was cluttered with discarded beer cans and an overflowing ashtray. Two worn-out armchairs and a couch which didn't match either of the chairs were the only other furniture. The carpet was stained and threadbare in parts. The house smelt of damp and decay.

The kitchen lay straight ahead. If anything it appeared in an even more unkempt state than the living room.

There were no sounds coming from upstairs. There didn't appear to be anybody else at home. The house was empty apart from the dishevelled young man that still stood holding the open front door.

'You on your own, Cathal?' Jo Roberts asked needlessly.

John continued to inspect the kitchen.

'Yeah,' came Cathal Murphy's muttered reply; he looked the young detective up and down, not quite knowing what to make of her. Then he hissed, 'What's it to you?'

'Just want to ask you a few questions, Cathal, that's all.' It was John who spoke, causing the young man to shift his gaze from one Garda officer to the other.

'In here, I think.' John indicated towards the kitchen, even though it was perhaps the grubbier of the two rooms; it did have a kitchen table and three wooden chairs which he thought might lend themselves better to an interview than the living-room furniture. Also, John dreaded to think what might lie in wait contained within the folds of the armchair covers.

'Do you have a warrant?' Cathal smiled, thinking that he could take back some control of the situation.

Jo looked at John to give the answer.

'Do we need one, Cathal?' he asked, fixing the younger man with a hard stare. 'Have you something to hide?' Then, turning to his colleague, he continued. 'Cathal here clearly has a problem with us being here. Don't you think so, Jo?'

The young DC smiled on hearing John address her by her Christian name for the first time.

'I wonder why that could be.'

'Maybe we should ask him.' Then, turning towards Cathal, she added, 'Perhaps under caution, down at the station.'

John smiled; the young constable was playing her part perfectly. 'Right, Constable, you put Cathal in the car, I'll wait here till the warrant comes through and then we'll interview him under caution.'

'That okay with you, Cathal? The car's outside.'

Cathal Murphy started to fidget, making it obvious to John that the young man probably did have something to hide. John guessed that it was probably only small amounts of some illegal substance or other, 'for personal use'. Likely at worst to, as before, lead only to a small fine or a caution.

But Cathal didn't know that.

Nor did he know that John and his partner had no interest in Cathal Murphy's personal habits, illegal or otherwise, at least not at present.

'Okay, okay.' Cathal's face gave away the fact that he'd lost the battle of wills, even before it had really started, and had resigned himself to the lesser of two evils.

'So, Cathal, are you happy to have an informal chat just with the two of us here at the house?'

'Okay.' Head bowed in submission, Cathal confirmed that he was.

'Jo, have look upstairs, I don't want any surprises.'

'There is no one up there,' Cathal said a little too hastily, making John think, *That must be where he keeps his stash.*

'Quick look won't hurt, though, will it, Cathal?' As John spoke Jo Roberts was already halfway up the stairs, pulling on a pair of plastic gloves.

The young man bowed his head and stuck his hands in his pockets.

John took the opportunity to make him stand facing the wall, then spun him around and give him a frisk to ensure that he hadn't any concealed weapon that might appear later.

Finding nothing, he waited for Jo to re-appear.

When after a few minutes the DC returned and, reaching the bottom of the stairs, she held up a small clear package containing a small amount of white powder.

'Now, what have we here?' John asked.

Cathal didn't answer.

John led the young man into the kitchen and then, with one hand on his shoulder, pressed him down onto one of the wooden chairs, before taking his own seat across the table. As the DC sat down beside her boss, John stretched his arm out and swept it across the table, removing the pile of discarded dishes and cutlery which crashed down onto the floor, many of the plates shattering on impact.

'Ow!' Cathal rose to his feet.

John reached across the table, grabbed him and pushed him back down into his seat. 'Sorry, Cathal, always been a bit clumsy. Still, it makes it easier to talk.'

Cathal Murphy slumped back into his seat in resignation.

'Okay, Cathal.' John leant across the table towards him. 'Tell us what you know.'

'Know? About what?'

John leant back and sat silently for a few seconds as Cathal Murphy looked from one to the other and back again.

'We are looking for the son of a diplomat who has gone missing.'

Cathal was visibly taken aback by John's words. Then he showed some signs of relief that the Gardaí didn't seem so interested in his drug habits. 'Sorry? Son of a missing diplo…? I don't understand. What's that got to do with me?'

'Do you know a Daniel Wilson?' John leant forward again, awaiting the reply.

'Er, yes? The American guy?'

'That's who we're interested in, Cathal. He's gone missing and we want to know if you know anything about it.'

'Why would I know anything?' Cathal stuttered.

'We were told that he was a pal of yours,' Jo Roberts interjected.

John looked up at the detective constable, a little annoyed at being interrupted.

'Who told you that?'

'Never mind, Cathal.' John seized control of the interview once more. 'Do you know him or not?'

Cathal Murphy shifted in his seat, as if struggling to decide what to say next, which answer would lead to the least hassle.

John thumped the desk to regain Cathal's attention.

'Okay, yes. I know him.' Cathal had winced at the sound of John's fist hitting the table, but the gesture had had the desired effect. 'But only slightly. He isn't a friend as such. I only knew him through other people.'

'What other people?'

DC Roberts reached into her breast pocket for her notebook and then retrieved a pen from inside her jacket. She flipped the notebook open and placed it on the tabletop, then waited, her pen poised, ready to record the details of others that may have been involved in Daniel's disappearance.

'He has a girlfriend.'

'A girlfriend?' John raised an eyebrow; this was confirmation of what the ambassador and the FBI man had thought, but hadn't been completely certain of.

'Yeah,' Cathal continued. 'Cara… something. Lives in a posh house on Donnybrook Avenue. Has a brother, I know him a bit better. We used to hang out together, but I haven't seen him for a while – went off to university, I think.'

'Okay, so tell me about this Cara.'

'Cara Williams.' He paused, then continued. 'That's her name – brother's Joe. Joe Williams. I think she was pretty keen on that Daniel fellow, the American,' he added unnecessarily. 'I always found her a bit clingy, but Daniel didn't seem to mind – he came across as a pretty cool guy.'

'So tell us about how you knew them.' John couldn't quite see the son of an ambassador being bosom buddies with the likes of Cathal Murphy. Except maybe for one thing – the small package that now sat on the table in front of Jo which Cathal kept glancing at.

Cathal shifted uncomfortably in his seat, confirming John's suspicions.

'Drugs? Was Daniel into drugs, Cathal?'

Cathal remained silent; he knew the score and didn't want to incriminate himself. 'Maybe I should have a lawyer,' he mumbled.

'Cathal, we haven't charged you with anything… yet.'

At that point and exactly on cue, Jo Roberts picked up the small package of white powder and waved it under Cathal Murphy's nose.

It seemed to have the desired effect, which was reinforced when John repeated that they weren't really interested in Cathal and his habits; they just wanted to try and find Daniel Wilson.

'Okay, okay. Yes, Daniel used to get a bit of blow from me now and again – his girlfriend got him into it, I think.'

'Anything stronger?'

'Possibly, I don't really know.'

John waved the package of powder in front of Cathal Murphy's nose. 'What will we find if we send this to the lab for analysis, do you think, Cathal?'

Again the younger man shifted uncomfortably in his seat. 'Okay, but if he did do other stuff he didn't get it from me.'

'Why not, Cathal? You seem to have a supply. Maybe there's more in the house. Perhaps we should ring for a search unit. What do you think, DC Roberts?'

Just as the younger detective was attempting to retrieve her phone from her jacket pocket Cathal Murphy suddenly leapt to his feet and made a run for the kitchen door.

John extended his leg, tripping Cathal up just as he attempted to make his way past him. Cathal Murphy landed in a painful heap on the floor.

Jo Roberts pulled him to his feet and roughly, more forcefully than John would have expected from a young woman even of Jo's physique to muster, and shoved him back into his seat.

'You were saying, Cathal?' said John, apparently totally unfazed by the attempted escape.

Cathal Murphy glared angrily at him and shrugged his shoulders. At first John didn't think Cathal was going to say anything more, but then: 'Okay, maybe he got some blow from me. But actually only a little.' He was almost pleading. 'I didn't like the guy. Okay?'

'Didn't like him. Why?' It was Jo that spoke first, but John didn't mind. Cathal Murphy was in retreat and he was going to be a bit more forthcoming whoever did the questioning.

'He thought he was better than us, that's why.'

'Surely you must have encountered that attitude before, Cathal?' John leant forward into the younger man's face.

'Yeah, but he looked down on us, thought he was the bee's

knees, but I heard he owed money to other people that he got his shit from but he didn't cough up for a lot of it. I heard he was in big trouble. The guys he owed money to, you don't mess around with. If you know what I mean.'

'Like who?' John was properly interested now.

'Oh, no. Not a chance, Mr Guard.' Cathal had regained some sense of self-control. 'I give you those names, I'm a dead man walking. So do your worst. I don't care anymore.'

John and his subordinate looked at each other, but John knew that Cathal had gone as far as he would and they would have to find out about the others he had implicated in other ways.

At least there now was this girlfriend as a starting point.

chapter five

John slept badly that night. He had tossed and turned, mulling over the day's events. Daniel Wilson wasn't quite the innocent young man that his father seemed to believe he was. Sanders, despite John's dislike for the man, had been right. Daniel had been mixing with the wrong crowd.

He had decided though to pursue things a bit further before passing on what he'd learned to the ambassador or even to DCI O'Brien. No harm in holding off till things were a bit clearer, he had rationalised. Finally, having got things ordered in his head, he had drifted off into a light sleep.

When he awoke, he rubbed his face and his weary eyes and sat on the edge of the bed. *Strange*, he thought; his face felt numb. He rubbed it again; the right side felt different. He could feel his fingers touch his cheek, but it was like an anaesthetic. It felt numb and peculiar, definitely different from his left side, where the sensation felt entirely normal. He nipped his cheek. No pain, just a mild pressure sensation.

He got up and went to the bathroom. He looked in the mirror. He made faces at himself. No, his face moved normally. It just didn't feel right.

'Must have slept awkwardly,' he reasoned, speaking to his reflection. 'Probably go away later.'

He went back to the bedroom and got dressed.

He was about to head out to the station, but by now his face felt worse. Now it was really starting to annoy him, so he turned back, shutting the front door behind him, and pulled out his mobile. Scrolling through his contacts list he retrieved his GP's number and dialled it.

The call was answered after a few minutes.

He explained the problem and asked matter-of-factly simply to make an appointment. The girl at the other end of the phone had obviously been trained in medical triage because she quickly said that the practice kept slots free for emergencies.

'An emergency?' queried John.

Sensing his concern, the girl at the other end of the phone quickly added, 'I don't know if this is one,' in an obvious attempt at reassurance. 'But it could be.'

John was worried now. 'What do you mean, could be?' he asked before the telephone operator could explain any further.

'Well…' She hesitated. 'Those symptoms could be a stroke… I'm not saying it is a stroke,' she added quickly. 'It's just that we've been told to make sure that the doctors see patients with certain symptoms as quickly as possible.'

Now John was really worried. 'When can the doctor see me?' he asked a bit shakily.

'We have a free slot at nine thirty, if you can make it.'

John looked at his watch – 8.45. 'I'll be there.' He hung up and headed for his car. Knowing where the surgery was, he reckoned it would only take him about thirty minutes max. to get there depending on the traffic, but he didn't want to be late and risk missing the appointment. Not after what the GP's receptionist had implied.

As he set off, his mind in a whirl, he dialled the station's number on his mobile, cursing the fact he didn't have hands-free in his car; he placed his mobile phone on his shoulder and then leant over, trapping it between shoulder and ear. When the call was answered he asked for Jo. He drove on impatiently while waiting to be put through. Finally, when he heard her voice at the other end of the call, he simply told her he had an appointment and would be a bit late. He didn't explain or expand upon the nature of the appointment and happily Jo didn't ask.

She did aske what she should do until he got there.

He said that realistically he didn't know how long he'd be. He really didn't. So he told her to see what she could find out about Daniel and perhaps the girlfriend. Visiting Daniel's school might be a good starting point.

Halfway to the surgery he realised that if he was having a stroke the last thing he should be doing was driving a car. He ignored the thought and drove on as quickly, but also as cautiously, as he could.

He arrived at the GP surgery at ten past the hour. After checking in, he sat somewhat nervously in the waiting area.

He didn't have to wait long; the receptionist had obviously alerted the doctor to John's arrival and he was ushered into the consultation room without much preamble.

'Mr McDaid?' the doctor enquired without looking up from the case notes in front of him. 'We don't see you here very often,' he continued before John could even confirm his identity.

'Try to keep away from the medical profession as much as possible.' John tried to hide his rising dread of what the doctor might say next.

The doctor then swivelled around in his seat, bade John to sit and introduced himself: 'Dr Finlay,' adding, 'No jokes, please, I've heard them all.' He extended his hand, which John shook.

'So what seems to be the problem? The girl who made the appointment was a bit sketchy on the details, I'm afraid.'

John went on to explain that he had woken up with the facial numbness and that it was still there and hadn't gone away – if anything it had got a bit more pronounced.

The doctor rubbed his chin and thoughtfully went through a list of questions, simply confirming that there had been no previous illness of any significance, that John was reasonably fit, didn't smoke, though perhaps drank a little over the recommended daily intake.

After the initial interview the GP led John over to the examination couch and asked him to take off his jacket, shirt and tie, and to lie down on the couch. After the inevitable blood pressure check and sounding of heart and chest the GP moved on to John's face. He asked him to sit up on the couch facing him.

'So where is the numb feeling? Draw it out on your face as best you can.'

John drew a line around the area of numbness: from the right side of his forehead down the middle of his nose along his chin, though missing a piece at the angle of his jaw where it actually felt okay then around the back of his ear and round his forehead and back to where he had started.

Then he tried to explain: 'It was there when I woke up – that was the first time I noticed it. But then it was really only the cheek area that was affected. Afterwards it seemed to gradually spread to the whole side of my face. Well, it was spreading, but as soon as I made the appointment with you it actually seems to have stopped and hasn't really got much worse.' Then he added, 'But not any better either.'

'And what time did you first notice it?' the doctor asked.

'I got up about seven thirty, had a shower. That's really when I first noticed it, especially when I was brushing my teeth.'

'Did the gums feel numb?'

'Yes, I think that's what brought it to my attention. But it was definitely confined to my cheek and the inside of my mouth then.'

'And it spread?' The doctor stroked his chin.

'Definitely. Yes. But slowly. Now as I've shown you it seems to cover nearly the whole right side of my face.'

'So,' the doctor looked thoughtful, 'you first noticed it at around 7.30 and obviously it might have been there a bit longer as you were asleep, yes?'

It was a rhetorical question, so John didn't answer.

The GP looked down at his watch. 'It's now 9.30-ish. So it has got gradually worse over a couple of hours?' Then he added unnecessarily, 'At least.' He paced around the consulting room for a minute or two as if in thought, then returned to the bedside. 'Good,' he said, looking John in the face. 'That's good.'

'Good?' asked John, aggrieved, and rapidly moved to sit up on the couch and confront the health professional. 'What do you mean, good? What's wrong with me?' he asked, trying to supress the feeling of anxiety that tightened in his chest.

'Relax. Relax.' Dr Finlay placed his arm on John's shoulder and eased him back onto the couch. 'What I mean is, that you have not had a stroke.'

'But the girl on the phone...?'

'Yes, she's trained to pick up on certain symptoms, but while initially, yes, the facial numbness might suggest a stroke, I can reassure you that it isn't.'

John wasn't immediately convinced. His face gave away his continuing concern.

'Let me explain,' said the doctor calmly, again placing his hand on John's arm. 'A stroke comes on like that.' He clicked his finger. 'It does not come on gradually. Gradually, like the way you have described.'

'So it's not a stroke?' John slumped back, relieved, but then the anxiety returned. 'So what is it, if it's not a stroke? What is wrong with my face?'

The doctor took a small step back and then, looking John directly in the eye, to convey sincerity. 'You've heard of Bell's palsy?'

John paused and then confirmed that he thought he had.

The doctor went on to explain. 'A Bell's palsy is due to some inflammation in the facial nerve. It affects the face and the face only. It comes on like you've described over a few hours or even days and the way the face is structured, one nerve supplies one side of the face, the other facial nerve supplies the other side. So when one nerve is damaged in any way only one side of the face is affected.'

'So it's a Bell's palsy?'

'Well…' The doctor hesitated. 'Not exactly.'

'Sorry, I thought you said—?'

'I used the Bell's palsy as an analogy,' the doctor quickly interrupted John's attempted reasoning.

'An analogy?' John looked at the doctor, now somewhat perplexed.

'Yes, an analogy, because most people have heard of Bell's palsy. It affects one side of the face just as I've explained. But the difference here is that a Bell's palsy is inflammation or damage to the facial nerve, which is the seventh cranial nerve—'

'Sorry, I'm not with you. The seventh—?'

'Bear with me. There are twelve, what we term, cranial nerves on each side of the face and head. They each do different things mostly to the face and the senses thereof. The facial nerve supplies the muscles of the face. So, any damage to that nerve causes a facial paralysis on the affected side.'

'Whoa, hold on a minute.' John started to rise to his feet. 'Facial paralysis? I haven't any weakness in my face. It's numb, that's all.'

'Please sit down, Mr McDaid, and let me explain.'

John sat back down, but he could feel anger rising in his chest; he didn't quite know what to make of what he was being told.'Carry on,' he eventually said, taking a deep breath.

'So, no, you have no facial weakness, that's correct. That is because in your case it is not the facial nerve that is affected.'

'But you said—?'

'I know what I said.' Now the GP was being a bit more direct.'I said it was an analogy, an analogy because most people have heard of a Bell's palsy. But as I explained, the facial nerve is the seventh of twelve nerves that supply each side of the face. The seventh nerve, the facial nerve, supplies the muscles of the face. In your case it is not the seventh nerve that is affected. It is the fifth cranial nerve, the one we call the trigeminal nerve.'

'The tri... gem... what?' John asked concernedly.

'The trigeminal nerve. The trigeminal nerve controls sensation. The sensation or feeling of one side of the face.'

John was still a bit confused.

'What I am saying is that a stroke is caused by one part of the brain being starved of oxygen when a blood vessel is blocked.'

'But how can you tell it's not a stroke without tests?'

'Because of your history, that's the description that you gave, and by my examination of your face.'

John still looked unconvinced.

So the doctor continued. 'Firstly, the area that's numb matches precisely the area supplied by the trigeminal nerve. It misses out the angle of your jaw, for example. A stroke would affect the whole of one side of the face...' then he paused before adding, 'usually.'

'What do you mean, *usually*?' John started to get up again. 'Do you mean you're not certain?'

The doctor waved his hand.'Please sit down, Mr McDaid.

That is only part of the reason that I am convinced that you haven't had a stroke.'

John remained standing, gripping the desk, anxious to hear what the GP had to say next.

'The main reason that I don't think you've had a stroke...'

John was all ears as he gradually once more sank into his chair.

The GP continued once John was seated again. 'The story you gave me, it's not that of a stroke.'

John looked at the doctor quizzically.

The GP continued. 'You told me that your facial numbness came on gradually. Over a couple of hours, you said?'

John nodded in affirmation.

'A stroke,' the doctor leant forward to emphasise the point, 'a stroke is, as I said, due to the blockage of a blood vessel. Yes?'

John nodded.

'As the blood vessel is blocked suddenly, usually due to a clot, the symptoms come on suddenly as well. One minute fine, the next...' He thumped the desk to illustrate his point. 'Like that. Bang!'

He leant back in his chair and folded his arms across his chest. 'That is not how the problem with your face started, is it? You told me it was there when you woke up but then it evolved over a couple of hours. Yes?'

'Okay. Yes, that is how it happened.' John paused for breath, relieved to hear he hadn't had a stroke after all. But then reality kicked in again. 'So, if it's not a stroke, what is wrong with me?'

'I think you have inflammation of the trigeminal nerve,' the doctor asserted.

John still did not appear totally convinced.

'At the moment your face feels numb, because the nerve isn't working, but I suspect it may actually get a bit worse before it gets better.'

'What do you mean, worse?' Now John was worried again. 'The numbness will spread?'

'No, no, it's already done its worst that way. The numbness already affects the whole area supplied by the nerve. No, what I would be concerned about that as the inflammation starts to settle the sensation will start to return.'

'That's a good thing, isn't it?' interrupted John.

'Yes, but...' The doctor hesitated, spotting the level of concern returning to John's expression. 'As the sensation returns it is not unusual for the numbness to be replaced by facial pain.'

'Pain?' John queried.

'It's called trigeminal neuralgia, though sometimes referred to as tic douloureux. Have you ever heard of that?'

'I've heard of a tic,' confirmed the patient.

Before John could continue any further by way of explaining what he knew of a tic, the doctor continued. 'No, that's not quite the same thing... Well, it is... but it isn't, if you know what I mean.'

John shook his head, indicating that he had no idea what information the GP was trying to confer.

'Let me explain.' The doctor tried to assume a calm, reassuring tone, sensing John's growing unease. 'Trigeminal neuralgia – or, as I said, sometimes called tic douloureux is due to inflammation or sometimes something irritating or pressing on the trigeminal nerve—'

'Something pressing on the nerve?' John almost whispered.

'A blood vessel usually. Nothing sinister, I can assure you.' Again the doctor paused to let his words sink in, before continuing. 'So what you have described to me is undoubtedly a problem with this nerve. Not a stroke.' He felt the need to re-emphasise the point about it not being a stroke.

'So what happens next?' John still wasn't fully convinced

but was prepared to take the doctor's word for it. At least for the time being.

'As I said, the likely outcome will be that the numbness will gradually subside.' Then he quickly added, 'Without any medical intervention.'

Taking a moment to absorb the doctor's words, John heaved an audible sigh of relief, but then asked, 'So, how long will it take to go away?'

'Mmmm… that's the difficult bit, I'm afraid. A nerve palsy usually comes on fairly quickly.' Then, realising that he might confuse his patient again, he quickly added, 'By "quickly" I mean over hours or even days, but not suddenly, like a stroke.' He felt the need to re-emphasise one more time the 'not suddenly' part of his explanation. Then he said, 'But…'

'But?' John sat forward again.

'Yes, I'm afraid recovery is generally slower. Nerves invariably do heal but slowly – I think we are probably looking at a number of weeks or even months.'

'Oh God, you mean I've got to put up with this dental anaesthetic feeling for months?'

'I can't be specific, I'm afraid. What will be, will be. But honestly I do believe it will improve by itself in the long run.'

John fidgeted in his seat, not quite certain what to ask next.

'Also,' the doctor continued.

'What now?' said John becoming anxious once more.

'It may well become painful.'

'Painful?'

'I'm afraid so. As the numbness lessens it is very likely to be replaced by some pain. The douloureux bit of the name comes from the French for painful.'

'And the tic bit?' asked John.

'A tic, as in a twitch, usually in response to the pain, I'm afraid.'

'Okay, so what sort of pain is it?' John tried to act manfully, unafraid of any forthcoming pain.

'Most people describe the pain of trigeminal neuralgia as a sudden stabbing pain, a bit like needle.'

'And this may go on for months?'

'I am sorry, yes, and sometimes even longer.'

John visibly slumped. 'That's just great. Thanks, Doc.'

'Hold on, John.' The GP had used John's first name deliberately, probably to try to console him. 'I can't give you anything to lessen or take away the numbness, but we can treat the painful aspect of the condition.' Then he hastily added, 'The treatment for the pain is very effective, trust me.'

'What sort of treatment?'

'Just tablets.'

'Painkillers?' John was wary of painkillers; in his professional life he'd come across too many people addicted to painkillers.

'Actually no. Not painkillers.'

'What then?'

'The medication I'm going to prescribe...' He reached across the desk for his prescription pad and then a pen, before continuing. 'These meds are very specific for neuralgia and very, very effective.'

'What sort of tablets are they?' John asked, still unconvinced.

'Actually, they started life as drugs to control epilepsy but later it was found that they were actually better at treating neuralgic pain than the epilepsy, so that's their main use now.'

'What's it called?'

'We used to use a drug called carbamazepine – actually we still do, but it can cause a little drowsiness so now we use a drug called gabapentin. Gabapentin is really effective and has very few side effects. That's what I'm going to prescribe for you.' He started to scribble on his pad.

Almost to himself and still looking down at the prescription he was writing, he said, 'Three hundred milligrams, one tablet. Three times per day.' Then he tore the sheet off and handed it to John.

John thought he had heard of gabapentin before. He thought it was a drug that some of the addicts in the area took. He queried it with the doctor.

'That is true, John, but honestly, taken correctly there is no real risk of addiction. Trust me on that.'

'Any side effects to expect?'

'Again, truthfully, I'd be surprised. But if you notice anything come back and see me straightaway. In the meantime make an appointment for next week for me to see you and make sure that it has stabilised, not got any worse.'

The doctor rose from his seat and guided John to the door; the consultation was clearly over.

*

Back sitting in his car John experienced a mixture of emotions. He had been reassured and was relieved, but he remained a little perturbed by the diagnosis and the possible future painful outcome.

Then he had a thought: at least the numb feeling in his face and the worry over a potential stroke had completely distracted him from the stiffness that still persisted in his leg.

Then, he cursed himself that he'd actually forgotten to mention his leg problem to the GP while he was there. But then he rationalised that the doctor wouldn't really have been interested in a muscle strain anyway, especially when he was dealing with a potential stroke. But then, he wasn't? Was he? Or was he? And just not telling him. 'Oh, shut up,' he said quietly to himself.

By the time he reached his office the facial sensation had

at least stabilised – it was certainly no worse, despite his inner turmoil.

Jo Roberts was waiting for him to arrive. She rose from her desk as he had made his way to his office and had followed closely behind him.

John manoeuvred himself around his own desk and, with a wave of the hand, waved her into his office.

Brimming with enthusiasm, she started to speak before John had properly settled into his own chair. 'I think I've found her, sir.'

'Found her? Who?' John was still distracted by the odd feeling in his face. He was pleased to note, however, that his voice sounded normal and that his junior hadn't seemed to notice anything about it or indeed his face either.

'Daniel Wilson's girlfriend.'

'Good work. Tell me.'

'Cara Williams. She's seventeen, lives on Lynn Hall Place, number 26.'

'I thought Cathal the scumbag said she lived on Donnybrook Avenue?' John replied, turning around to face her as he opened the door to his office.

'Lynn Hall Place is just off Donnybrook Avenue, sir,' she said as she followed him through the outer office space.

John got up again and walked around back and forth across the office before retrieving some papers from his briefcase and then seating himself down again. Jo Roberts stood awkwardly, still hovering near the open doorway.

With a flick of the hand, John summoned her to sit down opposite him. 'What do we know about her?' he asked matter-of-factly.

'Not much, I'm afraid. Daughter of a local accountant, apparently. Quite well off, by all accounts… if you'll excuse the pun.' She smiled at her own joke.

'Aren't they all? Would have to be, to live just off Donnybrook Avenue,' John interrupted, apparently unamused. 'Haven't come across a poor accountant yet, have you, Constable Roberts?'

'Is that a chip I can see on your shoulder?' asked Jo Roberts somewhat flippantly.

John, again not quite catching the humour in the remark, made a move to look at his left shoulder, but quickly caught himself on, realising what she meant.

'Ha, ha, Constable. Very funny. No, but just maybe we chose the wrong profession.'

'Or the wrong partner,' she replied.

'Eh, what do you mean?' John asked, his interest piqued.

'Well, by all accounts, Mr Williams didn't make his money, or at least all of it, through his work.'

'How then?'

'It seems he works for a large import/export company.'

'So?'

'He married the owner's daughter. His father-in-law is Gerard Martin—'

'The Gerard Martin?' John butted in before his subordinate had finished speaking.

Impressed that her boss knew him, or at least had heard of him, she added, 'Yes, the Gerard Martin that owns five or six big companies specialising in anything from manufacturing to overseas marketing. He's worth something in the region of three hundred million Euros if the newspapers are to be believed.'

'Whooo,' whistled John.

'Well,' the young constable continued, 'this Cara Williams' father is not only married to Gerard's daughter,' she looked down at her notebook to confirm the daughter's name, 'Felicity, but he also works for at least one of his father-in-law's companies.'

'Hence the house off Donnybrook Avenue?'

'And the apartment in Davos. Oh, and the villa somewhere in southern Spain.'

'Davos, as in that exclusive ski resort in Austria?'

'Switzerland,' she corrected him, thinking that clearly, his knowledge of geography wasn't in the same league as his knowledge of the local well-to-dos.

'Okay, I get the picture.' He spoke now with a hint of tetchiness in his voice, a little annoyed to be corrected by his junior, or perhaps more so by his own error. 'So tell me about the daughter...' then he added, 'Cara,' making sure this time he didn't make any mistake.

'Pretty girl, but not that clever, so her teacher says.'

John rubbed his face again; still that numb feeling persisted. 'Go on,' he encouraged her. 'So you visited her school?'

'The school allowed me to talk to some of her friends. Cara wasn't there. Apparently she hadn't come to school the last few days – flu or something, the teacher said, though I got the impression she didn't really know why she hadn't attended.'

'Couldn't have got wind of our investigation, I don't suppose?' John asked.

'Possibly. The teacher seemed to know why I was there. The school itself had had some concerns themselves. They knew, for example, that Cara was going out with Daniel – he was actually a former pupil. By all accounts they met at the school shortly after he came over from the States. Also, the embassy had already made some enquires and that Sanders chap had already visited the school.'

'Had he indeed? He didn't share that information with me,' John added, a little annoyed that he hadn't actually formally questioned the FBI man. He allowed himself a small smile; after all, he had that to look forward to.

'Anyway, it seems that it was common knowledge that Cara

was keen on Daniel and they seemed quite close, although a couple of her friends weren't so sure that Daniel reciprocated Cara's feelings. According to the girlfriend's classmates Cara liked to get her own way. A bit spoilt, they thought.'

'Nice friends,' John reciprocated.

'Anyway,' Jo continued, 'she's not been to school since around the time Daniel went missing.'

'Run off together?' John asked, mainly to himself.

'It's a possibility, I guess. But her parents haven't reported her missing, at least not to us.'

John leant back in his chair.

Jo continued. 'Do you think we should pay her parents a visit?'

After only a moment's hesitation, John pushed his chair roughly backwards and rose to his feet. 'I think so, don't you? Let's go.'

He was already halfway across the office heading for the door.

chapter six

Thirty minutes later the two Gardai officers stood outside the large detached house that was Cara Williams' home. John stood with his back to the door admiring the long, tree-lined sweep of the drive they had just driven up to reach the house itself.

The noise of the door being opened made him spin around.

A tall, bespectacled man regarded them inquisitively through the narrow opening between door and frame. 'Yes?' he asked somewhat brusquely.

John and Jo produced their warrant cards and proffered them towards the man's face. 'Garda officers. I am Detective Inspector McDaid; this is Detective Constable Roberts. May we come in?'

The man made no effort to open the door any further. Rather, he regarded them still with some suspicion before asking, 'What's it about?'

'Mr Williams?' John regarded the man. He appeared to be in his fifties, balding, with a jowly face and growing paunch.

The father nodded, allowing John to continue.

'We're looking for a missing child, Mr Williams. Can we speak to your daughter? Is she in?'

'What do you want to speak to Cara for?' The homeowner was still giving no ground but rather holding the door tightly, as if to prevent any unwanted intrusion.

'It's part of our investigations… sir.' Jo had spoken, adding the 'sir' in an attempt to appear deferential and placate Cara's father.

He paused and seemed to consider things momentarily before opening the door properly and stepping aside to afford the two Guards access to the house.

Both stopped just inside the door, thus allowing Cara's father to pass and lead them further down the hallway before ushering them into what appeared to be the main sitting room.

He bade them to sit down; both officers politely declined. Williams himself then remained standing also. Mrs Williams, Cara's mother, made a brief appearance but shrank back into the kitchen when her husband told her to.

He turned back to John and Jo. 'So tell me, what's this all about? Why do you want to see my daughter?'

'We are led to believe,' John leant forward, 'that she knows a boy that has disappeared. Is she here, sir?'

'She's upstairs. But I'm sure she knows nothing about it,' the father stated adamantly, before adding, 'I'll fetch her. But I want you to know, she's a sensitive girl. I won't have you upsetting her.' Then he added, quite forcefully, 'And I'm not leaving her alone with you when you interrogate her.'

'I think "interrogate" is a bit strong, sir,' Jo replied. 'We just want to ask her a few questions, that's all.'

With that the older man turned and made to leave the room. Jo and John exchanged glances as they listened to him slowly ascend the impressive wooden staircase that both had noted on their way to the sitting room.

The detectives continued to look at each other; both seemed acutely aware that for some reason Cara's father hadn't been surprised by the reason for their visit, nor, and perhaps more importantly, that he hadn't asked the disappeared boy's identity.

A few minutes later, the father reappeared, holding his daughter's hand firmly in his own. The daughter stood, partially shielded by his body in the doorway to the room. She remained there unmoving, staring blankly in turn at the two detectives in front of her.

John noted her pale complexion, her long dark hair which hung lankly from a parting on the crown of her head. She was dressed in a pair of long-sleeved trouser pyjamas. Pyjamas, which boasted cartoon characters, thus making them childlike and a little incongruous with the eighteen-year-old girl that wore them. Judging, however, by their wear, they were old yet well-loved and therefore, like a comfort blanket, a throwback to earlier days, and something which she had probably been reluctant to part with. Despite this somewhat bedraggled appearance, to John at least, there was there was something bewitching and attractive about her. It could have been her deep-set brown eyes; her face, even with no makeup, was beguiling, and her slim figure, even in those pyjamas, would have attracted any young man's attention.

'Cara was in bed. She's not been well,' her father explained.

Could explain her absence from school, thought John.

As her father led her into the room, both John and Jo noticed that she limped slightly.

'Have you hurt yourself, Cara?' Jo asked, concerned.

It was her father who answered: 'Twisted her ankle playing hockey at school a few weeks back, nothing serious. Nearly better now, pet, isn't it?'

His daughter nodded her affirmation as he led her over to an armchair to seat her down.

'Cara.' It was Jo who spoke again. John did not interrupt,

figuring that the young girl was perhaps more likely to respond to a young female than to himself.

The girl shifted her gaze to Jo alone.

'Cara,' Jo continued, now having gained her attention, 'we want to ask you about Daniel.'

At the mention of his name the young girl glanced anxiously up at her father.

'Oh, him,' her father answered. 'Waste of space if you ask me.'

John took a step forward. 'Actually, Mr Williams, it wasn't you we wanted to ask, it was your daughter.' He knelt down to face the young lady.

She trembled visibly as he did so.

'There's nothing to be afraid of, Cara, we simply want to find him if we can. His father is worried about him.'

Cara glanced back at her father, who made a move to approach the pair but was stopped by Jo's outstretched hand.

'Now, Cara,' John continued, as her father stood still a few feet away. John looked her straight in the face and she turned away from her father and met her gaze.

Now that he had her attention, John continued. 'So, Cara. You know Daniel Wilson. Yes?'

She nodded her affirmation.

'Do you know where he is?'

Cara Williams fidgeted in her seat and then looked back up at her father, who nodded at her.

'No.' She shook her head. 'No, I don't know where he is.'

'Are you sure?'

Her father took a step forward again. 'She's just told you she doesn't know.' He sounded angry.

John turned to face him. Even though he was still on his knees and therefore was towered over by the older man, the look on John's face told him instantly that his interruption was not welcome.

Cara's father backed off.

Turning again towards the seated girl he lowered his voice a little and asked again, 'Are you sure?'

The young woman nodded, but tears started to well up in the corner of her eyes.

'Somebody told me that you were his girlfriend. Is that true?'

Again she nodded. One of the tears started to run down her cheek.

'So when did you last see him?'

'We were supposed to go to a party, but he never showed up.'

Jo got up and stood behind John. 'Would that be a party with Cathal Murphy and his mates?'

John glanced back at her in a warning. Her inexperience was showing. He hadn't wanted to give away any information, such as their awareness of Cathal, his chums and their habits, at least until Cara had mentioned them herself. Then he could have compared their stories to see if they matched. But now Cara would have concluded that they knew about Cathal and his connections and may become a bit more cautious in what she said, especially with her father hovering around.

'Yeah, he was there. I think.' She admitted nothing more.

'The party was Saturday, a week ago?'

'Something like that, yes.' Again she glanced up at her father, who by now was starting to pace back and forth across the room.

'Please sit down, Mr Williams.' Jo realised the distraction he was becoming to his daughter so led him to an upright wooden chair at the back of the room.

'And Daniel didn't turn up?'

'Yes, we'd arranged to meet there. Dad didn't like Daniel. Thought he wasn't right for me. So I arranged to meet him there rather than let Daniel come to the house.'

'That true, Mr Williams?' John swivelled around to face the now-seated father.

'As I said, in my opinion the boy was a waste of space.' He attempted to rise from the chair but was stopped from doing so as Jo stepped forward to block his path. Sitting back down again, he continued. 'That boy.' He paused momentarily. 'That boy had every advantage and he was just throwing it all away.'

'What do you mean, Mr Williams?' John was intrigued. 'Throwing it all away?'

Cara remained unmoving in her seat, staring at the floor.

Her father thought for a moment then continued. 'He was flashy, the son of a US diplomat. Had it all. Apparently top of his class at school... or at least he said he was. Then he started to hang out with that bunch of reprobates. Lost all interest in school and trying to get on in life. Just wanted to drop out. No ambition. No drive. By all accounts he was even into drugs. Then he got Cara involved. I could see that he was going to destroy her life too. He was dragging her down to his level. Cara's a good girl. She's got a good home here. Like her brother she was going to be a success in life, then along comes this Daniel Wilson and his chums and things start to fall apart.'

John looked from father to daughter and then back again. 'But I thought it was actually your son that knew Cathal Murphy?'

Cara Williams threw him a warning glance then buried her head in her hands.

'What?' her father almost shouted.

Obviously Cara's father hadn't know that his son had dealings with Cathal and his gang before Daniel had come along and that it was through him, not Daniel, that Cara had become involved.

'My son's a good boy. In fact he's at university. He'll make something of himself, mark my words. Not like that Daniel.'

'So you didn't like Daniel?' John hardly needed to ask the question; he already knew the answer. He turned back to Cara Williams. 'But you were going out with him, behind your dad's back?'

Cara nodded meekly.

Her father threw up his hands in surrender.

'But you have no idea where he is now?'

The tears were flowing freely down both cheeks as she shook her head.

*

Back in their car, the two detectives stopped at the end of the drive to compare notes.

'What did you make of that?' asked John.

'Well, the father clearly doesn't like Daniel,' Jo replied, looking out at the road.

'That much is obvious. I got the impression, though, that we didn't get full story from them. I thought that the daughter, at least, knew more than she was telling us.'

'Like things she didn't want her father to hear?'

'Probably.'

'So, you think she knows why Daniel has disappeared.'

John restarted the car, gripped the wheel and made to move off. He didn't reply to the question, preferring to remain silent, engulfed by his own thoughts. He looked left then right and manoeuvred the car out of the driveway and onto the road.

chapter seven

Jo sat across from John at his desk.

They were trying to recap and decide where to go next.

'We have to assume that Daniel's missing, not as that guy Sanders thinks, just run off for a while – not to do so leaves us open to criticism if it turns out something has happened to him.'

'Agreed,' confirmed Jo.

'If he turns up – all well and good, we've not lost anything but a few days' work.' After a moment's thought, John added, 'Okay, where should we go from here?'

It was almost a rhetorical question, but Jo answered anyway. 'I think, sir,' she added the 'sir' to make sure she got John's attention, 'that the young ones are the most likely to be able to shed some light on Daniel's disappearance. Perhaps we should start with them.'

'I agree. We haven't talked to his brother. Jake, wasn't it? And I would like to get Cara Williams on her own, or at least away from her father. He seemed to be quite controlling and I don't think she could say everything in front of him.'

'Maybe we should get Cathal in as well?'

'I doubt he'll tell us much.' John hesitated. 'Unless…'

He paused in thought and then added, 'We can get him on something first.' Rising from the desk, he grabbed his jacket as if to leave and then turned back to face Jo. 'I'll have a word with the local drug squad – I'm sure they can get something that'll allow us to bring him in.'

Jo nodded in agreement.

'In the meantime have a word with the embassy, see if you can set up a meeting with Daniel's brother.'

'Will do.'

*

Jo arranged the meeting and at the appointed hour, John and Jo arrived at the US embassy and were quickly shown through to the ambassador's office.

John smiled at Mandy as she offered them a chair each and then retreated to her own desk in the anteroom. As she left she reassured them that the ambassador would be with them directly.

John bit his lip. He didn't relish meeting the ambassador again – it was his younger son that he wanted to see – but realistically he knew that was unlikely to happen without his father being present.

After a few minutes the door opened again and in strode the ambassador, followed closely by Sanders. Behind the two of them trailed a youth who shuffled along looking nowhere but the floor.

'Mr McDaid.' It was Sanders who spoke. 'Good to see you again. Any news?'

'Not yet, sir.' John made a point of directing his answer to the ambassador himself, trying his best to ignore the FBI man's presence. 'We've conducted some enquiries, but nothing substantial to report as yet.'

The ambassador was clearly disappointed by John's response but maintained an air of authority.

'As we said on the phone, we just wanted a word with Jake, if that's alright with you, sir.'

The youth who had maintained his distance and still stood a little further back, partially shielded behind Sanders' body, flinched at the mention of his name.

'I wonder, sir, if we could talk to him alone. If that was alright with you?'

'I… I really don't think that's appropriate, Inspector. He's only a child, you know.'

Again the youth shuddered, but it was more of a shrug this time – probably at being called a child.

Jo suddenly interrupted, trying to defuse the situation before any escalation could occur. 'What if Mr Sanders stays?'

The ambassador again hesitated and glanced over at the other American.

Sanders nodded, indicating that, if required, he could be the 'responsible adult'.

John realised that Jo's intervention would indeed be helpful. Jake was more likely to open up if his father wasn't in the room, and although John didn't warm to Sanders it did seem a reasonable compromise.

Eventually, the ambassador acceded to the request and moved to leave the room. As he did so he turned to Sanders and fixed him with an expression that made it clear to the FBI man he was to protect his younger son at all costs.

John pulled the other chair around from behind the desk and suggested that Jake sit down.

The three that were seated were in a semi-circle, John and Jo either side of the teenager. Sanders remained standing, taking up position a few feet behind his charge.

Jo smiled at Jake. If anything was going to disarm him, John thought, it was a smile from his younger colleague.

Jake sat upright in the chair but tried to keep his gaze fixed on the floor, only occasionally glancing up at the two Gardai officers.

John noticed, though, that when he did so it was mainly in Jo's and not his direction.

Jake's face, still bearing the spots of adolescent acne, remained impassive. His blond hair hung limply from a crude centre parting. He wore a check shirt, jeans and worn plimsolls. From the pictures John had seen of his older brother, it was Daniel, despite his youthful appearance, who had inherited his father's strong, handsome features.

'Jake, tell me about your brother,' Jo said.

'Er, what do you want to know?' came the reply.

'What was he like? Was he happy here? Did he get on with your father and the other people in the embassy?'

'He was my brother, what more can I say? I think my father was a bit disappointed in him, though.'

'Why do you say that, Jake?'

'He was always the golden boy, but when he told Dad he didn't want to go to university, he wanted to do his own thing, it didn't go well. That's why he took the gap year – it was a sort of compromise: Daniel got some time to do what he wanted, Dad thought he'd change his mind and go to uni after all.'

'Jake, do you know anything about Daniel's disappearance?' It was John who spoke.

The young man stiffened and shuffled his feet back and forth on the floor. He didn't speak.

'Jake...?'

Finally, looking up, he spoke, though almost in a whisper. 'No. All I know is we were going to a party, but Daniel didn't show up.'

'Did you go to the party, Jake?'

'Yeah, I went. He was supposed to meet me there. But he never showed up.'

'Why didn't you go to the party together?'

Jake again tried to avoid any eye contact. 'Don't know.'

'Jake, I think you do.'

Sanders took a step forward, sensing that John's questioning was hardening. John immediately shot him a warning glance and the FBI man relented, moving back to his former position.

'He said was going to talk to somebody before the party – that's all I know.'

'Who was it, Jake?'

Jake just stared at the floor and shook his head.

'Was it Cara? Jake?'

Jake raised his head and met John's gaze for the first time. It was obvious to John that Jake had thought that he hadn't known about his brother's relationship.

'Her? Might have been, but I don't know.'

'You knew he was going out with her, though?'

'Yeah, I liked her, I thought it was quite serious. Sometimes I found her a bit clingy, but Daniel didn't mind. I think he enjoyed the adoration.' He smiled at the thought but then paused and added, 'I think he was a bit scared of her father, though. From what Daniel said her father had warned him off a couple of times.'

'But you're not sure it was her Daniel had arranged to meet up with before the party?'

'No. Mainly because she was at the party. I saw her there and she looked pretty upset, probably because Daniel wasn't there. I didn't speak to her, though.'

'Okay, so it wasn't Cara he was going to meet up with – are you sure you don't know who it was?

'I thought that he might be seeing someone else and he

was keeping it from Cara. I did think something was going on. I thought that he was keeping secrets from me as well as Cara. He had been acting funny, being a bit cagey about things recently, which wasn't like him.'

'Cagey about things. What sort of things?'

Jake seemed to think about it, pausing before replying, 'He would go out, but he wouldn't tell me where he was going or what he was doing. Then there was the money...' He stopped suddenly, realising he had let something slip that he shouldn't have.

John noticed Sanders stiffening in the background. John ignored him. 'What money, Jake?'

Jake hesitated; he glanced around at the FBI man behind him.

'Mr Sanders, like myself, is only here to help find Daniel, Jake.' He tried to reassure the teenager.

Sanders nodded in agreement.

Jake looked back to face John. 'I don't know where he got the money. All I know is he said he needed it.'

'So where is this money now, Jake? Did he have it with him when he disappeared?'

'I think so. I knew where he kept it. I looked shortly after he went off and it isn't there now. That's all I know.'

'So you really have no idea where he is, Jake?'

'Well,' again there was hesitation in his voice, 'I know that he was in contact with Emily shortly before he went missing.'

John and Jo exchanged glances. 'Who is Emily?' Jo asked.

'Our sister,' he replied.

Once again Jo and John looked at one another. There had been no mention of a sister previously.

'Tell me about Emily, Jake.'

'Um... she's our older sister. She's twenty-three. Mum had her before she met Dad.'

'So she's your half-sister?'

71

Jake nodded and then continued. 'She's a bit of a black sheep of the family. Dad doesn't approve of her behaviour, or the company she keeps. He rarely, if ever, mentions her.'

That would explain why neither of us have been told of her existence, thought John.

Jake carried on. 'Daniel, though, he'd tracked her down and been in touch with her. I know they'd been in contact quite frequently over the last few weeks.'

'So where does Emily live?'

'She's still in America. She lives somewhere in New York, I think. She left home a long time ago and Dad certainly didn't want her here. "Ruin his good standing," he said.'

A thought occurred to John. 'Could Daniel have gone to see her? Could he be in the States?'

Jake seemed to think about it for a minute or two. 'It's possible, I guess. I know he was never really happy here and his mood did pick up recently around the time he found Emily.' Then, as an afterthought: 'Maybe that was what the money was for.' Jake swivelled around to face the FBI man. 'You mustn't tell Dad. He'll be furious. Please.'

Sanders remained stony-faced.

*

After John and Jo felt they had gleaned all they could from Daniel's brother, they let him leave. As Jake closed the door behind him, John turned to Sanders and asked him if he could utilise his contacts to try and trace the sister and explore the possibility of Daniel having returned to the States.

'I'll get his dad to see if his passport is still here,' Sanders said as he turned to leave the room and seek out the ambassador once more.

'That's a start, anyway,' said John to no one in particular.

After a few minutes when John and Jo said nothing to each other but simply exchanged glances, the ambassador re-entered his office, closely followed by the FBI man.

'It's gone,' he stated bluntly.

'The passport?' John queried needlessly.

The ambassador nodded before continuing. 'I kept all the family's passports in a small safe in my office. Daniel's passport's not there.'

'You checked?'

'Yes, just now. It's definitely gone.' The ambassador started to pace across the room distractedly.

'Daniel knew the combination?' Jo asked.

'He did. Yes. I kept other paperwork and stuff in there. There were a few things of his kept in it.'

'What sort of other things?'

'Well, he had an expensive camera and sometimes if he was going on holiday he'd store his laptop in it.'

'And those things are still there?'

'The passport's gone from the safe and I can't find his laptop anywhere.'

'You said he would put his laptop in the safe if he was planning on going somewhere?' Jo asked.

'Sometimes. Yes, he would. Though like many teenagers he wasn't keen on being separated from it so often he'd take it with him. You know what young people are like.'

Jo, being not much older than Daniel, understood exactly what he was saying.

'There's more.' The ambassador moved around behind his desk and sat down. 'Once I found that the passport was missing I looked around his room. He kept a holdall under his bed. It's gone too. And I think some of his clothes are missing.'

'So he might have planned to run off, as Mr Sanders thought?'

The ambassador looked up, surprised. 'Sanders…?'

It was obvious to John and Jo that the FBI man had not previously voiced those suspicions to his boss.

John then directly engaged with the FBI man and asked him to explore the possibility that Daniel had returned to the States, though he made a deliberate point of not mentioning the errant sister.

Agent Sanders nodded his understanding.

chapter eight

The call came straight to John's mobile. He had been sitting quietly at his desk, a cup of coffee in one hand whilst reading through some unrelated reports.

'Hello?' he barked, a little annoyed at being disturbed.

He looked at the screen and, noting the American code on the incoming call, he dropped the files and put the coffee cup down gently on the desk, being careful not to spill any over the papers in front of him.

Sanders was quick to get to the point. 'We tracked down the sister. It took my colleagues a while to find her.' Then he added, by way of explanation, 'Apparently she moves around a lot. Currently, she's currently living in a tenement, in a rundown area of New York. Co-habiting with some heavy-metal guitarist.'

John detected a hint of disapproval in the tone of the agent's voice. 'Have you talked to her yet?'

'My colleagues have.'

'And…?' John grimaced; trying to get information from Sanders was like trying to get blood from a stone.

'They told me she hadn't seen him, denied any contact with him recently.'

'That's not quite what Jake said.'

'I told them that.'

'What did they say?'

'Really, they didn't want to take it any further. Told me they thought it was a waste of time.'

'Do you think she might be covering for him? We know they were in contact despite what she claims.'

'It's possible, I guess.'

'Given that his passport's missing, some clothes and a holdall are gone, and he has some money. He's gone off somewhere, he must have.'

'Okay, Tom.' He used the agent's first name in light of the favour he was about to ask. 'My boss has made this boy's disappearance a top priority given who he is. I suspect your boss has similar if not greater feelings about it.'

'Yep, the ambassador rings my superior on a daily basis.'

John suspected that the FBI were bending the chief superintendent's ear on a regular basis too, hence the priority given to John.

'Okay, Tom, do you think you could fix it for you and me to go see the sister for ourselves?'

'You mean go to New York?'

'I hardly think she's going to volunteer to fly over here and see us. Do you?'

Sanders paused. John could almost hear him thinking about the proposition. 'Okay, I'll talk to the ambassador. Given his concern, I think he'll probably be okay with it.'

'Great.' John smiled at the prospect of a trip, albeit a short one, to America's most vibrant city.

'Can you organise the travel arrangements and set up the meeting with Emily?' John bit his lip as he asked the question. If Sanders made the travel arrangements, hopefully the embassy would meet the cost. He didn't fancy his chances if he had to ask the chief superintendent to cover the expenses for the trip, especially given recent cutbacks.

Again there was a brief silence at the other end of the line. Then John detected an audible release of breath, which he hoped, was one of resignation. 'Alright, I'll get back to you. Leave it with me.'

'Hear from you soon.'

John was about to hang up, when the FBI man added, 'I'd rather take your young colleague with me, though.'

I bet you would, John thought as he smiled across at Jo seated further down the office.

She looked back at him with a questioning look.

John simply smiled and hung up without replying.

chapter nine

John rubbed the side of his face. The numbness was definitely easing; it was less intense and the sensation was starting to return, albeit slowly. However, the doctor had been right: as the dull feeling lessened, he now experienced short, lancinating stabs of pain. Each only lasted less than a second, but they were sharp and severe enough to momentarily make John stop in his tracks, particularly if there were a short series of bursts in a row.

Jo had noticed her boss involuntarily grimacing. She had commented once, asking him what was wrong, but had only received a gruff dismissal in response. She didn't ask again.

John had noticed that the pain would often kick off if he rubbed his face or even if he chewed some food. Suddenly, though, a spasm of pain shot up his face, nothing stimulating its appearance this time. He cursed silently and waited for it to pass.

He was annoyed with himself that he still had the doctor's prescription in his pocket, having initially dismissed the need for any medication. He made a mental note to get to a chemist whenever he could.

After a few minutes the pain disappeared and John relaxed.

Jo pretended not to notice that there had been any change in her boss's demeanour, given the previous dismissal

'I think it might be an idea to talk to Daniel's former teachers. What do you think, Jo?' he asked.

'Absolutely, sir. There does seem to be a lot going on with this young man before he disappeared.'

Without further need for conversation, John unrolled his shirtsleeves, buttoning them at the wrist and pulled on his jacket.

'Come on then, let's go.'

*

Daniel's school was only a mile or so from the Garda station and, given the time of day, it didn't take the pair long to drive there.

Unannounced, they presented themselves in front of the school secretary. She had been relatively easy to locate by simply following the signs from the school entrance to the headmaster's office.

Having introduced themselves and proffered their warrant cards John requested an interview with the headmaster.

Looking up from her desk, the secretary fixed the two detectives with a cold stare and the beginnings of a frown.

After a moments confrontational silence finally she spoke. 'This is most irregular,' she squinted at the warrant card, 'Inspector McDaid.'

'Mr Houston is a busy man. He has a full schedule today. In fact he's teaching the lower sixth in fifteen minutes.'

John wasn't going to be bullied, even by a woman clearly used to acting as her boss's gatekeeper. 'We have had a report of a missing teenager.' Then he added, a little needlessly, given where they were, but certainly emphasising the point, 'A former pupil at this school until quite recently, we believe.'

The secretary, John guessed, was in her late fifties, her hair cut in a bob but with a dyed dark reddish and unnatural tinge. She was dressed, John thought, if a bit unkindly, a little younger than her years, in a verdant green dress stretching down below her knees and a large and chunky wooden beaded necklace hanging loosely around her neck.

After a moment's consideration, the secretary seemed to back down, albeit reluctantly, at this information. She was clearly used to shielding her boss from unexpected interruptions, and, John thought, quite proficient at it.

She rose slowly from her desk, still looking sourly at the pair, before turning and knocking at the headmaster's door behind her.

John tried to reassure her: 'We won't keep him long.'

Nonplussed, the secretary spoke briefly with the still obscured occupant of the room but then turned back to them and ushered them in. As John and Jo moved to pass her she backed away; Jo, looking back, noted her quietly withdrawing to her earlier position, once again acting as gatekeeper to the inner sanctum.

As they entered the office, the headmaster rose from behind his impressive mahogany desk in greeting, then indicated a couple of chairs for them to sit in.

The headmaster was a man in his early sixties, slightly rotund but with a fresh, smiling complexion and not quite the authoritarian figure that John had experienced from his own school days, nor quite what he had expected having met the headmaster's secretary.

Once introduced and after a brief handshake, he repositioned himself behind his desk and asked, in a generally friendly and disarming way, 'What can I do for you officers?'

John, before replying, noted the bamboo cane hanging from a small hook on the wall behind the headmaster. *Perhaps,* he thought, *Mr Houston wasn't quite as benign a figure as he liked to portray.*

'It's concerning Daniel Wilson,' John confirmed.

'Ah, Yes. I thought it might be. His father's people have already been in touch.'

By 'his father's people' John guessed he meant Sanders or one of his cronies. He exchanged a look with Jo.

'Daniel's gone missing,' John confirmed.

The headmaster nodded and then asked how he could help.

'We hopefully won't keep you too long, I know you have a class to get to—'

'Don't worry, I've sent asked Mrs Perry to ask if one of the other teachers who's on a break if they can go down and hold the fort. I'm sure they can think of something to occupy them until I get there.'

John had little doubt that Mrs Perry, even after the very brief encounter he had had with her, would make sure that somebody gave up their break time to sort the headmaster's class out.

'Can you give us any background on Daniel?' Jo asked.

'I didn't know him that well, but I did try to keep an eye on him.'

Before John could speak the headmaster continued. 'I taught him in only one class, mathematics, not his best subject, if truth be told, but I did hear that he was particularly interested in art. From all accounts he was quite good at it.'

'You said you tried to keep an eye on him?'

'Yes, his father had asked me to,' came the reply, a bit defensively.'I believe he was a bit worried about him.' He went on to explain, 'His mother had died relatively recently, you know, and not long afterwards his father had brought Daniel to live over here.'

'I understand,' sympathised John.

'Yes, it can be very hard for a teenager, losing a parent and then losing all your friends as well.'

'How did you find him, Mr Houston?' asked Jo.

'Initially, I think he found it difficult, but then he seemed to make some friends and things improved.'

'Cara Williams? She was one of his friends?' continued Jo.

'You're well informed, Ms… Er?'

'Roberts.'

'Yes, Ms Roberts, they seemed quite close. She was in the class below his. Daniel's mood and demeanour certainly seemed to improve when she came on the scene.'

John leant forward to interrupt. 'Daniel's brother Jake said that he thought Daniel might be seeing somebody else?'

'I don't know anything about that, I'm afraid. He always seemed happiest when Cara was around.' He paused, as if gathering his thoughts. 'Or at least it seemed so.'

'You seem to question how just how happy he was?' John was intrigued.

'Well, in the last couple of terms at St Columba's Daniel had become more withdrawn, preoccupied. His schoolwork had certainly tailed off.' The headmaster leant forward across his desk to access his computer keyboard and then, with a few deft strokes, brought up a spreadsheet on the screen and turned it towards the two officers. He pointed to a line on the spreadsheet: 'See.'

John and Jo squinted to see what he was indicating.

Realising their difficulty making out what he was indicating, he clarified for them: 'You see here?' He pointed again. 'Daniel, when he first arrived a year or so ago, we had to put him into one of the first-year of the leaving certificate classes, when given his age, his peers, would all be a year ahead, in their second and final year of the course.'

'How did that go?'

'Well, despite all that, Daniel seemed to do well and in fact he was near the top of the class at one point. Then...' He paused.

John and Jo moved closer still.

'Here,' the headmaster continued, realising he had their full attention. 'His marks started to fall off. Then there was absenteeism. See here, a number of days off. No explanation. We did send a message to his father, but we didn't get a response. To be brutally honest I thought his father was maybe part of the problem.'

John forward. 'Why do you say that, Mr Houston?'

The teacher hesitated, then as if making his mind up, he replied, 'I probably shouldn't say this, but...'

'But?' John pushed him.

'In any meeting I had with Daniel's father it was quite clear that his and Daniel's perceptions of life after school differed widely.'

John encouraged him to continue with a small nod of the head.

'The father clearly thought Daniel should pursue a professional career. Go to university, study law and emerge as a lawyer or barrister, or something equivalent.'

'And what did Daniel want for himself?' Jo asked.

'He knew that he had the ability, we knew it too, to go to university. But he didn't seem to want to go down that route. I think he lost heart – that's why his classwork fell off.'

'What do you think he actually did want to do, Mr Houston?' John took control of the conversation again.

'As I said his marks fell off at school, but in the end he did get reasonable leaving certificate results. He could have got into a university, not a top one, but a university nonetheless.'

'But he didn't go?'

'No, I talked to him. It was clear during the conversation that Daniel had, at least at that time, not intended to follow in his father's footsteps. He regarded himself as a free spirit. If he liked anything it was his art. Given time and the encouragement he might have gone to art school, but his father wouldn't hear of it, thought it a complete waste of time and money. In the end they had agreed that Daniel took a gap year to try and sort his head out. I think that was probably a good idea. I would have liked to hear how it was going, what Daniel was up to, but we lost touch. I suppose he thought he'd left school behind him and didn't want anything more to do with us.'

'His father did say that he thought he'd become more unsettled again recently, but he didn't know why,' Jo added by way of explanation.

'We have heard something about drug use. Do you know anything about that, Mr Houston?'

The headmaster looked aghast. 'Certainly not.' He straightened and gripped the desk. 'We do not – I repeat, not – tolerate drugs at St Columba's. If Daniel got into drugs it must have been after he left the school.'

'Mr Houston, we are not trying to suggest anything.' John tried to ameliorate the teacher. 'We have been told by other witnesses that Daniel might have experimented with drugs at one time.'

'I don't know anything about that. We have a zero-tolerance policy on drugs at St Columba's. But we all do have to recognise that young people these days do get up to things, things of which we may not approve, but in their own time.'

It was clear to John that the headmaster was trying to put some distance between the establishment for which he was responsible and any wrongdoing.

'I do accept what you are saying, Mr Houston, but can I

ask, in your experience, could dabbling with drugs account for sudden changes in mood?'

The headmaster sat back in his seat and released his grip on the desk. After taking a few minutes in thought, he replied, 'Yes, Detective Inspector, I think that that can happen.' But he quickly added defensively, 'In theory, of course. There was no way that we could have or would have suspected Daniel of dabbling in drugs when he was with us.'

John and Jo exchanged a sceptical look.

'Is there anybody else you think we could talk to?' asked John.

'Miss Bailie was his form teacher. She would probably know him as well as anybody here.'

'Could we talk to her?'

'I'll ask Mrs Perry to see if she's available.' He rose and left the office to see firstly if his secretary had accomplished her mission in getting his class covered.

On returning he confirmed, 'You're in luck. She on a free period – Mrs Perry is going to ask her to come over.' He had remained standing near the door as he spoke. 'Look, I better go and sort this class of mine out. You can wait for Miss Bailie in my office if you like, but I'd better go.'

Despite his offer, he remained standing by the door for a few moments as if debating whether he actually should leave the two detectives alone in his office.

Making his mind up, he turned to leave before swivelling around and adding, 'I'll get Mrs Perry to bring you some tea, or coffee if you prefer.'

'Tea would be fine,' replied John, thinking to himself that Mrs Perry didn't strike him as the type to offer refreshments to unheralded visitors.

The two sat in silence and it was a few minutes after the headmaster had left that the headmaster's secretary pushed the door open again and entered the room. She was carrying a tray bearing two cups, a jug of milk and a small plate containing two digestive biscuits.

'Compliments of the headmaster,' she said stiffly. She set the tray down on the headmaster's desk in front of them and turned to leave.

Before she could do so, John got up to hold the door open for her, but he also moved so as to block her path. 'I don't suppose you can shed any light on Daniel Wilson's disappearance, Mrs Perry?'

She regarded him stiffly, clearly annoyed at the question. 'It's not my place,' she said quietly, trying to manoeuvre around him.

John held his ground. He suspected that Mrs Perry knew a lot more about what went on in the school than her boss did. He suspected she was a nosey kind of person and that it was she who kept the headmaster up to date with the day-to-day running of the daily timetables, the activity of the teachers and pupils alike. She would, after all, have access to all areas and not, as Mr Houston would, cause people in her vicinity to be careful in their words and actions. Secretaries, even ones as formidable as Mrs Perry, would often be invisible to other employees, regarding her simply as one of their own.

Mrs Perry refrained from trying to fruitlessly sidestep the detective and stood, as if pondering what to do next. Finally she spoke, fixing John in her gaze. 'All I know – and this goes no further, you understand – that Daniel was a nice young boy. Or at least he was when he first arrived. He even started going out with a girl from the school.'

'Cara Williams?'

'That's her.'

'He seemed happy?'

'At first, yes. But later I didn't think things were right.'

'What do you mean, not right?'

'I saw something.'

'You saw something?'

'What was it you saw, Mrs Perry?' added Jo, trying to back up John's line of questioning.

Before she could answer a young woman appeared in the outer office and approached the door where John and Mrs Perry were standing.

'Ah, Miss Bailie,' muttered the relieved secretary, switching her gaze and looking over John's shoulder.

John stepped aside, allowing Mrs Perry to leave. As she did so, she made a point of introducing the newcomer. 'Miss Bailie, Daniel's form teacher.' Then, turning to the younger woman: 'Miss Bailie, these are two detectives – they are here to investigate Daniel Wilson's disappearance.' Then she added, somewhat unnecessarily, 'He was in your class, I believe.' Without saying anything further the secretary took her leave, only briefly glancing over her shoulder towards John.

Miss Bailie was a petite brunette with a fresh, open expression; she was not John's perceived image of a form teacher. Certainly not one that he had encountered in his own school days. *Clearly*, he thought, *times have changed*. Miss Bailie, he was sure, was a woman that any impressionable young teenager might find it difficult not to hang on to every word that she said. But then he corrected himself, admitting that he was probably just being misogynistic.

'Call me Sarah,' said the young woman, extending her hand.

John shook it, noting the soft, warm skin. He couldn't help smiling as he did so.

Out of the corner of his eye he caught a glimpse of Jo rising from her seat, to also greet the young teacher. But as she did so she turned and fixed John with a quizzical gaze.

They all sat down; this time John took the headmaster's chair on the other side of the desk but sat back quietly to allow Jo to start the questioning. He had decided that the teacher could probably relate better to Jo than himself, being the same sex and nearer the young woman's age. Besides he had to admit he was happy to simply observe.

After around twenty minutes of questioning they came to the conclusion that the form teacher was not able to add any further information to what had already been said. She had confirmed Daniel's perceived change of mood but had no idea why this had occurred.

They let her return to her duties. John got up quickly to open the door for her and smiled as she exited; the young teacher returned the smile.

Closing the door behind her, John turned to his companion. Jo was scowling at him, arms folded in front of her.

'What…?' exclaimed John, arms outstretched.

'You know… Down, boy.' Jo got up and led him out of the office, striding ahead.

As they passed Mrs Perry's desk she sat impassively watching the two leave. John hesitated, then turned to face the secretary. 'In the headmaster's office you said you saw something?' He stood upright in front of her desk. Jo heard the question and stopped, listening, waiting for an answer.

The secretary, despite her previous controlling personality, seemed to diminish a little and squirmed in her chair. She took a few seconds to answer as if debating whether she should do so. 'Well, I really don't know if I should say.' She paused again. 'But the boy has gone missing.'

'Anything you can do to help, Mrs Perry, will be appreciated.' Jo spoke reassuringly from the outer office door.

'Well, I saw him having coffee with a girl one day…' She paused before adding, 'Not his girlfriend.'

'Not Cara?' John quickly asked.

'No, definitely not her. It was another girl. I was out shopping. I saw the two of them going into a local café. I recognised Daniel from the school. I didn't recognise her. I'm sure she's not a pupil at this school. In fact she looked older than Daniel.'

'And they were together, are you sure?'

'Definitely, they were huddled over a table in the café as I walked past. Deep in conversation.'

'Can you describe her?'

'Small, fair skin, dark hair. Actually quite smartly dressed. That's why I thought she was older than Daniel. Probably early twenties.'

'Smartly dressed, you say, Mrs Perry?' It was John who had once again taken up the questioning.

'Long coat, over a short dress, high heels. That's all I remember.'

'Anything else you noticed, Mrs Perry? Anything at all.'

'Not really, they just seemed deep in conversation.' She paused again before continuing. 'That's what annoyed me and why I remember it.'

'What annoyed you?' John leant over her desk.

The secretary shrank back. 'Well, he had a girlfriend, didn't he? Cara. She seemed so happy.' Then she added, almost as an afterthought, 'And I thought he was happy too. So I thought, why was he cheating on her? No good will come of it.'

'You are sure he was cheating on Cara?'

'As they left the café they walked down the road and they certainly seemed to have a lot to talk about. What else would he be meeting her for? Teenagers often have a thing about older women, don't they?'

John straightened up, and he and Jo exchanged glances, both wondering if there was anything else to ask the secretary.

Jo stepped forward. 'Did you ever see her again, Mrs Perry?'

'After Daniel had left school I thought I saw them together again a couple of times – each time Daniel seemed quite animated. The last time I saw them together they were standing outside a building on Abbey Street just before they disappeared inside.'

'When was that?'

'It was the afternoon before Daniel went missing.'

'And you've not spoken of this to anyone else?'

'Certainly not. It's not really any of my business, is it? But now the poor boy's disappeared I thought you should know.'

'You didn't mention it to Cara, his girlfriend?'

'No. I thought I should have, but no I didn't. Especially with her...' She stopped speaking; John thought he spotted a small, uncharacteristic tear in the corner of her eye. 'Maybe I should have said something. Maybe then Daniel wouldn't have gone off.'

'Why didn't you say anything to him or Cara?'

'It was not my place. I am not an old busybody, you know. He is an adult, what he gets up to is his affair. And besides, Cara's father...' She stopped in her tracks again.

'Cara's father?' John repeated.

After a few moments, the secretary regained her confidence and then spoke, still a little shakily. 'Have you met him?'

John nodded.

'Well, then you'll know. He's not the easiest man in the world to get on with. He's very protective, overprotective of his daughter in particular, if you ask me.'

'How do you know this?' Jo asked.

'Mr Houston has had a few run-ins with him. He's just burst in here, no appointment, demanding to see the headmaster over some trivial upset of his daughter, and I've come across him at parent-teacher meetings. To me he comes

across as quite threatening towards staff. Especially those
that he thinks don't praise Cara's school performance highly
enough.'

*

As they exited the school, John turned to Jo.

'A bit to think about,' he mused.

'And which particular interviewee are you thinking about?'
Jo laughed as she lowered herself into the car.

chapter ten

Back in the office later that afternoon, John sat, head lowered, elbows on his desk and head supported by his hands. He felt unusually tired for the time of day.

Must be getting old, he thought.

In the past he would have boundless energy, especially when investigating an intriguing and as yet unsolved case.

He yawned inadvertently. As he did so there was a sudden dart of pain up the side of his face. It made him wince.

He rubbed his cheek, but that only seemed to stimulate another spasm. Then another.

Reaching into his pocket he retrieved the capsules that the doctor had prescribed. He had been reluctant to take any, but now he thought he should.

Within half an hour the pain had subsided, though he still felt fatigued.

He resolved to go and see the GP again tomorrow.

As he mulled over things, he became aware of Jo standing on the opposite side of his desk.

'Do you think the time has come…?' she asked.

'Come for what?' John interrupted, a bit tetchily, annoyed by his tiredness and the facial pain.

'Sorry, just trying to be helpful.' Jo retreated, a little hurt by his tone.

John quickly replied, 'No, it's me who should be sorry. I'm just a little tired, that's all. I shouldn't have spoken to you like that. I'm sorry.'

Jo held her silence for a moment, then, seemingly forgiving him, she asked again, 'Do you think it's time?' Then she paused before adding, 'To run a poster campaign? *Missing person, have you seen this boy?* That sort of thing?'

John thought only for a few seconds. He knew she was right; they had to move things on. 'I'll talk to his father. I'm sure he'll agree.'

At that Jo turned to leave. As she did so John called after her, 'Sorry again.' He really had not meant to be so sharp.

Definitely time to see the doctor again.

He tried ringing the surgery and got the same receptionist as before. This time, however, she was not as forthcoming with an early appointment. Apparently, having misdiagnosed him on the previous occasion, she wasn't going to be caught out again. 'I have nothing available until next week,' she informed him. 'I take it you want to see Dr Finlay again?'

'I guess I should. He knows my case.' Then, sniggering, he added, 'Or at least my casebook.'

'Mmmm…' replied the receptionist, clearly not amused. 'Next Tuesday, 2pm.'

She didn't wait for confirmation and merely hung up, presuming that John would make time to be there.

As he put down the phone, Jo knocked softly on the frame of the open door to his office. John lifted his head and beckoned her in with cursory wave of his hand.

'The drug squad have arrested Cathal Murphy. He's down below.'

'That was quick.' John sat back in his seat, hands behind his head.

'Well.' Jo hesitated. 'It might have been something I said. I have a friend in narcotics.'

'Best I don't know,' John confirmed. 'Anyway, he's here now.' 'Do you think they'll let us speak to him?'

Jo nodded. 'But we need to be careful. I don't think their boss knows about our involvement. And I don't want to get anyone into trouble.'

'Discretion is my middle name.' John was already on his feet and making for the door. 'Second floor? I presume.'

Again Jo nodded and then turned to follow him.

*

The second floor of the Garda Siochana headquarters was the drug squad's domain. It was laid out much as any of the other floors but was inhabited by men and women who looked, dressed and behaved very differently from the regular Gardaí in the other divisions. John had always found it difficult to distinguish the good guys from the criminals, but he guessed that was the whole point of this division: to blend in and integrate with those who dealt and used illegal substances.

As the pair made their way across the outer office floor a large bearded man, in a checked shirt hanging over a pair of jeans that had seen better days, stepped out of an inner office and greeted them. 'Jo, good to see you. Hope they're looking after you upstairs.' He turned to John, extending his hand. 'DI McDaid, I've heard a lot about you.'

'All good, I hope.'

Without answering the question and as he released John's hand, he continued, 'I'm detective Inspector McGrath, Johnny McGrath.'

'Pleased to meet you, Johnny.' Then he continued. 'Jo tells me you have Cathal Murphy in custody?'

'We do indeed,' Johnny McGrath confirmed.

'Do you think it would be possible for us to have a word with him before you formally charge him?' John fidgeted as he asked the question; he knew that what he was asking was irregular.

'Mmmm...' The other man scratched his chin as if in thought, but then he turned slightly and winked at Jo. 'One good turn deserves another, I guess.'

It was Jo's turn to fidget.

'Where is he?' John was tiring of this subterfuge. He knew Jo had tipped McGrath off and McGrath had probably guessed that John already knew.

'Okay, I'll take you down to him.' Then, lowering his voice to make sure nobody else in the department could overhear what he said, he added, 'As I told Jo, you scratch my back, I'll scratch yours.' Again he winked in Jo's direction.

This time John noticed that Jo winced at the analogy.

'Let's go.' He turned and, gesturing for them to follow, he led them out of the office past the bemused looks of others present, and down the stairs at the far end.

'I've put him in one of the interrogation rooms and left him to sweat.' He looked down at his watch. 'He's been there about an hour, so he should be getting pretty fed up by now.'

Standing outside the interrogation room, the three observed Cathal Murphy through the one-way glass window. Cathal was sitting at a desk in the otherwise bare, grey monochromatic room which measured only about ten feet by ten feet. There was only one other person in the room, a uniformed Garda constable who stood stiffly by the door.

Cathal nervously chewed at his nails, inspecting each one in turn each after a few minutes' nibbling at them.

'He's all yours,' Johnny McGrath announced, turning to leave. 'You've got thirty minutes. No longer, mind. The inspector will be back by then.' And then he added, probably unnecessarily given the subterfuge so far, 'He won't be best pleased if he learns that I've let you interrogate one of our suspects before we've had a chance to do so ourselves.' With that he left the pair to get on with it.

As John entered the room, the uniformed constable stepped aside silently.

Cathal Murphy rose to his feet, gripping the desk and knocking his chair backwards as he did so. Anger was written all over his face. 'What have you arrested me for?' He shouted the question even though John and Jo were by now only feet away from him.

'Sit down, Cathal,' John replied calmly, taking his own seat across the table from the suspect. Jo followed suit and lowered herself into the seat beside John.

Cathal Murphy remained standing, leaning over the table, by now red in the face. He remained silent and motionless, apart from a small dribble of saliva, the consequence of his earlier outburst that slowly moved down from the corner of his mouth.

After a few minutes as John and Jo remained silent and simply looking back at him with blank expressions, Cathal Murphy seemed to realise the futility of his stance. He wiped the small patch of saliva away with the back of his hand and, albeit reluctantly, sat down once again.

'Look, Cathal, by all accounts we've got you banged to rights. Possession, with intent to sell.'

'Those drugs were for my own personal use,' Cathal interrupted quickly.

'Again, Cathal. You've got form.' John pulled a folded charge sheet out of his jacket pocket. It was one he had printed off earlier when Cathal Murphy's name had come up in the investigation.

'Let's see,' John mumbled, going down the list printed on the sheet. 'Possession of an illegal substance, supplying an illegal substance, possession again. Oh, I see here assault of a Garda officer while in the line of his duty, evading arrest... need I go on?'

Cathal just stared back, stony-faced.

John leant forward to confront Cathal directly. 'My guess, Cathal, is that you are looking at one to three years with all this previous.' He laid the sheet down on the desk so that the list of offences was visible.

'What do you think, Jo?'

Jo simply nodded, though she knew that despite the extensive list of offences it was unlikely that Cathal would face a custodial sentence given the small amount of drugs he'd been apprehended with. She also recognised, though, the game that John was playing.

'Look, Cathal, here's the rub.' He continued to lean forward to get even closer to Cathal, who by now was steadfastly looking down at the floor to avoid John's gaze. 'We are not really interested in the drugs.'

Cathal Murphy looked up quizzically.

'We are trying to trace that boy, the ambassador's son, Daniel Wilson, remember?'

Cathal nodded slowly.

'So if you can help us a bit with where he might be, we'll have a word with Inspector McGrath and see what we can do to help you. What do you think, Cathal? One good turn deserves another?' He glanced in Jo's direction, knowing he had used the same phrase that the other detective had used to acknowledge Jo's help.

Jo remained sitting passively, ignoring the comment.

Cathal shuffled his feet and drummed his fingers on the desk as if trying to come some kind of decision. Finally he looked John square in the face and said, 'Okay, if I tell you all I know you keep it to yourselves.' His eyes darted over to Jo as if to ensure that she was included in the deal. 'I'm no snitch.'

'We know that, Cathal,' replied John reassuringly. 'We just want to find this young man, that's all.'

Cathal seemed to retreat into thought once more. After a few moments he lowered his head and in a low and almost mumbling voice he spoke. 'I did meet this Daniel Wilson, the American guy.'

John nodded, encouraging Cathal Murphy to continue.

'I met him through Michael Williams – Daniel was going out with his sister.'

'Cara?' asked Jo, who had remained silent up to this point.

'Like I told you last time, yeah.'

'Last time you also told us that Daniel was into drugs as well, Cathal. Is that correct?'

'Yeah,' Cathal growled. 'So what? Most people our age are. There's no harm in that, is there?'

'Some people might disagree with that statement, Cathal,' John affirmed.

'Maybe so. But so what?'

Changing tack slightly, John asked, 'How well did you know Daniel, Cathal?'

Cathal lowered his gaze down onto the floor once more. 'I didn't really know him. As I said I'd only met him once or twice through Michael and Cara. I just knew him to see, that's all.'

John noticed that despite Cathal's attempts to avoid his gaze, he had blinked repeatedly as he spoke. From his years of interrogating criminals, John took this as a sure sign that Cathal was lying. There must have been more to their relationship that the younger man was admitting to.

'What about Daniel's father – he knew about the drugs, though, didn't he?' It was Jo who spoke.

John shot her a warning glance; her inexperience was showing again. He didn't want her to interrupt Cathal's flow. Just let him get on with it. That was the way to go. Keep your powder dry, don't let them know what you know until towards end of the interview, then hit them with the questions. That way you can detect any inconsistences and any obvious lies within their testimony.

'No idea,' Cathal replied defiantly.

Quickly John made a decision to keep pushing Cathal, so as not to allow him to clam up. 'Okay, Cathal. You know we can help you here. You help us, we'll do what we can for you.'

Cathal seemed to relent.

'Regarding Daniel's drug habit—'

'I didn't say he had a *habit* – he just used them now and again, that's all.'

'Yes, but Cathal, last time we talked you said Daniel owed money. So maybe it was just a bit more than once or twice?'

'Well… yes… but…' Cathal was blinking furiously now.

'Who did he owe money to, Cathal? Was it you?'

Cathal sat back; a look of astonishment came over his face. 'Whoa there. I don't deal drugs. No way. You're not pinning that on me.'

'In this charge sheet,' John turned the sheet around so Cathal could read it, 'there is at least one mention of "intent to supply".'

Cathal held his hand up, palm towards John. 'I was fitted up on that one. One of your colleagues wanted to teach me a lesson, because I wouldn't tell him who my supplier was, so he pinned that on me. I don't deal.' As he spoke he remained wide-eyed and didn't blink once.

John was inclined to believe him. 'So who did he owe money to?'

Once again Cathal slumped into silence.

The three sat in silence for a number of minutes. Jo now knew not to jump in.

Finally Cathal spoke. 'I didn't tell you this, okay?' He looked back and forth between John and Jo.

They both nodded their agreement.

'I heard that he bought some stuff from Paddy Boswell and his clan.'

'The Romany Boswells?'

'That's them. Most of us keep away from them. They're dangerous.'

'But not Daniel?'

'He was arrogant, I didn't like him much. He thought he was better than all of us, knew more than any of us. But the Boswells turned him over.'

'Turned him over?'

'I heard that they sold him some fake grass and when Daniel confronted them they denied it and threatened him to pay up or else.'

Cathal was in full flow now. John glanced at Jo to ensure there were no further interruptions.

'Anyways, they thought that he owed them money, but he was holding out. I think he thought that because they were travelling people they'd just move away before he'd have to pay them. I warned him. Told him, it didn't work like that. That those people don't do debt. He wouldn't listen.'

John sat back to think about what Cathal had just told him. Then after a few seconds more he asked, 'So what did he do with the money then? If he didn't pay off the Boswells?'

Cathal looked shocked. 'What money? I don't know anything about any money.'

John nodded at Jo, indicating for her to step in.

'By all accounts when he disappeared he had some money with him.'

'I don't know anything about any money,' repeated Cathal, who now sweated profusely. Then, after a moment's thought: 'Maybe he paid off Paddy Boswell after all.'

After a few more perfunctory questions, John felt he'd got all he could out of Cathal Murphy. He swivelled around in his seat and waved towards the glass mirrored window behind him, indicating that McGrath and his team could now have Cathal back.

'You'll put a good word in for me?' pleaded Cathal.

John didn't reply but nodded his affirmation.

chapter eleven

Back at the station John and Jo weighed up what they knew and tried to decide their next move.

'We could talk to the Boswells,' suggested Jo.

'We could, but to be honest I don't think we'll get much from them. It's highly unlikely that they'll admit to suppling drugs to Daniel and less so to having anything to do with his disappearance. We'll put it on the to-do list anyway, I guess. Any other thoughts?'

Jo paused for a moment in thought then replied, 'We could try and find out where he got that money he was seen with.' Then she added, 'But where would we start?'

As they continued to share their thoughts, there was a loud rap on the door.

'Yes,' shouted John in reply somewhat irritably, annoyed at having his chain of thought interrupted.

A young detective stuck his head round the door. 'There's an American chap here to see you, Inspector. Won't take no for an answer.'

John rose from his desk and opened the door. Sanders, the FBI man, was standing at the far end of the open office space looking around impatiently. Spotting John he waved and then unbidden started to make his way past the jumble of desks. The young detective moved to block his progress, but John restrained him, putting a hand on his arm.

'It's okay. I know him. I'll talk to him.'

With that the younger man withdrew and John ushered Sanders into his office.

Walking back around his desk and sitting himself down opposite the FBI man, he glanced at Jo, who had got up to give the American her seat.

'So what can I do for you, Mr Sanders?' John asked.

'It's more what I can do for you, Inspector McDaid,' Sanders replied, smiling smugly.

'Oh, yes?' asked John. 'What's that?'

'Well, you asked about going over to New York.'

John regarded the other man quizzically.

'It's on. The ambassador says if you think it will shed some light on his son's disappearance then he's prepared to sanction it.'

'That's good news.' John couldn't help smiling at the thought of a trip to the Big Apple, work or not. 'When can we go?'

'I thought the sooner the better, so I've booked flights for tomorrow. Then back after the weekend. Suit you okay?'

John thought for a moment and then consulted his phone diary. 'Yep, should be okay. You can hold the fort here, can't you, Jo? I'll clear it with the inspector, though as he's not paying for it, should be okay.'

After Sanders had gone through the arrangements and confirmed that Daniel's sister had indeed agreed to see them, he got up and left, simply nodding at Jo as he made his way out of the inner office.

'Well, there's a turn up for the books.' John whistled, leaning back in his chair.

'Would you like a towel, sir?' asked Jo, looking down on him.

'A towel?' John looked bemused.

'To wipe the smug smile off your face.'

'Oh, ha, ha. All in the line of duty.'

'If you say so, sir.' Jo was unconvinced.

John decided not to pursue the conversation any further, rather turning attention to matters in hand. 'I'll take the opportunity to push Sanders to see if he or his colleagues can shed any light on that money that Daniel was supposed to have. He couldn't have had much opportunity to get it from anywhere else but inside the embassy. Now that Sanders knows about it, I'll bet your bottom dollar that he's investigated it. Hopefully I'll be able to get some info on it from him.'

'What will I do while you are off gallivanting?'

'Hardly gallivanting, Detective Roberts.'

'You know what I mean.'

'Let's be professional about this. Why don't you try the Boswells anyway, despite what we said before?' But then he quickly added, thinking better of it, 'Take uniform with you. The Boswells are not likely to be the friendliest people you are likely to meet.'

'I think I can handle it.'

'Just be careful, that's all I'm saying.'

'Message received and understood.'

'When I get back, depending on what the sister says, we'll have another go at the girlfriend and his brother, Jake. That is if we don't find him shacked up over there, of course.'

chapter twelve

John was up early the next day. He packed a small carry-on packed with sufficient supplies to last him the few days he was to be away. A change of underwear, a couple of clean shirts and some toiletries. John was not a man unduly conscious of his appearance.

He reached the airport in good time to check in but found that Sanders had beaten him to it and was standing waiting for him in the departures hall. The American made a point of looking at his watch, pulling his sleeve up to emphasise the action. 'Cutting it fine, aren't you?'

'That's us Irish – we like nothing better than a bit of queuing,' he said over his shoulder as he moved to join the sneaking queue at the Aer Lingus check-in desk.

Sanders looked at him unappreciatively, then stepped forward, tapping him on the shoulder.

John turned to see Sanders pointing to a nearly deserted desk at the far end of the check-in area.

'What?' asked John.

'Not here. Down there,' indicated the FBI man again.

'But that's reserved for business…?' Then, after a pause: 'You mean we're travelling business class?' John struggled to suppress his excitement. As a humble Garda officer he'd never had the opportunity of an upgrade before. But he didn't want Sanders to necessarily know that.

John heaved his bag over his shoulder and exited the crowd, circumnavigating the group of people that quickly pushed forward in an attempt to claim the space he had just vacated.

A smile from the check-in girl as she accepted the offered boarding pass and he turned to re-join his American colleague to make their way to the business lounge before departure.

Arriving at the lounge and being again greeted by an unaccustomed smile from the attendant, John realised why Sanders had been impatient for his arrival. The lounge offered free food and drinks to sustain them through at least the initial part of the flight until the on-board service kicked in.

John, though technically on duty, suddenly felt that he was going to enjoy this trip.

* .

Arriving into the John F Kennedy International Airport and as the plane manoeuvred onto its parking bay, John had time to reflect on the journey, but more importantly on the reason for the trip. He had deliberately and with considerable self-control declined the offers of on-board alcoholic drinks. Sanders did similarly but, John suspected, with less effort and willpower than he himself had exerted.

Tired and exhausted, John felt the jet lag starting to click in; he disembarked and made his way through the airport, security and customs checks. Those for visitors to the States being somewhat tighter than those for returning US citizens, he found Sanders waiting for him in the arrivals hall already clutching a half-consumed mug of coffee.

'What kept you?' he asked, a smile on his face.

'Your compatriots,' John replied somewhat wearily. 'They seemed to actually think I might want to stay here.'

Sanders didn't rise to the jibe. Rather, he simply turned dropping the cardboard coffee cup into a nearby rubbish bin and strode towards the exit. 'Come on, no time to waste. We'll take a cab and check into the hotel, then we've an appointment with the local cops,' he looked down at his watch, 'in just over one hour.'

As the taxi made its way slowly through downtown New York, negotiating the heavy city traffic, John stared at the rows of skyscrapers that made up the central areas of New York. They were as he suspected how New York should look but were actually in marked contrast to the more modest two-storey houses that populated the city suburbs which they'd passed through on the way from the airport.

The hotel was the Broadway Inn, but not like any inn that John knew from home. It was a brown-bricked cube of five storeys in height, surmounted by a further but slightly smaller cube of another five storeys, which itself was topped with what looked, as John bent his head back and squinted, trying to take in the entire structure, like a penthouse.

Sanders pulled the luggage from the car boot – or trunk, as he called it – dropped John's case on the sidewalk and made his own way into hotel reception, leaving John to pay the cab driver.

As the two, now reunited, stood in the hotel check-in queue, Sanders explained the hotel was one that his department frequently used to put up interns and visitors as it was comfortable and functional if not the most high class of hotels in New York. John simply shrugged; it wasn't as if they were here for very long and he hoped in any case that they wouldn't be in the hotel much anyway.

As they reached the top of the queue, John watched his American companion sign the register but make the point that the tab was to be picked up by his department. He then took the key card from the receptionist and moved off towards the lift. John stepped forward, putting his hand out expectantly. The receptionist gave him a quizzical look.

'Sir?' he asked.

'My key card, please.' John requested politely.

'Mr Sanders has it, sir,' came the reply, pointing towards the FBI man, who was waving at John to follow as the lift doors opened. It was then John realised he was sharing with Sanders – not a scenario he relished.

They didn't speak on the way to the twelfth floor. Sanders stood upright, just back from the doors as the lift ascended; John lurked just behind him.

The room was pleasant enough and boasted spectacular views over the city. John dropped his bag on the floor beside the bed nearest the window and then threw himself onto the bed itself. He was feeling more and more under the effects of jet lag. It was just after 6pm here in New York, but 11pm back home.

He was about to have a snooze, when Sanders, clearly more used to dealing with long-haul travel, shook him and said, 'No time for that. We need to go and see the detective that interviewed the sister. We'll leave her till tomorrow, but I'd like to hear what she told the police here first, so that we're ready for her.'

John wearily threw his legs over the side of the bed, rubbed his eyes and rose to his feet.

'Anyway,' Sanders added, 'staying awake till New York night-time is the best way to beat jet lag.'

John just stared back at him and then, somewhat reluctantly, followed his new partner out through the door and back down the corridor to the lift.

Out on the street again, the traffic noise was deafening. Streams of cars were making their way along the surrounding streets. The majority of the vehicles seemed to be the famous yellow New York taxis. Despite the apparent plethora of taxis Sanders, who had made his way out to the centre of the roadway and now stood, somewhat precariously, John thought, trying but failing – or at least having some difficulty – in hailing one. Most, if not all, appeared occupied. Finally, though, one did pull abruptly across the inner lane of traffic and onto the kerbside opposite John. This was to the obvious annoyance of the driver just behind the cab who had been making his way slowly along that inner lane. His horn sounded loudly and the driver yelled some obscenity that John couldn't quite make out, at the taxi driver.

John opened the car door but waited for Sanders to pick his way back across the lines of traffic before getting in himself.

Sanders barked, if a bit breathlessly, the address of the NYPD station to the driver through the Perspex shield that protected him from unruly customers. The driver turned and looked at them sceptically as if asking himself why two probable police officers were hailing a cab perhaps wondering, more importantly, would he get paid for the journey?

After a painfully slow trip – though, to be fair to the driver, he did take every possible shortcut and route to dodge the traffic snarl-ups – they reached the dirty grey exterior of the police station where their meeting with the detective was to take place. As they exited the cab, Sanders offered cash to the driver but waited demanding a receipt. 'For administrative purposes,' he explained.

Expense claim more like, thought John, now regretting that he hadn't done the same with the driver from the airport, which had been a considerably more expensive journey.

They were greeted at the front desk by an NYPD

unifoirmed officer who was even larger than Sanders himself, though the slight paunch might have suggested that he was not quite in such good shape. The bulky policeman eyed the unlikely pair up and down suspiciously: a tall, well-built man in a tight-fitting yet expensive suit with a distinct overbearing and self-confident appearance, accompanied by a smaller and more dishevelled character who tended to hang back to the side and slightly behind his partner. John had consciously let Sanders take the lead in this part of the investigation at least.

Sanders introduced himself, producing his FBI identity card for confirmation and stated that they had an appointment with a Detective Brown. The policeman lifted the phone from his desk, still eyeing the pair with some suspicion. The NYPD clearly didn't relish a visit from the FBI.

After a few minutes of hanging around in the waiting area a middle-aged balding and moustached man appeared from an inner office and greeted them warmly.

'Come through, come through.' He ushered them back into the inner office. The desk officer watched them leave, still unconvinced of their bona fides.

The detective noticed John glaring back at the large man at the desk. 'Don't worry about Davis – he's suspicious of everyone that comes here. I think they pay him to be like that. Keeps the troublemakers out.'

As the three sat round the detective's desk it was Sanders who was first to speak. 'Inspector Brown—'

'Ethan, please.'

'Okay, Ethan…' replied Sanders, if a bit reluctantly, wishing to keep the interview as formal as possible. 'Tell me what the sister said.'

Ethan Brown rolled his shirtsleeves up, revealing thickly hairy arms; he then leant back in his seat and related details of his interview with the sister, occasionally referring to some notes he had made at the time. 'So essentially,' he concluded, 'she denied that he had come over here or, in point of fact, that she had had any recent contact with Daniel.'

'Well, we know that the last bit's a lie. We have his phone records and he definitely contacted her. We also know he had a sum of money – we think he might have bought a ticket to New York. My colleagues back home are looking into that possibility. I think we do need to see her ourselves.'

Then, as an afterthought: 'Do you want to come with us? Might make it look more official. She knows you're NYPD.'

The detective was already pulling on the cheap, dirty brown jacket that had been loosely hanging over the back of his chair. He had never had any intention of allowing the FBI man to run roughshod in his jurisdiction.

Leaving the station by the rear entrance Ethan Brown led them through the caged-off car park situated to the rear of the main building before stopping beside what John noted appeared to be a fairly dilapidated car but one of undoubted American origin.

Noting John's quizzical look, Ethan Brown explained, 'In our line of work it doesn't pay to have a flash car. Wouldn't stay flash long – not in this neighbourhood, anyway.' He climbed in, adding, 'Don't worry the engine's sound. She'll get you there and back.'

A little reluctantly, John lowered himself into the backseat, whilst Sanders rode up front with the detective.

With a roar the engine fired and then, somewhat enthusiastically – perhaps a little too enthusiastically for John's comfort as he struggled to fasten his seat belt – the car lurched forward as Detective Brown gunned the car out through the car park gate and out onto the side street before forcing his way into the main stream of traffic on the main road that led across the front of the station. Some of the oncoming cars hooted their displeasure at Brown's tactics but were simply greeted with a wave of the detective's arm as he leant out the driver side window to gesticulate to them.

'That's New York for you,' explained Sanders, turning around to address his Irish colleague.

Detective Brown remained nonplussed, clearly accustomed to making his way through the heavy downtown traffic.

'We're not in any rush,' John offered, as he became increasingly uneasy with the car's erratic progress.

'No. I know,' replied Brown, before leaning out of his window again and shouting something that John couldn't quite make out at another driver who foolishly had tried to edge his way into a gap that the detective had already decided was his own.

After what seemed an interminable time, yet which was really only about thirty minutes, Detective Brown who had spotted a car pulling away from the sidewalk suddenly swerved the car across two lines of traffic and attempted to ease the vehicle into it. John thought that their car was too big for the small gap that had been vacated; nevertheless, with some backwarding and forwarding Ethan Brown managed to ease the car into the small parking area.

Breathing heavily at his exertions, he explained that parking was a nightmare in this neighbourhood and you took any chance you could. The three eased themselves out of the vehicle and, while John and Sanders stood on the pavement, Ethan Brown shoved a note, 'Broken down', under the nearside widow wiper. 'Better than a car alarm,' he explained.

Emily Wilson lived two blocks away in a tenement in Brownsville, part of the Brooklyn area of New York. John sweated profusely, unused to the humidity of the city, as the three walked around the maze of very similar-looking buildings and through crowds of people, mostly young and often hooded with heads bowed as they made their way aimlessly along the sidewalk, often mostly in groups of four or five. They only occasionally glanced up at others, it seemed, simply to make sure that the other would step aside and let them through. To John at least it was an unusual scene – used to the Irish population as he was, this crowd seemed unfriendly at best, threatening at worst. Sanders and Brown simply strode ahead, unaware of John's discomfiture.

Ethan Brown stopped, almost knocking into an old lady coming the other way, and pointed to a building ahead. 'That's where she lives. Seventh floor.'

Sanders nodded and the three continued on towards the tenement.

The door was ajar; the lock hung loosely from its fittings. No one had made any attempt to repair it. The hallway was dark and smelt of urine. John was unsure if it was cats' urine or human, but it probably didn't matter, both equally likely.

John pressed the elevator button.

Nothing happened.

He looked around at his colleagues, who simply shrugged, as if they expected nothing different, and turned to make their way up the stairs.

John wheezed as he tried to catch his breath on the seventh-floor landing. The sweat continued to lash off him; he rubbed at his forehead with a handkerchief. Sanders and Brown each smiled at the limey's discomfiture.

The door was opened on the third knock.

A female head looked out through the small gap that the door chain permitted.

'Emily Wilson?' asked Ethan Brown.

'Who wants to know?' came the reply.

'Detective Brown, NYPD.' He proffered his badge. 'My colleagues and I would like a word.' He made no attempt to introduce Sanders or John, letting Emily Wilson believe that they were also local police officers.

Emily Wilson looked suspiciously from one to the other, but then, probably reassured by the police badge, she somewhat reluctantly pushed the door closed. Reassuringly they heard the chain being taken off before the door opened again and she let them in.

The door opened directly onto what appeared to be the living room of the apartment. Blinds, half closed, hung limply from the two window frames at the far end of the room. The windows themselves overlooked some lower buildings adjacent to the tenement block that they were in. The somewhat grimy windowpanes admitted a dappled light, casting a partial shadow over a large sofa, which was the main piece of furniture in the room. The sofa itself was adorned with a large throw one which probably had once been white but was now a dirty grey in colour. A couple of electric guitars were propped up beside a television in the corner of the small room. Some damp articles of clothing hung from a drying rack near to the door.

She offered the three a seat on the sofa while producing a small leather-covered stool for herself. Ethan Brown lowered himself cautiously onto the sofa; Sanders and John decided to remain standing just behind their new colleague.

'I've already talked to the police,' asserted Emily quickly, her voice and manner defensive. Her accent, John noted, though unmistakably American, was very different from the accents of the native New Yorkers he had met already.

'Somethings come to light,' replied the New York detective.

'About Daniel?'

'Yes. These gentlemen,' he turned to indicate John and Sanders,'have come from Dublin because of new information.'

Emily Wilson looked quizzically from one to the other.

Detective Brown took up the mantle. 'You told my officers that you hadn't seen or heard from Daniel recently – that's right, isn't it?'

Emily Wilson shifted uncomfortably in her seat. 'Yes…'

'But that's not quite true, is it, Miss Wilson?' The detective leant forward to emphasise the question, then waited silently for an answer, letting her ponder on exactly how much her inquisitors knew.

'What do you mean?' she responded, defensively folding her arms across her chest.

It was John that picked up the conversation. 'We know he was in touch. His passport's missing and we know he had money.'

Daniel's sister paused as if in thought, then, clearly having come to a decision, opened up to her inquisitors. 'Okay, look, I may not have been completely honest with the other officers.'

'Yes…?'

'Daniel was unhappy in Ireland. He wanted to come home.'

'Unhappy?' It was John who asked; Ethan Brown glanced over his shoulder as if to point out who was in charge of the inquiry on his soil.

'Look. We were in contact,' Emily Wilson admitted. 'But only briefly.'

'And…?' Ethan Brown asserted his control.

'He did want to come over and stay with me, or so he said. He told me he had set something up. But he wanted to stay with me at least till he could sort something more permanent out. He told me it was some sort of business arrangement. That things were starting to look up and that he wouldn't need to stay with me for long. I have to admit I did think he was sincere, that he was really planning to come over. I was actually looking forward to seeing him. It's been a while…'

She hesitated, dropping her head, before adding, 'But he never arrived. He never did come.'

'What sort of business deal?' John interrupted, picking up on that part of the conversation. This was the first time anybody had mentioned any business dealings that Daniel might have had.

'I don't know. All I know is he was quite excited about it.'

'Did you get the impression that what he was talking about was legit?' Ethan Brown sounded sceptical. 'It's not often a nineteen-year-old gets offered a business opportunity in New York.'

'He was convinced about it – at least that's what he told me.'

'But he didn't give you any clue what kind of business deal it was?'

'No, sorry. I didn't ask. I was just glad that he was coming over. That he was finally getting his life sorted out. I know he found it difficult living with our father.'

'Did he tell you then why he didn't travel?' Ethan Brown leant forward towards Emily, who now was starting to cry.

John offered her his handkerchief, much, it seemed, to the displeasure of the New York policeman.

'He said he was going to come. He said that he had got some money from somewhere, but then I didn't hear from him again. He never came.'

'Some money? Did he say where he got it from?'

'No. But he was going to use it to get here. I got the definite impression that he was a bit worried about the money, though. I don't think that it was just being in Dublin or his father that upset him – I think there was more to it than that. He wanted to change his life, get a new one, get away from the embassy at least.'

'Why do you say that, Emily?'

'Just the way he was talking about things.'

'Did he mention drugs or a family called the Boswells?' asked John from behind Ethan Brown's back.

Emily Wilson took a few minutes to reply as if trying to remember her conversations with her half-brother. 'I don't think so,' finally she replied. 'All he said was that he wanted to get out of the country, to get away, and that he had the flights sorted.'

John glanced over at Sanders and nodded. It did seem to make some sense if, as had been already reported, Daniel did owe the Boswells money and didn't want to pay them despite, it seemed, now having the means to do so.

Going back to the original question, John asked again, 'Where do you think Daniel got the money?'

Emily Wilson was a little taken aback by the question, as if she'd not really given it any thought before.

'Would his father have given him the money? As pocket money, for example?' he continued.

'You must be joking.' Emily almost laughed. 'Him? He's a bloody miser. Never given me a cent and I doubt he'd have given Daniel any either.' Then she added, 'Especially if he thought Daniel was going to up sticks and come back to the States.'

'Why do you say that, Emily?'

'Our father – well, he's not my real father, anyway – is an overbearing control freak. He would have seen Daniel leaving as a sign of his own failure. Certainly he's never forgiven me for walking out.' Emily sat back and stared at the floor. Another tear rolled down her cheek.

'You've no idea then where the money came from?'

There was another pause, then: 'Actually I do remember one conversation I had with him.'

'Yes?' John inclined his head.

'It was a bit garbled, but he said something about somebody else at the embassy giving him the money.'

It was Sanders' turn to look interested. The FBI man interjected before either John or Ethan Brown could pursue the point. 'Do you know who at the embassy gave him the money?' Then, after a moment's thought: 'Or why somebody would give Daniel the money?'

Emily Wilson initially shrugged her shoulders, but then turned to face Sanders again as if she'd realised something. 'As I said, it was a bit garbled, but I remember him saying that someone at the embassy had done something, that he had something on this person and it was them that had given Daniel the money to leave.'

'So it was hush money?' John asked.

'I'm not quite sure what that is,' replied the young woman. 'But if it is what I think it is, then yes, it was probably to stop him telling anybody about what he knew.'

'Do you think that was why he wanted to leave? Did he think he was in trouble?'

'I don't know. All I know is he was glad of the money and he was going to use it to get himself over here.'

Now it was Sanders' turn to take over the conversation given that he felt it was now impinging into his area of the investigation. 'Do you know who this person that gave him the money was?'

'No, Daniel never said.'

'Or what Daniel had on him?'

'No, sorry. But as I said, I did get the impression that Daniel was blackmailing him. That it wasn't just a gift.'

'Why do you say that, Ms Wilson?' Sanders was growing more agitated at the thought of somebody at the American embassy being somehow involved in Daniel's disappearance.

'Well, why else would anybody in the embassy have given

him the money to get here? Especially as they would have known that it was in defiance of his father, the ambassador?'

Sanders nodded; he couldn't disagree with her logic.

After another short period of silence and reflection Emily Wilson continued. 'I think, though, it might have been at least part of the reason he wanted out.'

'Why do you say that, Emily?'

'It's just… it's just that when he mentioned it, and he only mentioned it once, he sounded a bit scared, that's all.'

Ethan Brown turned around and addressed the FBI man directly. 'Looks like something for you to investigate, Mr Sanders.' He couldn't quite keep the smile off his face, having uncovered something that neither Sanders nor his colleagues had not known about previously.

With that they took their leave, thanking Emily Wilson for her co-operation, if a bit belatedly.

*

The following day, seated in the back of a taxi on their way back to the airport, John turned to Sanders. 'Did you believe her?'

His chain of thought disturbed, Sanders looked around. 'Who? The sister?'

'Well, who else have we talked to?'

'Sorry, yes, I was just thinking.'

'About the money?'

'Sounds like it's something I need to follow up when I get home.'

'It does, but what about the sister's assertion that he wanted to leave Ireland for some job opportunity? Is that possible?'

'Well, he's an American citizen, he's nineteen – no reason why not.'

'But apparently he never arrived.'

'I don't know,' replied the FBI man. 'So the sister says. She could be hiding him, I guess. She might if she thought that somebody was after him.'

'I believed her,' asserted John. 'To me she came over as generally concerned about him and anyway, there wasn't really anywhere in that small apartment to hide a teenage boy.'

'I'll give Brown a call when we get to the airport and get him to put some surveillance on the sister. It can't do any harm.'

John nodded his assent, adding, 'And we can carry on investigations at our end.'

The two continued their journey in silence, immersed in their own thoughts on the way the two different yet interlinking aspects of the investigation were going to proceed.

chapter thirteen

Back in Dublin, jet-lagged and fatigued, made worse by a poor night's sleep, John had nevertheless reported for work the next day. The first thing he had done on reaching his office was summon Jo Roberts and ask her for an update on her visit to the Boswells whilst he had been away.

Essentially there was little to report. Visiting the Boswells on their current site led to them essentially denying everything. They denied knowing Daniel. They denied anything to do with drugs, stating that they were upstanding members of society, if a little misunderstood, often abused and the subject of prejudice.

Following this initial visit, Jo, undeterred, had secured a search warrant for the family's caravans and motor homes. Then, while enduring loud protestations with further claims of discrimination and police harassment, quantities of probable illegal substances, now awaiting analysis, were found, along with large sums of cash.

Paddy Boswell had been brought in for questioning but, as expected, nothing further was forthcoming and he had been released on bail awaiting the lab results.

So, given John's fruitless trip to New York and Jo's so far unrewarding encounter with the Boswell clan, the investigation appeared to have stalled. There was still no word of the missing teenager.

John sat slumped at his desk, surrounded by paperwork, paperwork that should have been dealt with weeks ago, but the distraction of the missing boy coupled with an inner feeling of fatigue had distracted John and led to this unusual, certainly unusual for him, apathy towards routine office matters.

The mobile phone in his pocket started to vibrate. Recovering his senses, he pulled it from his jacket and answered the call.

'Hello?' he answered without looking at the screen.

'Hello, is that Mr McDaid?'

'Yes, speaking.'

'You've got an appointment with Dr Finlay at two o'clock, haven't you, Mr McDaid?'

John looked at his watch. One thirty. It had completely slipped his mind. 'I'm really sorry. I had forgotten – I was caught up on a case. But don't worry, I'm just leaving now,' he lied. 'It will take me less than half an hour to get there... so I should be on time.'

'Don't be rushing, Mr McDaid. That's why I'm ringing. The doctor's had to go out on an urgent home visit, so he's asked me to ring around those patients on his afternoon list and see if some of them could come in later. Does five thirty suit you or would you prefer to leave it till another day? Dr Finlay said he would stay on and see those patients on his list he can't see right now if they can come in later.'

John breathed a sigh of relief; he did want to see the GP again, so the fact that he could despite his own folly, made him smile. 'Five thirty, I'll be there,' he affirmed.

He resolved to write the details of appointment down – not only the time but also all the symptoms he wanted to discuss.

John spent the rest of the afternoon trying to catch up on the mountain of paperwork that had built up given his distraction with the Daniel Wilson case. Finally giving up, he shuffled the remaining documents into a drawer and headed off to make the doctor's appointment.

*

Even now, in late afternoon, it was nigh impossible to find a parking space near the health centre. Eventually, as he drove back and forth he suddenly spotted a car which was about to pull out. As it left, John quickly manoeuvred his own vehicle into the space vacated, much to the obvious displeasure of the driver of another car, who had obviously also spotted the first car's departure.

The waiting room was nearly empty as he entered and took a seat. There was only one other occupant: an old lady sitting reading a book, her black leather handbag at her feet. Clearly Dr Finlay had either got back sooner than expected and already seen the bulk of his list or many of those who had to be rebooked had chosen another day.

'Mrs Spencer...' It was the GP who spoke, putting his head around the door to summon the other patient. Then, noticing John sitting patiently on the other side of the waiting area, he gave him a nod and indicated, to the clear displeasure of the older woman now teetering towards the consulting room with the aid of her walking stick, that he shouldn't be long.

After about ten minutes or so the other patient reappeared at the consulting room door, now clutching a prescription in her free hand. Dr Finlay followed and indicated for John to join him in his office.

Having offered John a seat the doctor sat down opposite him on the other side of the desk. 'Okay.' He looked down at his notes. 'You're back early, Mr McDaid. What can I do for you?'

John tried to gather his thoughts and explain things in an ordered fashion. 'There are a number of things I need to ask you about.' John noticed the look of displeasure spreading over the GP's face. Given the lateness of the clinic and the busy day, John guessed that 'a number of things' was the last thing the GP wanted to hear.

'Firstly, can I ask if the tablets are working?'

'Well, yes, they do seem to take the pain away within a short time, but that's only part of it, I'm afraid,' John replied, before continuing. 'The pain can still be quite severe and it seems to be coming more frequently, but also—'

Before John could reel out the other issues he wanted to discuss the doctor had leant forward over his desk and replied, 'I don't think that's unusual, Mr McDaid. In fact, I think we did discuss this possibility the last time I saw you. Things often get worse before they get better.'

John tried to remember if the doctor had in fact discussed this detail with him but was prepared to give him the benefit of the doubt. 'Yes, but there are other symptoms as well. Things I forgot to mention last time.'

The GP indicated for him to continue.

'Well, there's fatigue, I seem to be tired all the time—'

'Probably the tablets – they can do that, you know,' answered the doctor before John could finish his sentence.

'No, it's definitely not just the tablets,' asserted John, sitting forward to address the GP directly.

'And how can you be certain?' The GP smiled benignly.

'Well, for one, the fatigue was there before you gave me the pills and,' he continued, 'it's there whether I take the pills or not.'

'Tiredness is what we doctors term a non-specific symptom.'

John looked at him quizzically.

'By non-specific I mean it can be caused by a lot of unrelated things.' He then began to list things that he thought could contribute. 'Lack of sleep, over-working, long hours, depression—'

'It's none of those, I can assure you,' interrupted the patient. 'It has come on recently along with this dammed – sorry, excuse the language…'

The GP waved his hand as if to dismiss the word and bid John continue.

'This awful numbness in my face, the pain that goes with it and also the problem with my leg.'

The GP leant even further forward; it seemed to John that he now had the doctor's full attention. 'Your leg? You didn't mention any problems with your leg before.'

'No, you're right. I'm afraid I forgot and also I thought I might be wasting your time.'

'So what's changed your mind?' The GP was now clearly now intrigued by the array of symptoms being presented to him.

'The more I thought about it, the more I think they are all related.'

'Related? In what way?'

'Well, at first I just thought the leg problem was just a strain and was dismissive of it, but then I couldn't remember hurting it and there was no pain.'

'No pain? So just what have you noticed wrong with your leg?'

'This may sound strange.'

The doctor shook his head. 'Go on.'

'Well, it just doesn't seem to work right.'

'What do you mean, doesn't work right?'

'I limp. As if it's weak. In fact, it wasn't me who first noticed it, it was my son, and recently others at work have commented on it.'

'You said you thought all your symptoms were related. Why?'

'They all appeared around the same time. I've never had anything like this before. In fact, I've always been very fit and healthy.'

The GP consulted his notes again, this time to verify John's statement. Acknowledging the paucity of earlier consultations the GP again asked him to continue.

'Also when the fatigue is bad, the leg is bad, I limp more as if it's weak and the pain in my face kicks off.'

Now seeming convinced that there really was something going on with his patient, the doctor forgot about the unpaid overtime he was putting in and started to furiously scribble in the clinical notes. When he had written all that he wanted to at that time, he rose and ushered John over to the examination couch at the side of the consulting room. 'Better have a look at you, I think.'

John hesitated. He was a little taken aback by the GP's sudden change in tone, though pleased to be taken seriously.

'Sorry, would you mind slipping your trousers, shoes and socks off?' He added quickly, 'So we can get a good look at this leg of yours. Just the one? Or do you think both are affected?

'Just the one. This one.' John pointed to his left leg as he levered his shoes off and eased himself out of his trousers, pulling the socks off as he did so. John complied and then heaved himself up onto the doctor's examination couch. The GP looked John's legs up and down. John watched him do so.

'They look normal enough,' he said finally. Then, with a twitch of his head, he reached for the patient's right thigh and jerked it upwards. The whole leg left the table – not just the thigh but the lower leg and foot as well.

'Just relax,' said the GP.

'I am, honestly.'

The GP tried the manoeuvre again with the same result. Then he tried the other leg: the same thing happened. 'You seem a bit tense – you are tensing up your legs.'

'I don't think I am. Is that not supposed to happen, my leg rising when you lift it?' asked John, somewhat puzzled.

'Mmmm… not the whole leg. Never mind, we'll move on.'

Next the doctor asked John to sit on the edge of the bench and try to lift his legs in turn while the GP tried to prevent him.

The GP won.

John found that the GP's hand and arm were stronger than his legs.

'Mmmm…' The doctor scratched his chin. 'Lie back up again, will you, Mr McDaid?'

Reaching behind him the doctor produced a ball of cotton wool and then a small pin. He proceeded to ask John, who had been instructed to close his eyes, to tell him which object he touched him with.

John had no difficulty distinguishing the soft touch of the cotton wool from the prick of the needle.

Finally satisfied, the doctor confirmed that John's sense of touch was indeed intact. Moving quickly on he opened a drawer in his desk to produce a patella hammer, then, with his arm under both lower thighs, he gently lifted John's legs slightly upwards. With the slower, gentle movement John's heel this time stayed rooted to the couch.

Tapping each knee in turn, John was a little surprised by the forceful jerk of the reflex. 'Pretty good reflexes, eh, Doc?' he asked.

'A bit too good, I'm afraid,' was the muttered reply.

Now John was a bit worried.

To complete his examination Dr Finlay scratched the soles of both feet in turn with the tip of the patella hammer.

Both of John's big toes reacted similarly, rising to attention.

It was GP's turn to look a bit worried, though he was clearly trying to suppress his concern for the sake of his patient.

John, being trained to pick up on body language, was not oblivious to the GP's change in demeanour.

'Okay, up you pop. Let's see you walking.'

John did as he was bid and strode back and forth across the consulting room floor under the watchful gaze of the health professional.

'You're not limping at the moment,' finally the GP observed.

'No, it only really seems to happen when I'm tired or I've walked a long distance or sometimes when I run.' John thought that maybe the other man didn't believe him.

'Get your clothes back on, Mr McDaid, and we'll have a talk.'

Sitting once again at the GP's desk, John waited patiently as the doctor once again filled out his notes.

Finally looking up from his paperwork, the doctor paused as if gathering his thoughts. Then he spoke, with a more sympathetic tone than John had detected before.

John was worried again.

'There does appear to be a problem with your legs, Mr McDaid.'

'No, only the left leg,' John corrected him.

'I'm sorry. No, both appear to be a bit weak. Granted, the left more so than the right, but the right is definitely weak as well.'

'Are you sure?' asked John, more in hope than expectation.

'I'm afraid I am. Yes. You see, when I tested the strength in your legs my arm appeared to be stronger than your legs – legs plural.'

'Maybe I wasn't trying hard enough?'

'In my opinion you were, and normally the leg muscles are much stronger than the arm muscles – they have to keep you upright, after all. Yet I was able to push your leg down when I asked you to keep it up. I shouldn't really be able to do that.'

'You haven't been weight training, I don't suppose?' John tried to deflect his growing anxiety.

'No, sorry,' the doctor continued with a more serious tone, ignoring John's attempt to lessen the mood in the room. 'And then there's the reflexes—'

'My reflexes? I thought they were pretty good?'

'A bit too good, I'm afraid,' interrupted the GP before John could continue.

'So what is wrong with my leg? Sorry, legs?'

'Actually your legs are, in point of fact, alright.'

John looked quizzically at the doctor. 'But you said—'

The doctor interrupted before John could continue his questioning. 'Your legs are okay, but I think the problem – that is, why you limp, why you think your legs are weak – is not so much something inherently wrong with the leg muscles, but rather in getting the messages down to your legs to tell them to work properly.'

'Getting the message down…?' John was definitely confused now. 'What do you mean, not getting the messages down to my legs?'

'I think the problem is in the spinal cord.'

John remained silent, waiting expectantly for further explanation.

'The spinal cord.' The GP turned to point at an anatomical chart on the wall. 'See here?' He pointed to the row of back bones running down from the skull. 'This is your spine.' He ran his finger down the line of the bones. 'It is not just a line of bones that keep you standing upright; inside the spine there is a river – a tunnel, if you like – in which runs the spinal cord.'

John looked at the chart, his attention now captivated.

'The spinal cord carries messages to and from the brain down to the individual nerves that stretch out from the spine. These transmit to carry feelings or sensations back up to the brain and then, of course, messages down from the brain to the muscles to make them work.'

'Okay, got it. I understand. Like a power line or telecommunications conduit.'

'Exactly.'

'So, what is wrong with my spinal cord?' John leaned forward expectantly.

'Put simply,' the GP responded, 'the messages seem to be being disrupted. The leg, or legs, appear weak because the messages from your brain aren't strong enough to get the muscles working hard enough.'

'Why is that then? What's wrong with the spinal whatsit? What is wrong with me?' John asked plaintively.

'To be honest with you, Mr McDaid, I'm not sure. There are quite a few things that can cause a problem like yours. It could be a disc pressing on the cord or some problem within the cord itself. This needs further specialised tests, I'm afraid.'

'So when can I have these tests?'

'I am going to have to refer you to a specialist for these, I'm afraid. I don't really have the access or the expertise to order the tests that are necessary.'

'A specialist? What sort of specialist?'

'A neurologist. They specialise in this sort of thing. They will get to the bottom of it for you. I'm sure of that.'

John realised that the GP was trying to be helpful and reassuring, but he still couldn't completely suppress his growing feeling of fear and uncertainty.

'Okay.' He tried to come over as in control. 'How soon can I see a neura… ologist…'

'A neurologist,' the GP corrected him. 'There may be an issue there.'

'An issue?' John was even more worried now.

'I'm afraid so. Firstly, neurologists are only based in major teaching hospitals and secondly, there are actually a shortage of neurologists in Ireland. So they can have quite long waiting lists.'

'Oh God.' John slumped in his seat. 'You mean I'm stuck with this till I see him?'

'Look, I will do my best to get you seen and this sorted out ASAP,' the doctor affirmed.

John had a thought; he pulled himself upright again. 'I'm in the Guards and we all have a private medical insurance scheme. I'm sure it will cover this sort of eventuality. Would going privately to see the specialist be possible and would it speed things up?' he asked hopefully.

'Actually, yes, it might. I know quite a few neurologists, though not all, do see private patients and their waiting lists are, obviously, much shorter.'

'Can I go private then?' he said, before adding, 'Even if the scheme doesn't cover it, I need this sorted and I'm willing to pay anyway.'

'Leave it with me, I'll see what I can do.' The GP got up and, with his hand on John's elbow, he guided him out of the office, the consultation complete.

Before retreating back into his consulting room the GP called after John, who was making his way, if somewhat shakily, through the reception area. 'Make sure my receptionist has your phone number so they can get in touch as soon as I've confirmed the private appointment.'

John nodded his assent.

chapter fourteen

John sat at his desk and pondered the current situation. Some time had passed and they were no further with the investigation. It seemed, and most of the witnesses confirmed it, that Daniel was unhappy and had wanted to leave. He had taken his passport, so the most likely scenario seemed to John was that he had left Ireland completely. Yet, although professing to wish to stay with his sister in New York, at least if the sister was to be believed, he never showed up. So just where did he go?

He turned things over and over in his mind trying to think of a useful strategy to take things forward.

He waved at Jo to come over.

'Daniel Wilson. We seem to be stuck at the moment.'

Jo nodded in agreement. There was little she could think to say.

'Have we got anything back from the lab on the analysis of the drugs found at the Boswells?'

'I haven't heard anything. I'll give them a ring. They should have got something back by now. But even if they do prove to be what we think they are, it doesn't necessarily link the Boswells to Daniel's disappearance.'

John scratched his head. 'No, but at least we can pin something on Paddy Boswell and his clan.' He leant back in his chair. 'It's hard to see, though, where to go from here. Daniel just seems to have disappeared into thin air. We're told nefariously that he wasn't happy here or that he was in some trouble, but all we know is that he seems to have left on his own accord, he did, after all, pack a holdall and take his computer, passport and some money.' Another thought: 'Talking of the money, Sanders said he'd pursue that angle. Again, I don't suppose you've heard anything from him either?'

'No,' Jo confirmed.

'Leave that one to me,' replied John.

Jo went back to her desk to phone the lab.

Moments later, still clutching the phone but with her hand over the mouthpiece, she gestured to John to come over. 'Yes, Dr Chadwick, I have him here now.' She handed the phone to John.

'Inspector John McDaid here,' he affirmed.

'This is Alan Chadwick, Dr Alan Chadwick.' The other introduced himself. 'You sent us some white powder. Powder that you picked up in a raid, I understand.'

'My colleague retrieved it, yes,' John corrected him.

'That's as may be,' continued the scientist. 'You were right to be suspicious of it.'

'So it is an illegal substance? Jo was pretty sure it was cocaine.'

'Exactly. She was absolutely correct. It is indeed cocaine.'

'Good to know, thanks, Doc. We'll bring the suspect in again.'

'Hold on, I haven't finished yet—'

'Sorry, what did you say?'

'I said I haven't finished yet. There's a bit more to it. You see, it's not pure cocaine.'

'Not pure? What do you mean?' John was intrigued.

'We found that it was mixed with something, something else, we're not absolutely sure yet but it seems to be some sort of laundry detergent, ground up and mixed with the pure cocaine.'

'A laundry detergent? That sounds a bit odd.'

'It's actually quite common in the illegal drug industry. Some agents, like caffeine, detergents or even some laxative agents, are often added to the cocaine to bulk it out, mainly so the seller can get more money from less cocaine. The additives they use are usually a white powder that is visually indistinguishable from the real thing. Usually the agents they use are not particularly dangerous. Though in saying that they are not generally something that you would want in your body. Using the detergents, though, can actually result in harm – there is some evidence that detergents can build up in arteries and cause dangerous blockages in the heart, brain or liver.'

'So we suspect that the Boswells were padding out their drugs to cheat people into shelling out for a diluted mixture rather than the real thing?'

'Cutting cocaine like this is, as I've said, not an uncommon practice, but as to whether your suspect added the mixer or was selling the drug illegally, that's beyond my remit. I'm afraid that's for you to find out, Inspector, not me.'

'Okay, that's very helpful and does give us a start. Tell me, can you identify exactly what the agent added to the cocaine was?'

'Good point, Inspector. If we can it should almost be like a fingerprint, helping you to identify the batch it came from.' He paused.

John could hear the rustle of papers being rifled through as if the scientist was checking his notes.

'We should be able to,' finally he continued, 'given a bit

more time. All I can say is that we have identified pure cocaine cut with an ethoxylate. But which one and how much per gram of cocaine we can find out. As soon as we have the results, I'll let you know.'

John replaced the receiver and turned to Jo. He related the gist of the conversation, much of which Jo had either overheard or deduced anyway, but it was good to recap.

'So we have one line of enquiry anyway. We know Daniel knew the Boswells. We've been told that they supplied him with drugs and we know the Boswells do have drugs on site. I wonder if Daniel might have been into something stronger than just blow after all. I think we need to talk to Daniel's brother Jake again. He knew Daniel took drugs but he didn't mention anything about cocaine.' After a short pause for thought he added, 'Maybe the girlfriend as well, see if she knows anything about Daniel's drug habits.'

*

Back once more at the embassy, John and Jo sat in an anteroom and waited. They had asked to see Daniel's brother 'just for some clarification', they had indicated. When the door opened, though, it wasn't Jake that entered, rather it was the ambassador himself, who pushed his way into the room past the security guard that was maintaining a vigil just outside the room. He appeared red-faced and somewhat flustered.

'You've interrupted an important meeting,' he blurted out. 'I can only spare you a few minutes. Any update on Daniel?' he asked, breathing heavily; he had obviously rushed over from the aforesaid meeting and was not a man accustomed to sudden exertion.

'It wasn't actually you we wanted to talk to, sir. It was your other son, Jake.'

'Jake. Why? What's he got to do with it?'

'Just a bit of clarification on a few things he'd mentioned to us previously.' John did not think it wise to mention the fact that the clarification sought was concerning Daniel's possible drug habit. 'As regards Daniel's disappearance, we do have a few leads, but as yet no sign of Daniel himself.'

'I hope you are putting all your resources into finding him. He's only a young boy, after all... and given my position...' He didn't finish the sentence but looked back and forth between John and Jo.

John nodded reassuringly. 'We are doing all we can, I can reassure you on that point, sir.' Then he paused as if thinking for a few seconds before continuing. 'As we have you here, sir, we believe Daniel made a conscious decision himself to leave – can you think of any reason why he should do so?'

The ambassador's face turned a deeper shade of red and he puffed a few times before replying, 'Certainly not. I don't know quite what you are implying, Detective, but Daniel was happy here. I don't know of any reason why he would want to take off. That's an absurd suggestion.'

'Well, sir, he did take his passport, some money and clothes with him when he went missing. So it is a line of enquiry that we do feel obliged to pursue.' He remained silent for a couple of minutes to allow the ambassador to digest their assertions.

'Do you know of any reason that Daniel might have wanted to run away?'

The ambassador backed off and thought for a few minutes. Then he looked back and forth at the two detectives and admitted, 'Well, we did have words a few times. Mainly about his behaviour and the company he was keeping.'

'Company?' It was Jo who spoke. John glanced at her; he thought it better to let the ambassador continue uninterrupted.

'Yes, I got some reports from our security people – they're pretty sharp, you know – and again, given my standing here, they do keep a pretty close eye on us.'

'What sort of reports did you get?' John decided to push the ambassador further than he was likely to admit to voluntarily.

'Well...' He hesitated before continuing. 'I heard he was seen in the company of some travellers and there was some mention of drugs. I confronted him with it. We had a bit of a set-to, if truth be told.'

'When was this, sir?'

The ambassador moved around behind his desk and sat slowly down. With his head bowed he uttered quietly, 'Just before he went missing, actually.'

'Sir, do you think that argument could have been instrumental in Daniel's disappearance?'

The ambassador slumped lower into his chair. 'It's possible, I suppose, but to be honest I don't think so. We were always having arguments. He's a teenager. I was the same at his age. Rebellious. You know what it's like.'

'Was the argument about drugs?' John pushed the point.

'To a degree, yes. I'd found some cannabis in his room, but we've all done that, haven't we, Inspector?' the ambassador asked hopefully.

John just nodded. He had to agree that most teenagers these days had experimented with drugs one way or another.

'Nothing harder? Cocaine, for example,' Jo interrupted.

The ambassador was taken aback. 'Certainly not,' he replied forcefully, turning to face the younger detective. 'He wouldn't get involved in that. No, definitely not.'

'So what was the argument about then?'

'It was more about the people he was seen with, rather than any drugs he might have bought from them. I was worried, and I have to say my security team were worried about his associating with them.'

'These people, do you know who they were?'

'Sanders will know more details. The team report to him and then he passes it on to me. All I know is that the group they were most concerned about were a bunch of travelling people.'

'The Boswells, by any chance?'

The Ambassador looked at John quizzically; he seemed alarmed that the Irish detective knew the family but also relieved that the Gardai seemed to be looking in the right directions.

'Yes,' he confirmed, nodding. 'Exactly. I take it you know them?'

'We are following a line of enquiry which does include the Boswells. So yes.'

'On another point,' John continued, taking advantage of the understanding he now seemed to have established with the older man. 'We have had reports that when Daniel disappeared he had some money with him.'

'Money?' interrupted the ambassador.

'Yes, sir, by all accounts a fair amount too. Do you have any idea where he would have got the money from?'

Again the ambassador looked stunned. 'I really have no idea. I gave him some pocket money, of course, but he didn't have a job or anything...' He hesitated, before continuing. 'Given what we've just talked about, I was very careful to not let Daniel any access to undue amounts of cash.'

They were interrupted by the door being pushed open.

Jake leant cautiously into the room.

'Jake, these Guards want a word with you, I believe.' The ambassador seemed now to be more accepting of John and Jo's presence and their ambition to continue to examine every angle of his son's disappearance. Even if some of it was disturbing and upsetting.

Jake slunk into the room and sat down on a chair near the window.

John and Jo pulled up two chairs to confront him. John glanced around at the ambassador, who was reclined in his own chair and clearly making no effort to leave.

John weighed up the options. He would prefer to interview Jake on his own. He was sure that Jake might be more forthcoming if his overbearing father was not present, but it was clear that the ambassador himself had resolved to stay and, given Jake's age, he was entitled to be accompanied by a responsible adult. John just wished that that adult wasn't the ambassador. But on reflection there was probably little he could do about it. So he began the interview.

He started with a few simple questions in order to try to get the younger man's confidence.

Jake stated that he didn't know where Daniel was or why he left.

John mentioned their sister, but again, Jake asserted that he didn't know about any thoughts that Daniel had had about going to stay with her.

He spoke quietly but, it appeared to John, truthfully. John resolved to push the conversation onto more controversial issues.

'Jake, we know,' and, to reassure him, he added, 'and your father knows, that Daniel took drugs.'

Jake glanced quickly over to his father, who remained sitting passively on the other side of the room. The ambassador nodded. 'I know, son. Tell them what you know.'

John indicated his thanks to the ambassador and then continued. 'Daniel smoked pot, yes?'

The young man fidgeted in his chair, then lowered his head and quietly, almost too quietly, he muttered his confirmation.

'Tell me, Jake, did Daniel ever use any harder drugs?'

Jake looked up, a questioning expression on his face. 'What do you mean, harder drugs?' he asked.

'Well, cocaine, for example.'

The younger man looked to his father for support. 'Absolutely not. I would have known. He never touched anything like that. I swear.' Again, he switched his gaze over to his father, almost pleading for support.

The ambassador rose to his feet. 'I think maybe you should leave, Detective. We've both told you that Daniel was not involved in serious drug-taking. Clearly you are upsetting Jake, so can you just go?'

John turned to face the ambassador, who still stood behind his desk. 'Just one more question.'

'Go on then,' the ambassador relented.

Turning back to Jake, who sat, head bowed, unwilling to look at John, he shuffled his feet back and forth as he gripped the seat of the chair with both hands.

'Jake, you told us Daniel had some money with him when he left. Is there anything more you want to say about that?'

Again Jake looked over at his father but this time with a look of real trepidation, one that he tried to hide; although he suppressed it quickly John had picked up on it.

'Money? No, I just thought he'd got hold of some money from somewhere. I didn't know where he got it – Dad doesn't really splash out on us.' He looked over at his father for confirmation.

'Maybe we should leave it there, Detective. I think Jake's had enough for one day.'

John was sure that Daniel's brother knew more about the money than he was admitting. The look that had spread over his face at the mention of it had convinced him of that, but his father's presence, and now the older man's insistence that the interview be ended, made John accept that some of his questions would have to wait for another day.

John turned to the ambassador once more. 'Can we see Daniel's room?'

'Sanders has already checked it. He told you, didn't he, that he thought some things were missing? Just some clothes and a holdall, as well as his passport from my safe, obviously.'

'Yes, sir. But we'd like to have a look anyway. If that's possible.'

The ambassador reluctantly rose from behind his desk, not able to think of any reason to deny the two Gardai their not-unreasonable request.

The ambassador led the two through the vaulted hallway of the embassy and then up two flights of a circular staircase to the floor where Daniel's former bedroom lay.

'He didn't let me in here very often. He was quite secretive.' Then the ambassador added despondently, 'Maybe I should have taken more interest.'

'Teenagers, in my experience, can be like that.' Jo replied reassuringly.

John looked at her. He couldn't quite keep the questioning expression off his face. What did Jo Roberts know about teenage behaviour? Then, he guessed, it probably wasn't too long ago that she was a teenager herself. Maybe she had things she had kept from her parents as well? Anyway, this wasn't the time or the place to question her.

The ambassador opened the bedroom door and then stood aside, allowing the two to enter alone. He remained in the corridor whilst John and Jo inspected the room.

The curtains were half drawn, allowing just enough light into the small room to give it a warm, reassuring feel. There was a single bed, a desk, a chest of drawers and a built-in wardrobe. It was frugal compared to the opulence of the other parts of the building that John had seen previously. He opened the wardrobe. Clothes hung haphazardly from a number of hangers, though a few of the hangers remained empty. A number of pairs of shoes were neatly arranged along the floor beneath. Again, there were a few spaces. John called to the ambassador.

'There seem to be a few hangers lying empty – is that why Sanders said that he'd taken some clothes with him when he disappeared?'

The ambassador put his head around the door. 'I told him that my recollection was that the wardrobe was completely full, so he drew that conclusion, yes.' He retreated to the corridor once more.

'Seems a reasonable assumption.' John turned to Jo, who was standing looking at the wall above the small single bed. 'What are you looking at?' John asked when she hadn't responded to his assertion about the missing clothes.

'The picture,' she replied.

'The picture? What about it?' He turned to join her gaze. A single painting hung above Daniel's bed.

'Can't you see, John?' She glanced around at him.

'See. See what?'

'It's his.'

'Of course it's his. This is his room, isn't it?'

'That's not what I mean. Look here.' She pointed at the bottom right-hand corner of the painting. 'Look at the signature. Here.'

John leant forward and squinted at the small area with writing at the bottom of the canvas.

'D. Wilson. Do you see it?' Jo continued.

John nodded and then stood back to take in the whole picture. 'It's quite good, isn't it?'

The picture was a of a woman's head and shoulders. Not

a natural life portrait but a stylistic, almost surreal portrayal. It was striking in its effect. The woman was young and beautiful; she was painted side on, but with her head turned as she looked over her left shoulder towards the artist. The effect was powerful and hard to ignore as the model's eyes seemed to follow any other observer around the room. The woman's mouth was slightly open, highlighted by the bright red lipstick she wore. In her left hand she held a cocktail glass to her mouth. The shoulder of that arm, the closest part of her anatomy to the painter, sported a tattoo of a flower. *A rose,* John thought.

As he looked at the painting he couldn't help but think that the subject was somehow familiar to him, though perhaps that was just the effect that the artist wanted to achieve.

'It is certainly memorable,' agreed Jo.

The ambassador, hearing their conversation, again leaned around the door frame.

'He had a talent,' he said as he looked past the detectives towards the picture, then lapsed back into his own thoughts once more.

There was another smaller, but no less thought-provoking, picture hanging over the desk. This time of a man and a small boy walking away from the artist. Only their backs could be seen; they wore matching suits of an old-fashioned style and the older man sported a flat cap whilst the son, or at least John presumed it was his son, was bareheaded.

The ambassador looked up again and, seeing John admiring the other picture, observed, 'His ladies are better, I think. I don't quite know where got the ideas from, though. I'm sure he never met any women who looked like that.' He pointed to the original portrait.

'They are very good, though,' added Jo. 'I'd buy one for my flat.'

John looked at the two pictures again. He had to agree: they would undoubtedly adorn any household, adding vibrancy and style.

The ambassador looked back and forth between the two canvases. 'That was his dream. He wanted to be an artist.' He paused briefly, engulfed in his own thoughts. 'I suppose I should have encouraged him.'

John looked at Jo. Neither could think of anything to say.

Then the ambassador continued. 'Rather, I put him down. Told him there was no money, no future in painting. Encouraged him to concentrate on his schoolwork, go to university and get a proper job. Maybe I did drive him away.'

'His work is good, though. Could I take a photo?' John bit his tongue, realising he probably hadn't said the right thing.

The ambassador didn't seem to take any offence, but rather, seemed to perk up a bit. 'Go ahead, I'm sure Daniel would be flattered.'

As John pointed his phone to capture at the woman's portrait, the ambassador continued. 'There's more of his art in the summerhouse at the back of the building if you want to see it. He had quite a lot, actually. The summerhouse is quite dry and dark. Nobody really uses it, so he stored his work there. I think he dreamed of opening a shop or something and selling them.'

Without waiting for a reply, the older man turned and made his way down the stairs. He walked slowly and stooped, as if he carried the world on his shoulders. The talk of his son and his realisation of the young man's talent and obsession, which he had admitted to not supporting, seemed to weigh heavily upon him.

The two detectives followed him down to the ground floor, into an expansive sitting room and then, opening two large garden windows, they found themselves standing in a well-maintained walled garden.

They could hear street noise behind the walls, but any view was precluded by the height of the brickwork and the less attractive barbed wire that topped it. *One of many deterrents,* John supposed, looking around, *to keep out unwelcome intruders.*

At the bottom of the secluded lawn stood a small, white, wooden shed-like structure. To call it a summerhouse was a bit of an exaggeration. It did have a small, porch-like area, which John supposed you could sit out on, but the rest of the building was really just a storage cabin. Its single window was shuttered and closed.

The ambassador whirled around and made to go back into the embassy.

'Sorry, forgot the key, I'll just be a moment.'

John and Jo made their way slowly across the lawn to the summerhouse, admiring the shrubbery and the plants that surrounded them, placed mainly at the foot of the wall which had clearly been lovingly tended.

'Aren't they marvellous?'

John wheeled around to find the ambassador returned once more.

'The flowers, I mean.' He put out his arm and made a gesture around the garden.

'We have a magnificent man who does the garden,' he continued. 'Anyway, here's the key. Let's see if we can get in.' He strode forward, inserted the key into the lock and pulled the door open.

He froze.

'What the—'

John and Jo moved up behind him.

The ambassador was staring at the interior of the shed. Apart from a single discarded wooden box it was completely empty.

John and Jo pushed past. Entering the summerhouse,

a little shaft of light trickled through the shutter on the window; otherwise, the interior was gloomy and dark. They moved around the empty interior. The floor was dusty and John thought he could detect lines where paintings might have stood, protecting that small area from the dusty covering.

John looked at Jo and raised his arms in a shrug, not quite sure what he was looking at. They both turned to the ambassador, who seemed to slowly regather his composure.

'I don't… I don't understand,' he muttered. 'There were lots of his paintings here… lots. He kept them here.'

'I take it you haven't been in here since Daniel disappeared?'

'No, I'm hardly ever in here. It's Daniel's space. I respected that. There didn't seem to be any reason to come in here after he disappeared. I never suspected anyone would take his paintings. Oh my God. He'll be so upset if he finds out.'

'So you have no idea when the paintings were taken or where they might have gone?' John had quickly slipped back into formal Garda mode.

'No, none at all. You've got to help me find them,' the ambassador almost pleaded.

'Could Daniel have removed them?'

The ambassador seemed to consider the proposition. 'But why? He would have told me. Wouldn't he?'

'So you don't have any idea about the disappearance of the artwork? Is there anybody who might know when it was taken?'

The ambassador walked back and forth in the small room, stroking his chin as he did so. Finally he spoke. 'We can ask Doyle.'

'Who's Doyle?' asked Jo, moving forward to stand beside John.

'He's the gardener. He's here every day. He'll know something, I'm sure of it. I think he's still here. I saw him in the kitchen having a coffee earlier. I'll go fetch him.'

With that the ambassador whirled around and jogged back to the embassy, disappearing through the open windows.

John turned to Jo. 'What do you make of this?' he asked.

'Better wait to see what the gardener has to say, I think.'

John knew she was right. No point jumping to conclusions, though he already had a few possible options racing around inside his head.

The ambassador reappeared; trailing a short way behind was a small, bespectacled man, probably in his late sixties. He wore crumpled jeans and a worn, woollen jumper. The man looked apprehensively towards John and Jo, who now stood beside the open door which was the entrance to the summerhouse.

As they drew closer, the man whom the ambassador identified, unnecessarily, as the gardener, spoke. He had an north Dublin accent. 'I haven't done anything wrong, have I?'

It was the ambassador who spoke first, not giving John time to respond. 'The shed's empty. All my son's work. Where is it? Do you know anything about it?'

The man looked flustered and, before he could reply, the ambassador had repeated his questions, this time almost shouting them. It was clear that the loss of his son and now of his son's work was affecting him badly and he could no longer hide it.

John stepped forward and, taking the gardener aside, he spoke reassuringly to him. 'You're not in any trouble, Mr Doyle, the ambassador's just a bit upset. You know that Daniel's missing and now he's found the shed empty, his belongings gone – we just want to know if you know anything about it.'

Doyle took his time in replying, still not entirely convinced that he'd not get into trouble. He looked back and forth between John and the ambassador.

Finally, making up his mind, he spoke. 'I know that Daniel kept his paintings in there.'

'Yes?' encouraged John. *At least the gardener knows that*, he thought.

'He took them away himself.'

'He removed them. When?' The ambassador almost shouted at the older man, who instantly shrunk backwards.

'It was a few weeks ago. I helped him—'

Again the ambassador interrupted, even more loudly this time: 'You what? You helped him?'

Jo stepped forward to calm the ambassador and moved him away so that John could continue to question the cowering Doyle in peace.

'So just tell me then. What exactly happened?'

'As I said, it was a few weeks ago. Daniel said that he wanted to move the paintings. I knew that he had been in and out of the shed the week before, dragging crates in.'

'Crates?'

'Yes, he was boxing up the paintings as if to ship them off somewhere.'

'You saw this?'

'I did, sure as I stand here.'

'Why did no one else see what he was up to?'

'He was sneaky about it. Did it when nobody was about. He brought the crates in through that door there.' He pointed at a wooden door, partially overgrown but set into the brick wall. 'It opens up onto a back street behind the wall. Daniel had a key – I don't know where he got it, but he had a key, and he was the only one who ever used that gate.'

'Where did the crates come from?'

'I've no idea. I just know Daniel had a van – he brought the crates over in it, loaded the paintings into them and then we loaded them back into the van and he drove off.'

'We loaded them?'

'Yes, I didn't know, did I, that his father didn't know what he was up to?'

'Go on.'

'I was working in the garden one evening when I heard the van pull up outside then Daniel came in through that door. Got a bit of a shock, I did, I'd never seen that door opened before.'

'What next?'

'Then he starts trying to lift a crate out of the shed into the van, but I see that he's struggling, so I go over and help him, don't I? I didn't do nothing wrong, did I?'

'No, I can see you were only trying to help. How many crates were there?'

'Three, I think.'

'What happened after you got the crates into the van?'

'Daniel thanked me. I went back to my work and he shut the gate, locked it and then I heard the van drive off.'

'Was Daniel driving?'

'Oh no, sir. He was on this side of the gate. It was a lady. I only caught a glimpse of the back of her head when we lifted the crates in. It was her who took the van off.'

'Is that the last time you saw Daniel?'

'No, he wasn't in the van. He went back into the embassy and carried on as normal for the next few days. Then I heard he went missing, but it was a few days after he emptied the shed. I felt guilty, but I had nothing to do with him going off.' He stopped for a moment, then asked painfully, 'Should I have told the ambassador?'

'It's alright, you've told us now,' replied John reassuringly, adding, 'and anyway, as you say, he didn't go missing for a while after he took the paintings away. Thanks for your help.'

John let Doyle go back to his work and then, while Jo

looked on, he took the ambassador aside and explained what he had learned.

*

As they left the embassy and walked along the street to pick up their car before making their way back to the station. Jo turned to John and asked, 'What did you make of all that, sir?'

'Don't call me sir. It's John, okay?' John spoke tetchily. He apologised immediately, realising he was taking his frustrations out on the wrong person.

'We need to know why Daniel moved the paintings and where they are now. But that's not the only puzzling aspect to this case. I think Jake knows more about the money, for example, than he's letting on, I'm sure of it.'

'Why do you say that… John?' Jo asked.

'Did you see his expression when the subject came up? I'm sure if his father hadn't been there we could have got more from him. He knew about the money. I'm sure of it.'

'Isn't Mr Sanders supposed to be looking into that?'

'You're right. I'll give him a ring and tell him of my suspicions – maybe he can get more out of him.' John could feel the frustration rising again. 'There are other things we could have asked as well.'

'Other things?'

'Yes, I would have liked to know what he thought of his relationship with Cara.' He paused, then continued. 'And there's that other girl.'

'Other girl?'

'The one that secretary said she saw him with. What was that all about? And could that be the same girl that Doyle said was driving the van that took Daniel's paintings away?'

As they walked, John muttered, 'Curiouser and curiouser.'

chapter fifteen

The letter came through the letter box just as Niamh, who had stayed over, was coming downstairs. She picked it up and called up to John, who was in the shower.

'John, letter for you.' After a short pause, she looked at the envelope, turning it over in her hand. 'Seems to be from the Blackrock Clinic.' She put the letter down on the hall table and carried on into the kitchen to make them both a cup of coffee.

Hearing the words 'Blackrock Clinic', John quickly realised the significance of the letter. He towelled himself dry, threw on some clothes and made his way down the stairs, pulling on his shoes as he did so.

'What's the rush?' asked Niamh, putting her head around the kitchen door.

John didn't reply. He hadn't told Niamh about his GP appointments or his onward referral. He felt guilty about that. He had tried to rationalise his failure to do so, so that he wouldn't worry her, but realistically he admitted that maybe it was that he still felt their relationship wasn't strong enough yet – he hadn't known her that long, after all.

'Nothing. Just a busy day. That's all,' he lied.

He picked up the envelope and went into the living room to open it quietly on his own. He unfolded the contents and examined them closely. There seemed to be three appointments: one in the radiology department and one for something called neurophysiology. John scratched his head at that one; both of these were in the University hospital, and the other at the Blackrock Clinic for the consultant himself, one Dr Moran. The neurologist sported a number of letters after his name, MD PhD FRCPI. *To clarify his academic prowess, no doubt*, thought John. Also enclosed was a short, typed letter from the consultant's secretary explaining that the consultant had ordered an MRI scan and a neurophysiology investigation to be performed before the actual consultation as this would, he felt, speed things up. The MRI and neurophysiology appointments were at the beginning of next week and the consultation itself would be a couple of days later.

He decided to hide the details of the appointments from Niamh, at least at present. It may all be a fuss about nothing after all. He folded up the letters and put them in the inside pocket of his jacket out of sight. Then he joined Niamh in the kitchen.

Breakfast was nearly ready and it smelled good. She had prepared him sausages, bacon and a fried egg, an unusual treat.

He looked down at the plate as she placed it before him on the breakfast bar.

'What's this then?' he asked.

'Special treat,' she replied. 'You have seemed a bit stressed recently, so I thought you deserved it.' She placed a mug of coffee down beside the plate.

John tucked in without hesitation then, between mouthfuls, added, 'Thanks, I appreciate it.' He didn't add any more, certainly not disclosing any of the reasons for his current preoccupations.

Finishing breakfast, John kissed her lightly on the cheek and, feeling well satisfied, took his leave and headed for the office.

Making his way, albeit slowly, through the early-morning traffic, his mobile rang. Glancing down, he pressed the hands-free button and took the call. It was Jo.

'There's been a development.'

'A development?' he repeated unnecessarily.

'When I got to my desk this morning there was a message on my answerphone.'

'Yes? Who from?'

'Ethan Brown. He said that Daniel's sister had contacted him. He said that it was important. I couldn't ring him back, though.'

'Why not?' John wasn't thinking straight, hoping that this might indeed be the breakthrough they had been waiting for.

'Well, for one, they're five hours behind, so it's 4am there, and despite Ethan Brown's enthusiasm to pass on the information, I doubt he'll be at work yet.'

'Okay, smartass. I'll be there shortly and we'll ring him later.' He cursed the traffic snarl-up ahead under his breath.

*

Finally reaching his office he found Jo already there and sitting at her desk, a cup of black coffee on the desktop beside her.

He climbed in behind his own desk and waved for her to join him. Jo slid across on the wheels of her chair to sit opposite him across the desk.

'Any idea what Ethan wanted?' he asked.

'He didn't say. All he said was that something had happened and we should know about it.'

'Do you think Daniel's turned up at his sister's after all?'

'Mmmm… I'm not sure about that. I think he would have said in the message, don't you think?'

John nodded. Jo was probably right. It would have been simple just to say Daniel's turned up. He lapsed into thought.

Jo broke the silence. 'I'll ring him back at…' She consulted her watch. 'Just after lunchtime. American's usually start work quite early anyway. That'll be around 8.30am there. I'm sure he'll be in – he seemed quite keen to pass on whatever it was he wanted to tell us.'

'I'll leave it to you then,' John acceded.

Jo returned to her own desk.

John, with nothing else to do at the moment, decided to make start on some of the paperwork that had mounted up during the inquiry.

*

He hadn't really made much headway into the documentation, but he had started to feel a bit hungry – given the large breakfast that he'd consumed, he realised that time had flown by and that it was lunchtime and nearly time to contact his American counterpart.

As he turned things over in his mind Jo appeared at the end of the office area carrying, somewhat precariously, two cardboard mugs of coffee and two sandwich packs. Reaching his desk she deposited her burden carefully on it.

'Black coffee okay?' she asked, pushing one of the mugs towards him. 'I got one egg and onion, and one BLT – which would you prefer?'

'Either, you choose,' John replied, grateful to her for her thoughtfulness.

'I saw you buried in that paperwork, so I just took myself

off down to the canteen and fetched this. I thought you could do with something to eat.'

John decided not to tell her about his filling breakfast. 'Thank you,' he replied. He looked at his watch. 'Do you think we could give Ethan a go? It's what? Eight am there?'

'Umm… Perhaps give him half an hour.'

The two of them tucked into their lunch with some intermittent small talk between mouthfuls. John couldn't help admitting that he was growing more impatient to hear from the American and hence get things moving… hopefully.

The half hour passed slowly; the discarded mugs and wrappings cluttered John's desk.

Finally, unable to wait any longer, John took Ethan Brown's number from Jo, having decided to call him himself.

He dialled the number and listened to it ring with an unfamiliar ringtone.

After a few rings the phone was answered by a rather abrupt female voice. 'Yes?' she asked without introduction.

John quickly explained who he was, why he was ringing and, more importantly, that it was Detective Ethan Brown that he wanted to speak to.

'He's round here somewhere, I saw him a minute ago,' came the again abrupt reply, but this time John could hear the broad New Jersey drawl with which she spoke.

Then he heard the scuffle of her placing her hand over the microphone, but not completely, as she shouted across the office, 'Ethan, there's some guy with a funny accent on the phone. He wants to speak to you.'

John heard her hand releasing the phone. 'He's coming now,' she confirmed.

'Nice to speak to you,' John replied sarcastically.

There was no reply; rather, he simply heard the phone being dropped onto the desk and then a background noise he was familiar with: that of the hustle and bustle of a busy police department.

After several minutes the phone was lifted and Ethan Brown came on the line. 'Hi, John, is that you?'

'Certainly is – good to hear from you, Ethan. You've got some news, I hear.'

'Yeah, I rang last night, I forgot about the time difference…'

John glanced at Jo, who was trying to listen as intently as possible. His look suggested that that was Americans for you: totally focused on their own country and not really aware of the rest of the world. Why else would they have elected an otherwise unlikely 'America First' candidate to be president? But this wasn't the time to discuss politics.

'Hold on, Ethan, I'll put you on speakerphone – my partner Jo Roberts is here. She's part of the investigation as well.'

'Was that her voice on the answerphone? I did wonder.'

'We share an office, so yes, your call went to her line.'

'Sure sounds a sexy dame,' Ethan added.

'You're on speakerphone, Ethan.'

'Ahhh… Sorry about that.'

'Ethan, do you want to tell us what you've heard? I believe you said Daniel's sister was in touch?'

'Yeah, she rang me. Though to be honest I don't know what it means.'

'What did she say, Ethan?' John couldn't quite keep the growing irritation with the American detective out of his voice.

'It was something about some pictures – paintings, she said.'

'Paintings?' John sat upright in his seat; Jo leaned in towards the answerphone speaker.

'Yeah, couldn't really understand it'

'Understand what?' John was really quite irritated now.

'Well,' Ethan Brown continued slowly, a bit too slowly for the listeners at the other end of the phone. 'Well, she rang me and said that she'd got a call from some woman at a gallery. I think she said gallery – anyway, this woman wanted to speak to Daniel and when Daniel's sister said he wasn't there this woman simply said to tell him the paintings had arrived.'

'That explains a lot.' John had turned to Jo.

'It doesn't mean anything to me,' Ethan interjected. 'Care to explain?'

John took his time to explain Daniel's love of art and that he had stored some paintings at the embassy, but they had now disappeared. Ethan's talk to Daniel's sister meant that they had obviously been shipped to the States and were to be exhibited in a gallery there. This might explain Daniel's disappearance and why he might have needed money to ship the paintings and get himself over there.

'Are you sure, Ethan, that Daniel hasn't turned up at his sister's? He'd obviously planned to use her apartment, at least at first, as a base when he got there.'

'I'll find out,' Ethan confirmed. 'As you know we agreed to put the sister under surveillance since you were over, but I've not heard anything back. I would have thought I'd have been told if Daniel showed up. Anyway, I'll check.'

'Thanks, Ethan.' John ended the call.

chapter sixteen

The next day it had been confirmed from America that Daniel had definitely not arrived at his sister's apartment. Ethan Brown was, though, to pursue enquiries at the art gallery that had contacted Emily Watson.

Given the new information regarding the American link and while waiting for a further response from Ethan Brown, John and Jo had just started to discuss how to next proceed when John heard his name being called. John turned to see Chief Inspector O'Brien standing at the door to his inner office and beckoning to him.

John made his way across and was ushered into the chief inspector's office. O'Brien was not alone; the other man he recognised as Superintendent West, O'Brien's immediate superior. West was an imposing man: six foot three inches, but of lean build. His face betrayed his years of being in the Guards; it was creased and heavily lined. John knew that he was a man who had come up through the ranks. He knew his business and was not a man to be easily distracted.

O'Brien retreated to the back wall of his office

'Well, John, how's the investigation going?' the superintendent asked, dispensing with any preliminaries.

'We have a few lines of enquiry, but nothing substantial as yet, I'm afraid.'

'Look, John, I've had the Garda deputy commissioner on the phone – there's a lot of pressure coming down to find this kid, as you can imagine. Especially given who he is.'

John looked defensively at his feet. 'We think he might have gone back to America. There's a detective over there that we've been working with. I'm just waiting for him to get back to me.' John realised he was embellishing things a bit, but he felt he needed to demonstrate some progress or West might get him taken off the case, and he didn't want that to happen. At least not just when things were getting interesting.

He went on to explain his and Jo's findings to date.

The superintendent nodded silently at intervals, acknowledging John's assertions and possible explanations for the boy's disappearance. As they made to leave the office, DCI O'Brien made a point of closing the door behind them – no doubt, John surmised, to allow himself some time to put his own spin on John's investigation.

Returning to his desk, Jo looked at him quizzically.

After a moment's thought, he turned to her and suggested a recap of what they knew and, perhaps more importantly, what they didn't.

'There's a bit of flack being directed in the Super's direction,' he said by way of explanation.

After consulting and comparing notes it was John who took the reins. 'This America lead, it seems the strongest thing we have so far. Jake and his sister both intimated that he was going there, and then there is his artwork – it looks like it was shipped there. From what's been said so far his art was very dear to him.'

Jo nodded in agreement.

'Okay then,' John continued. 'We need to know more about his decision to leave, who knew about it and, more importantly, where he is now.'

'Maybe we should talk to his father and his brother again?'

'Mmmm, I don't think his father knows anything – he would have told us at the outset. Jake, now that's another matter. I bet he knew something. He and his brother were, by all accounts, quite close.' John paused, then, reaching for his notes, continued, 'To be honest, I'd probably leave a return visit to the embassy for another day. Daniel's father is bound to interrogate us and I'd prefer to defer that until we have something more concrete to report.'

Jo expression suggested that she could see the wisdom of this approach.

'So who else was close enough to him to have been aware of his plans?'

'Cara Williams?' offered Jo.

'Exactly. I think she deserves another visit.' He hesitated. 'I'd like to talk to her without her father present, though.'

Jo agreed.

'Right, what time is it now?'

'Three o'clock,' replied Jo, looking at her watch.

'If we go now we could get there by three thirty, traffic permitting. Chances are that the father will still be out at work.'

Standing up and pulling his jacket on over his shoulders, John made for the exit. Jo followed closely behind, pausing only to retrieve her phone which sat on top of her desk. She stuffed it into her pocket as she almost ran to keep up with her boss.

*

The traffic had been helpful, so only twenty-five minutes later they sat outside Cara Williams' house. John looked up the driveway.

'No car – hopefully we're in luck and he is at work. Cara, we know, has been off school and "poorly", so she should be there. Let's go.'

The two exited their vehicle and made their way up the short driveway to the front door of the Williams' house.

John knocked at the door. As he did so he glanced sideways at Jo, who shivered. 'Forgot to bring my coat,' she complained.

They didn't have long to wait. The door was opened by Cara's mother. John had met her only briefly at their last visit, she being summarily dismissed by her husband.

She appeared thin and frail. John had thought that she would be in her late forties, given Cara's age, but she looked much older. She wore an apron over a plain blue dress which hung to below her knees. The apron had flour stains down its length. John guessed that she been preparing a meal when they had disturbed her.

'My husband's not in,' she immediately informed them.

'It's not him we've come to see. It's Cara,' John asserted, taking a small step forward.

'I don't think Frank would like it. He should be here.' The woman looked frightened.

Jo stepped forward as well and, trying to be as reassuring as possible, she added, 'It's just a few questions. We won't keep her long. We'll be in and out before you know it.'

With that Cara's mother conceded and stepped back, allowing them to enter. She showed them into the living room while she remained in the hall. John heard her call to her daughter, who, John assumed, had remained upstairs in her bedroom – probably since their last visit.

A few minutes passed before Cara appeared in the

doorway; her mother stood behind her. Jo approached her and, though initially shrinking back, she allowed Jo to put her arm around her shoulders and guide her into the room. She still had a pronounced limp. As she helped the young girl along, Jo turned back to the mother, suggesting she should return to her baking, adding, 'Cara will be fine with us.'

To John's surprise the mother agreed to leave them to it and retreated to the kitchen.

Jo sat down opposite Cara, while John remained off to one side. They had agreed to leave the questioning to Jo, concluding that Cara was more likely to respond to her.

'Tell me about your relationship with Daniel, Cara.'

There was silence for a few minutes as Cara looked back and forth between the two detectives. Finally she started to speak. 'We were close, very close. We'd been going out together for nearly two years.'

Jo interrupted, 'You said you *had* been going out for two years, as if it was past tense. Do you mean you broke up?'

'Sorry, no, I meant we have been going out for nearly two years. It's just that he's gone missing, hasn't he?'

'Sorry, Cara, I didn't mean to interrupt. Carry on.'

'As I said, we were close. We had a strong relationship. We had plans.' A small tear ran down her cheek.

'What sort of plans, Cara?' Jo asked gently.

'We were going to get married. We'd discussed it. He loved me and I loved him.'

'What about your father, Cara? What did he think about you going out with Daniel?'

Cara stopped talking. She stared down between her legs, which she now gripped firmly with both hands.

'Cara?' John interjected.

Jo looked around crossly, clearly telling him to keep out of it.

'Cara?' asked Jo softly. 'Is there something you want to tell us about your father and Daniel?'

Cara lifted her head, tears now symmetrically ran down both cheeks and dripped silently onto the floor between her feet.

Jo remained silent and eventually the young woman started to open up. 'Dad didn't approve of Daniel. He thought that Daniel wasn't good enough for me. That he was going to mess up my life.'

'Mess up your life? In what way, Cara?'

'Dad always had high hopes for me. Being an only child didn't help, I guess.'

'What high hopes?' Jo encouraged her to continue. She detected a hesitancy in Cara's demeanour, indicating that she wasn't entirely happy with the way the discussion was heading.

After a moment's deliberation, in which she seemed to make up her mind to tell all, Cara continued. 'Dad wanted me to go to university. He knew that Daniel didn't and he thought Daniel would put me off going as well.'

'How did you know that Daniel didn't want to go to university?'

'We had discussed it. Daniel's father was like mine: he was pushing and pushing Daniel, but Daniel was adamant that he wasn't going.'

'How did your father know that Daniel had other ideas than going to university, Cara?' Jo was still encouraging her to continue.

'We were here talking about the future and our plans – I think Dad overheard us. He burst into the room and threw Daniel out. He said if Daniel didn't leave me alone he'd take it into his own hands to make sure I'd never see him again.'

Then, as if realising what she had said, she quickly added, 'He didn't mean it, though, it was just a figure of speech.' She looked pleadingly into Jo's face.

John, taking in what the young girl had said, asked, 'What do you think your father meant by he'd take it into his own hands?'

Cara Williams simply shook her head.

So John continued, 'Did you see Daniel again after that, Cara?'

Cara Williams looked about the room as if to ensure that nobody else was present, then admitted, 'Yes. But we had to see each other secretly. Daniel never came here again. We'd meet up at school before he left. After that we'd try and meet at friend's houses, parties or downtown as if we'd bumped into each other out shopping.'

'And your father never found out about the relationship?'

'No, I don't think so.'

'You don't sound absolutely certain, Cara.'

There was a long pause before she answered, 'There was one time…' More hesitation.

'One time what?' John leaned forward, struggling to keep the tetchiness out of his voice.

'One time. We were together in the park. The one around the corner. We'd agreed to meet up. We were just sitting on a bench holding hands, talking about this and that, when I heard something behind me in the bushes.'

'What did you hear, Cara?'

'It was just a rustle. I turned around and it stopped. I thought it was just some animal, but then I saw somebody, a man in the field behind the bush. He was walking away from us. I couldn't see his face, but…'

Jo and John said nothing, sensing that Cara wanted to continue.

'I thought that it might be Dad, that he'd seen us. I was scared. But when Daniel looked he said it wasn't and that I was just paranoid.'

'Did your father often go to that park, Cara?'

'He did, he often went for a walk there. To clear his head, he said.'

'So it could have been your father behind the bush?'

'No. Daniel said it wasn't so it couldn't have been, could it?' The two detectives looked at one another.

'We shouldn't have met there, I know that. Too close to home. Anyway, I was too scared to go there again, so we never did.'

John was about to say something when he heard a car pull up in the driveway. He got up to look out the window.

It was Cara's father. John watched him, red-faced, jump out of the car, slamming the door behind him and pacing purposefully towards the house. John checked his watch; it was only approaching four o'clock, so he guessed that Cara's mother had rung him and he'd leaped immediately into the car to return home.

John turned around and had to tell Cara that her father was outside.

Cara shrank back in fear. She got up, making to leave the room and return to the sanctuary of her own bedroom.

She was intercepted in the hallway by her father, who had burst in through the front door.

Cara froze. All this was witnessed by John and Jo, who, by now, stood in the doorway to the living room.

The man's face was suffused with anger, but it was obvious that this anger was directed not at his by now cowering daughter but at the two detectives beyond.

'How dare you come to my house and interrogate my daughter without permission?' he roared angrily.

'Just a few questions, Mr Williams.' John tried to ameliorate him. 'That's all.'

'How dare you?' he repeated, but he didn't move. He simply stood stock still in the hallway glaring at them.

Cara slunk past and made her way sheepishly upstairs.

John took in the figure that confronted them. He noted the man's posture, his obvious anger, but noted that he'd made no move to physically confront them, thinking the better of it – they were Gardaí, after all.

He motioned to Jo and the two of them moved to leave. Cara's father made no further attempt to obstruct them and stepped back onto the driveway to allow them to pass.

John could feel his hard stare still burning into his back as he climbed into the car. He looked in the rear-view mirror and watched Cara's father disappearing inside the house and the front door being slammed shut behind him.

'Nice man,' observed Jo.

John didn't reply; he remained deep in thought, as they pulled away from the kerb.

chapter seventeen

The weekend passed uneventfully; the investigation seemed to have stalled and there was still no sign of Daniel. On Monday morning John rang Jo to explain that he probably wouldn't be in till later in the day. He had his medical appointments, but he didn't share that with Jo.

'In the interim, you could check out that limp that Cara Williams has.'

'Why?' asked Jo.

'Just a hunch, that's all. See if it happened the way she said it did. A hockey injury.'

He seemed to sense Jo's scepticism at the other end of the phone.

'I just want to be sure that it's nothing to do with Daniel's disappearance, that's all.'

'In what way?' Jo was obviously still sceptical.

'Could they have had a fight, for example? Look, just check it out, okay?' John immediately regretted his tetchiness; he recognised that it was probably, at least in part, due to anxiety regarding the tests he was to undergo that morning. 'Sorry,' he said. 'Just a bad day.'

'I'll call her GP,' came the curt reply before she hung up.

After the call John felt bad for upsetting his colleague, and as he thought so he came to the realisation that by not telling Niamh about the hospital appointments he was probably going to upset her too. He made a decision and called her down from upstairs.

As she entered the kitchen she immediately picked up on his worried expression. 'What's up?' she asked, trying to be cheery.

'Sit down, I've something to tell you.' He indicated the stool on the other side of the breakfast bar.

Now she looked worried.

'You know I went to see the GP?'

'Yes, but you told me everything was alright.'

'Well, it was and it wasn't.'

'What do you mean?' Now she was really worried.

'He's sent me to the hospital for some tests and arranged for me to see a neurologist,' John stated candidly.

'Was that what that letter from the hospital was about? The one you told me was nothing to worry about?'

'Actually, yes. I'm sorry, I should have told you sooner.'

John went on to explain the nature of the tests and, more importantly, that they were that day. Then, despite John's protestations, Niamh insisted that she accompany him to the hospital.

'There's no need.'

But she wasn't going to be dissuaded.

*

Parking at the University hospital was a nightmare. Stuck in a seemingly endless queue for the main car park John was quite glad that Niamh had come along; he was able to abandon the car and leave her to try to get parked while he made his way to the radiology department. He told her he'd see her there.

The MRI unit was housed in a separate building a little away from the main hospital complex, thus making it easier to find. On entering, he noticed a plaque on the wall indicating that the building had only been opened relatively recently by the local TD, the member of the Dáil Éireann, the Irish Parliament. *That explains its independence from the main hospital complex*, he surmised.

Having checked in he sat in the small reception area waiting to be called. Niamh arrived before he was summoned. She appeared out of breath, having run from the car park to try to get there before he went in for the test.

'Got lucky,' she explained. 'Just saw a car pulling out of a space as I got through the barrier. Beat two others to it.' She smiled. 'Anything happening yet?'

John was just about to reply when a young woman in a white uniform called his name.

Niamh rose to accompany him.

'Sorry. It's patients only, I'm afraid,' the young woman stated matter-of-factly.

Niamh reluctantly returned to her seat and sat back down. She gave a small wave to John, who acknowledged it.

Following the radiography nurse he was shown into a small cubicle and asked to undress and put on a surgical gown. The gown tied at the back but gaped, exposing his backside; he stretched behind him to hold the gown together and avoid embarrassment.

Before exiting the cubicle, the radiography nurse handed him a sheet of paper which he was asked to read and sign.

Glancing at it he realised he was essentially to declare that he was not aware of any reason he could not have an MRI scan – in particular that he had no metal about his person. Querying this with the nurse, she informed him that an MRI was a magnetic resonance scan; in other words, it used powerful magnets. Any metal, such as a knee replacement, when inside the scanner, would heat up due to the magnetic field.

John happily returned the form now signed, confident that there was no reason to make any significant declaration.

The nurse led him into the scan room and indicate for him to climb up and lie down on a flat surface at the mouth of the scanner.

Doing as he was bid he stared at the scanner itself; it looked just like a tunnel barely wide enough to admit him. A voice spoke to him over a speaker and John turned to see two doctors waving to him from another room behind a large Perspex window.

The doctor who spoke instructed him on the procedure to follow. He would be moved into the scanner itself; it would be a tight fit, but he was not to struggle or move. The scanner would be noisy and the scan itself could take anything up to twenty minutes to complete.

John gave them a thumbs-up to indicate that he understood. The nurse left the room and, now alone again, he lay back down and within a few seconds the trolley moved mechanically forward on its runway and into the scanner itself.

They weren't kidding, he thought – it was a tight fit and very claustrophobic. John closed his eyes and then the scan began. He was engulfed in a loud noise like a pneumatic drill. The combination of the enclosed space and the ferocity of the noise made for an uncomfortable experience.

Finally, however, the nose abated and the trolley rolled silently back out of the scanner.

The nurse re-entered and helped him down before leading him back towards the changing room.

As he exited the scan room, the voice over the speaker congratulated him on his perseverance and informed him the scan would be forwarded to his neurologist.

From what was said there was no point John querying any results at this stage.

After getting dressed, he pulled back the curtain of the cubicle to find the nurse waiting for him. 'I think you were to have another test today, Mr McDaid?'

John remembered that he was indeed to have something else done. He hoped it wouldn't be as uncomfortable as the scan he'd just endured. 'Some electrical test, I think,' he replied with some trepidation.

'Thought so – neurophysiology, I think you mean.'

With that she led him out of the radiology department to be reunited with Niamh, and before leaving him the nurse explained carefully to him the route they needed to take to get to the neurophysiology lab.

John decided that he didn't quite like the term 'lab'. It seemed to imply to him some form of experimentation. As they walked Niamh asked about the scan.

'It wasn't too bad,' he lied. 'I have to wait for the results, though – they didn't tell me anything.'

They followed the nurse's instructions, making their way without further discussion and within minutes stood outside a door labelled 'neurophysiology'. John knocked the door tentatively.

'Mr McDaid?' said another young woman who stuck her head around the door. 'We've been expecting you. Come in.' And then, as an afterthought, she asked, 'How was the scan?'

John didn't reply. The young woman, dressed in a white jacket and blue trousers – *a uniform but not quite a nurse's uniform*, he thought – seemed to understand as she made no further enquiry.

Once again Niamh was left to sit and wait in the corridor outside as John was admitted to the inner sanctum.

This time there was no need to disrobe; he was simply sat

down at a desk, beside which stood some sort of machine with wires wrapped around it.

The neurophysiology assistant, as she described herself, carefully unwrapped the wires and proceeded to fix the pads at the end of each to John's head, arms and legs.

She took her time, ensuring that each wire and pad was in its correct position, checking and rechecking them several times.

Having completed her task, she turned to leave but not before informing him that the neurophysiologist would be along shortly and that he was not to touch, never mind dislodge, any of the wires that now adorned parts of his anatomy.

John sat and waited patiently. After only a few minutes an older man of Asian descent entered and introduced himself as Dr Khan, a consultant neurophysiologist.

Dr Khan then slowly and professionally explained the procedures to follow. Detecting John's worried look, borne at least partially from his recent uncomfortable experience in the scan machine, the doctor tried to reassure him. 'There will be no pain – at worst a little tickle where the electrodes are attached.'

John didn't like the word electrodes, but there was little he could do now but nod his head to indicate he understood.

Dr Khan then sat himself down on the opposite side of the free-standing machine into which all John's wire were connected.

At first he was directed to place his head on a support and look straight ahead at a screen. The screen flashed intermittently. John was relieved at the simplicity of the procedure; it was over in minutes.

'That's it?' he asked.

'Oh no. Not yet, that was only the visual evoked potentials.'

John didn't really understand but didn't ask.

'I have the sensory evoked potentials to do now,' the doctor continued.

Then, without any further warning, John felt something in his leg, then the other one and finally at his wrists where the pads were attached. It wasn't exactly painful, but each time Dr Khan flicked a switch the uncomfortable sensation returned.

After what seemed like an age, Dr Khan stood up, consulted the screen of the computer that sat on a table and was connected to the electrode machine. 'That's it. All done. I'll forward the results to your neurologist and he can discuss them with you when he sees you.' Then, just to be sure, he added, 'You have an appointment, yes?'

John assured him that he did. He tried to elicit some information about the tests he'd just undergone, but Dr Khan was unforthcoming, simply replying offhandedly, 'Your doctor will have to put these results with his own thoughts and any other tests you might have before he can reach a conclusion. It's not for me to comment. Ms Christie will disconnect you and you'll be free to go.'

The assistant had quietly re-entered the 'lab' and now stared to remove the wires and electrodes from John's limbs.

When he had wiped off the sticky gel that had attached each electrode with some alcohol wipes the assistant had offered him, he consulted his watch and decided to return to work.

He exited the lab and was reunited with Niamh, who had waited anxiously for him. John simply shrugged; at this point, there was nothing else to tell her. He'd drop her off and then go and see if Jo had any news for him.

chapter eighteen

As he walked back into the office, Jo looked up.

'I wasn't actually expecting you back, John,' she said, looking at her watch.

'I told you I'd be late but that I would be in. Anyway, we've still a lot to do. Talking of which, did you manage to get hold of Cara's GP?'

'Yes, I did, but bit of a dead end, I'm afraid.'

'What do you mean, dead end?'

'Well, it seems her injury was exactly as she said it was. Her GP was a bit reluctant at first to divulge any information, but when I explained the seriousness of the investigation, she decided to co-operate.'

'And…?'

'Well, she had received a discharge letter from the local A&E. It seems that Cara had twisted her ankle playing hockey, just as she told us. She was examined and underwent an X-ray. Nothing broken, just a ligament strain, so they simply strapped her ankle, gave her some painkillers and told her to keep her weight off it for the next couple of weeks and no more hockey for at least six weeks.'

'So you don't think the injury was anything to do with

Daniel's disappearance? She couldn't have been lying about how it happened.'

'No,' Jo stated firmly.

'Why so certain?' John asked.

'Timing was wrong, it actually happened and was documented in the GP records before Daniel went missing.'

'Okay, you've got me there,' admitted John. 'So what else is new?'

'Better news. Sanders thinks he's found Daniel's holdall. The guy who looks after the embassy gardens apparently found it tucked away in the shed. It was hidden behind some of his tools. He took it to Sanders.'

John encouraged her to keep going.

'I've asked him to bring it over ASAP.'

'So is he sure it's Daniel's missing holdall?' he said, trying to keep the excitement out of his voice.

'From the description and the contents, I would say pretty likely. That's why I asked him to get it over here. To be honest, I don't think he was too keen. I got the distinct impression that he wanted to investigate it himself. I managed to persuade him that that would be inappropriate. That this was an ongoing Garda inquiry.'

'Well done, good work.'

The two detectives then sat patiently, trying to occupy themselves until the desk sergeant rang through to say that a burly American had just dropped off something for them in reception.

John was first to his feet. 'I'll go and fetch it,' he announced as he exited the office.

Jo sat down and waited patiently for his return.

As John appeared in the doorway, he was already examining the contents of the holdall. 'Sanders didn't hang about,' he announced, trying not to look too pleased that

Sanders had obviously taken Jo to heart and decided not to interfere. But then checked himself, suspecting that Sanders hadn't bothered hanging around because he already knew what was in the holdall.

'Looks like we're in luck,' he said, setting the bag down on Jo's desk. 'It definitely fits the description of Daniel's holdall and the contents seem to match what was reported missing.' He pulled out some clothes and set them on the desk, then he pulled out a computer from the bottom of the bag and passed it over to Jo.

'Bingo,' he exclaimed, holding up a passport. Looking inside, he reported, 'It's Daniel's alright. Here, look.' He turned the open page to let Jo see, and there was Daniel's photograph and details.

'Is this good or bad news, John?'

On reflection John couldn't make his mind up. It was a breakthrough right enough to have retrieved the bag and Daniel's belongings, but Daniel was still missing, and now missing without his possessions. Could the bag suggest a more worrying aspect to the case?

'Let's see what else we've got.' He continued to rummage through the bag. 'What's this?' he suddenly announced.

Jo peered into the bag just as John pulled some money and papers from inside pocket that he had just unzipped. He laid the contents on the desk in front of Jo. But he quickly lifted the money back up again and began to count it.

'There's nearly €100 here as well as a similar amount in dollars.' Now, where did he get that from?' he asked to no one but himself.

'Do you think Sanders has already been through it?' Jo asked.

'Bound to have been. I wonder, though, did he notice that inside pocket?' He pointed to it again. 'I nearly didn't. Anyway,' he continued, 'I don't think he would have removed anything, not knowing that if we found out that he had, we could charge him for perverting the course of justice, and that certainly wouldn't look good on his CV. So what else have we got here?'

Jo had started to look through the paperwork that John had laid down beside her. She held up a booking confirmation for an Aer Lingus return flight, Dublin to New York. The outward journey was scheduled for the day after Daniel had disappeared.

Jo scanned the paperwork. She circled the booking reference and said she'd contact the airline to see if Daniel did in fact take the flight.

John, though, didn't seem to be paying attention; he seemed engrossed in one other piece of paper.

'What is it?' asked Jo.

'Some sort of receipt.'

'A receipt? For what?' Jo stood up to look over his shoulder.

'Look. Look here.' He unfolded the receipt and held it up between the two of them. 'It seems to be a receipt from a shipping company for the transportation of artwork as a part load in a container being shipped trans-Atlantic to New York.' Then, turning to the second page of the detailed printout, he whistled. 'Five hundred euros. Received, to cover cost of shipping.'

'So that means Daniel must have had the best part of €1,000 for his flight tickets, the money in the bag and the cost of shipping his paintings,' Jo interrupted while thinking to herself. 'So the reports we got about Daniel having some cash were true, but just how did Daniel get hold of that sort of money?'

'Maybe we do need to talk to Sanders again.' John continued to rummage through the bag but didn't come up with anything more than a few toiletries and a pair of trainers.

Jo had returned to her desk to re-examine the computer. 'Its password-protected,' she reported after a few minutes.

'Get somebody in IT to have a look at it. I'm pretty sure some geek down there will be able to break into it.' Then, as an afterthought, he added: 'Tell them it's urgent.'

John returned to his own desk and pulled up a chair. The holdall, which by now seemed to have given up all its secrets, sat in front of him. He was deep in thought, trying to piece together the meaning of the abandoned bag and the significance of its contents. Finally, seemingly making his mind up, he lifted the phone and dialled Sanders' mobile.

The call was answered immediately.

John thanked him for handing over Daniel's holdall and confirmed that the contents did indeed suggest Daniel was intending to travel to his sister's but that they didn't know as yet if he had actually gone, but it seemed unlikely. However, listening to Sanders' brief acknowledgement of the information that John was imparting, he formed the impression that the FBI man already knew most of what John was telling him, suggesting that he had taken time to examine the holdall and its contents himself before handing it over.

Before he could broach the subject, he noticed Jo waving at him.

'Hold on,' he said into the phone.

Jo was shaking her head.

'What?'

'I'm on the phone to Aer Lingus,' she said, holding one hand over the receiver. 'I gave them the ticket reference and Daniel's details. They say their database indicates that he did request a boarding pass, but as far as they can tell he never travelled. They're going to double check, but it doesn't look like he went.'

'Did you catch that?' He spoke into the phone.

Sanders confirmed that he had. 'So he was going to the States as we thought. You know the paintings are already in New York. To my thinking,' he continued, 'it does look like he was all set to travel and meet up with them in that gallery.'

John felt obliged to continue, even though Sanders may have already gleaned as much if he did indeed probe the holdall's contents himself. 'It looks like Daniel paid for the shipping of his paintings himself, or at least he had the receipt. He also seems to have purchased his flight tickets and we found about two hundred Euros in cash inside the holdall.'

'I wonder where he got all that money?' Sanders asked, a little unconvincingly, as if trying to imply that this was all news to him.

'I was hoping you'd tell me,' John replied quickly.

'I'm on it,' Sanders promised.

'While you are at it, as it does look like Daniel was at least intending to travel to the States and was bringing his paintings with him, can you appraise your contacts over there of these recent developments and see if they can follow up on them?'

'Sure,' replied the American. 'I'll get back on to Ethan Brown and update him, see if he can't come up with something more at his end. Maybe that gallery girl knows more than she's letting on. I'll let you know what he comes back with.'

Sanders was about to hang up, when John quickly added, 'Can you get him to send a description or, even better, a picture of that girl across to us?'

'Why do you want that?' asked the American quizzically.

'Just a hunch,' John replied.

Jo looked at him, smiling. 'Just another hunch, eh?'

chapter nineteen

At the request of his colleagues in Dublin, Ethan Brown decided to visit the gallery that had contacted Emily Wilson the following morning.

He parked a couple of blocks away and walked around to the premises. The gallery itself was a small building in a reclaimed and increasingly fashionable area of downtown New York. Its frontage was narrow and simple. The door to the gallery stood beside a full-length glass window, behind which was a display of a single picture supported on an easel.

Pushing open the door and making his way inside, Ethan noted that the area seemed deserted: no prospective buyers at this early hour, he guessed. The walls were hung with rows of artwork. These appeared, at least to Ethan's untrained eye, to represent many different genre and styles.

As he stood and looked about a door opened at the far end of the gallery and out stepped a tall, smartly dressed man in about his early fifties, Ethan calculated, and he was generally a good judge of such matters. The other extended his hand to Ethan; the handshake was accompanied by welcoming smile, but one a little too white not to have been manipulated by a local orthodontist.

'Adam Bradford,' he offered. 'Proprietor of these humble premises.'

Ethan, by way of reply, reached into his jacket pocket and produced his badge, which he held out for Adam Bradford to see.

'And what can I do for the NYPD?' he asked, his body language becoming a little more defensive.

'Do you know a Daniel Wilson?' Ethan asked quickly, not giving the owner any chance to prevaricate.

'Errrr... Yes... and no.'

'Sorry, Mr Bradford, I don't quite understand. Do you know him or don't you?'

'No, I don't actually know him as such. We've never met. But his paintings are here – they arrived from Dublin a few days ago. We had agreed to display and hopefully sell some for him.' Then he added, 'They're quite good, actually.'

'Did you know that he's gone missing, Mr Bradford?'

'Adam, please.'

'I prefer, if you don't mind, to keep things formal, Mr Bradford. This is an important investigation.'

The gallery owner, not used to members of the police visiting his premises, conceded the point.

'So did you know he'd gone missing?'

'He was supposed to be here when we opened the exhibition, but when we tried to get hold of him at the address he gave us, apparently he hadn't arrived there yet.' After a short pause he continued, 'Nothing's happened to him, I hope?'

'We don't know, I'm afraid. Just that he has disappeared from home – his father's the US ambassador to Ireland, but I suppose you knew that?'

Adam Bradford shook his head, but Ethan thought he caught just a glimpse of a small smile starting at the corner of the other's lips, probably suddenly realising that any publicity generated by the disappearance of his new-found client –

especially one so well connected – could only enhance the opening of his forthcoming exhibition.

Ethan Brown frowned at the other's obvious cynicism.

'I really know nothing about any disappearance. It was my daughter, anyway, who organised all the details.'

'So just how did a gallery in New York come across the artwork of a student in Dublin?'

'He sent us photos of his work. He is actually from this neighbourhood, so he knew about us and he said he'd want to exhibit them here rather than in Dublin. I got the impression when I talked to him on the phone that he actually wanted to come back home. Anyway, I thought his stuff was quite good and we arranged a visit to see them, in the flesh, so to speak.'

'I thought you said that you hadn't met Daniel?'

'I hadn't, or rather I haven't. I've never met him.'

Ethan looked puzzled.

The art dealer continued. 'You see, I wasn't the one who travelled to Dublin. I don't travel well, actually. I especially hate long flights.'

'So who did go?'

'My daughter, Babs – sorry, Barbara, she hates being called Babs, but old habits die hard.'

'Your daughter?'

'Yes, Barbara now works for me. She completed an arts degree, but work's hard to come by. I needed an assistant and she was available and happy to join the firm. We've been working together now for a couple of years.'

'So it was your daughter Barbara who went to Dublin, met up with Daniel and arranged to bring the paintings over?'

'Absolutely.'

'So who paid for the shipping?'

'I'm afraid we have a policy, Mr Brown.'

'A policy?'

'Yes, a policy. It is entirely the artist's responsibility to get his, or her, work to us. Especially if they are a young and unrecognised one.' He paused, smirked and added, 'Now, if Vincent van Gogh asked us to exhibit some of his work, we might, we just might, make an exception.'

Ethan Brown made a point of looking slowly around the small exhibition area, before replying, somewhat dryly, 'Unlikely, I'd say.'

Adam Bradford held his tongue.

'So, Mr Bradford,' Ethan continued. 'Is your daughter here? I like a word with her if I may.'

'She's just popped around the corner to the deli to fetch us a cup of coffee and a snack. She should be back any minute, if you'd care to wait.' The offer was made, Ethan felt, somewhat hesitantly. Adam Bradford probably didn't welcome the presence of an NYPD officer in his gallery for a moment longer than necessary.

Ethan Brown used the opportunity to look around the walls to take in the variety of artwork on display. Adam Bradford hovered impatiently behind him.

Within a few minutes the door to the gallery was thrust open and a petite, slightly hassled-looking young lady shoved her way in, holding the door ajar with her elbow as she tried to cling on to two beakers of coffee and a paper bag containing two doughnuts.

She was about to say something when she suddenly noted Ethan's presence and stopped in her tracks.

Ethan guessed she was in her mid-twenties; her dark hair had been tousled by the breeze which blew continually down the street outside.

Before Ethan could introduce himself, Adam Bradford did it for him. 'Barbara, this is Inspector Ethan Brown…' he paused for effect, 'from the NYPD.'

Ethan was impressed that the gallery owner had read his details from his badge completely. A skill of appraising the minutia of the art world, he guessed.

Barbara Bradford stopped in her tracks; she let the glass door close slowly behind her. Then, looking directly at Ethan, she asked, 'Why are the police here?' Although she'd been looking at Ethan, the question was aimed at her father.

'Routine enquires, dear. Nothing to worry about.'

Ethan turned to glare at the other man, who visibly shrank back. 'Ms Bradford, do you know Daniel Wilson?' It was the same question he'd asked her father moments before.

The look of shock suggested a different response would be forthcoming.

'Yes. Yes, of course I do.' She looked back to her father. 'Haven't you told him, Dad?' She turned back to Ethan. 'I went over to Dublin to meet him. He'd sent us some photos of his work. Dad and I agreed, they looked promising, so I went over there, talked with Daniel, agreed to exhibit them here in the gallery for him and came home to wait for the pictures to arrive… They're in the back. We didn't want to start to exhibition without Daniel being here. Isn't that right, Dad?' She turned back to her father for confirmation.

Her father nodded. 'I've already explained this to the officer.'

'He was very enthusiastic about the idea of exhibiting them here in New York,' Barbara Bradford continued. 'We had met up a few times, had coffee, discussed the options, etc.'

'Like him having to pay to get them shipped?' asked Ethan sceptically.

'Standard practice,' her father interjected tetchily. 'As I've already explained.'

'It was all a little bit odd, though,' Barbara Bradford continued.

'Odd? In what way?'

'Well, when I asked to see the paintings, we had to sneak into the embassy by a back entrance – happily the guard recognised him, but it turned out that they were stored in a kind of shed, not in the embassy itself, and we had to look at them in there.'

'From what I've heard, his father didn't really approve of him wasting his time doing paintings,' Ethan explained.

'So he was doing all his work on the quiet?' Adam Bradford asked incredulously. 'Certainly, we didn't think he was wasting his time. Did we, Babs?'

His daughter shrank a bit at the reference to her childhood handle before answering. 'Absolutely not. He had – sorry, has a real talent. We felt privileged to be the ones to first display them to the public. Didn't we, Dad?'

Again her father nodded. 'Barbara,' he had obviously noticed his daughter's reaction to being called Babs again, 'has an eye for this sort of thing and when they arrived I couldn't have agreed more with her. They are good – very good, in fact.'

'So what happened after the paintings arrived?' Ethan asked.

'We waited for him to contact us on his arrival, but when we hadn't heard anything I asked Barbara to ring his sister – she was the one who knew him, after all – and he had told her that he had arranged to stay with her for a while. But she hasn't seen him either – isn't that right, Barbara?'

'What's happened to him? Dad, do you know?' she asked almost pleadingly, sensing that something was wrong, especially now that the police were involved.

Ethan stepped closer to her to explain. 'It's just that it seems he's gone missing. The Garda in Dublin have asked us if we can see if he's turned up this end.' After a short pause for thought, he added, 'It doesn't look like he has.'

Ethan Brown turned to leave; he didn't think there was anything further he could learn from the father and daughter, at least at this time. But before leaving he did ask that if they thought of anything or, more importantly, if Daniel did make contact, whether they could let him know. He pulled a card from his pocket and handed it to Adam Bradford.

'My contact details are on that,' he affirmed.

Then, just as he pulled the door open, as if he'd suddenly remembered something, he let it go to allow it to close once more. 'Sorry, Ms Bradford. Would you have a photo that you could email to me?'

Both father and daughter looked at him quizzically.

'My colleagues in Ireland have requested one. Just to eliminate you from their enquiries. My email address is on the card.' He exited the gallery, noting, as he glanced back, the bemused looks of the pair.

chapter twenty

The email from Ethan Brown pinged its presence onto John's computer.

He was already sitting at his desk, so he opened it immediately. Scrolling down, he read it avidly. The email contained a report of the interviews with the Bradfords; the details were accompanied by Ethan Brown's own opinion that father and daughter were telling the truth and were as mystified by Daniel's disappearance, as was everyone on this side of the pond.

There was also an attachment to the email which contained a digital photograph of Barbara Bradford, the girl that had travelled to Ireland and met up with Daniel to sign him up for the New York exhibition.

He summoned Jo over to his desk. He re-read the email to her.

'Another dead end?' she asked.

John didn't reply straightaway; he was still trying to put together all the facts that they did know to try and determine which ones they didn't yet know.

'Well,' he finally answered. 'It does confirm and explain some of what we know, but it doesn't really seem to get us any closer to where Daniel is now.'

He printed out the photograph of Barbara Bradford, retrieved it from the printer next to his desk and handed it to Jo. 'Take this round to that headmaster's secretary – what's she called?'

'Mrs Perry.'

'That's right, Mrs Perry. Ask her if this could be the girl that she saw Daniel with, the one she thought he might be cheating on Cara Williams with.'

Jo looked down at the image. 'Will do. The photo does seem to fit the description that she gave us. I'll go see her and give you a ring.'

'Thanks, Jo.'

After Jo had left, John returned to the mountain of neglected paperwork. It hadn't seemed to have shrunk in size despite his earlier efforts.

Head down, slouched over the desk, sleeves rolled up and the will to live all but deserting him, he was suddenly aware of his desk phone ringing.

'Hello?'

'DI McDaid?'

'Speaking.'

'Hi, it's Ronnie Graham here.' Then, after a slight pause in which the caller realised that the pair didn't know one another and that his name would mean nothing to the other, he added, 'From the IT department. You sent us over a computer?'

John immediately straightened up and replied, 'I did. Have you got some news for me?' he asked hopefully. He recognised that the investigation badly needed some good news.

'Well, I suppose it depends what you mean by good news, but I've bypassed the password and we can access all the information that's stored on the computer. To be honest, it doesn't mean a lot to me – there's nothing illegal or even dodgy as far as we can see, but what's there might mean something to you.'

'Indeed it might. I'll be right over.'

He pulled on his jacket, remembering to take his mobile with him in case Jo rang; he reached across the desk for it and stuffed it roughly into his inside pocket, making his way out of the detectives' office and downstairs to the IT department.

The IT department was exactly as one would have expected it to be: rows upon row of individual desks, each cluttered by an array of electronics, but the central area was dominated by laptops or notepads of various sizes and shapes. Behind every computer screen John could just make out the top of an individual's head. All were bowed, vision intently fixed on the screen in front of them.

One of the heads near the back of the room popped up at the sound of the spring door closing nosily behind John.

An arm appeared beside the head and waved at him. 'DI McDaid?' the head called.

John made his way over to the man who spoke. As he did so he noticed that many, if not most of the individuals within the IT department, were quite young and all too completely engrossed in their computer screens to take any notice of him as he passed.

'Mr Graham?' John asked, probably unnecessarily, as no one else had as yet even acknowledged his presence.

'Ronnie. Please. We don't hold on formalities down here.'

Ronnie Graham looked a bit older than the others in the department. However, John guessed, he was probably a lot younger than he looked. His mannerisms were undoubtedly those of a younger man, but his features were dominated by a prematurely balding head.

Ronnie Graham noticed John trying to work out his age. 'It's just that my parting's got a bit wider over the years, that's all,' he explained.

John smiled and suggested they get down to business.

Ronnie flicked the laptop open. 'What would you like to see?'

'Let's start with his emails.'

The IT man opened the Gmail account and revealed a long list of incoming emails. A lot seemed to be junk, but a few caught his eye. There were a number to and from his sister in New York; they scrolled through these.

As John read each one in turn, Ronnie expressed his opinion. 'Looks like he was heading to New York.'

'That's what we've been told, and these emails seem to suggest that that was indeed his intention.'

There were other emails from the Bradford gallery and these too confirmed that which they already knew and backed up what they'd been told.

Further down the list of emails was the correspondence and booking with Aer Lingus; the reference number looked the same, as far as John could remember, as the one found separately in the holdall.

Ronnie went into the Aer Lingus booking and located the boarding pass that Daniel had requested and probably printed out. Jo had already confirmed, though, that Daniel had not boarded that particular plane. Delving back into the emails and also the computer's memory, there did not appear to be references to any other flight or flights from Aer Lingus or any other carrier.

'I've accessed his online banking if you're interested,' announced Ronnie after giving John time to process the information displayed on the laptop's screen.

'Yes please,' John confirmed.

Ronnie flicked the mouse from side to side, scrolling around the screen and tapping it intermittently.

Finally, up came Daniel's digital bank statements.

'All pretty boring stuff.' Ronnie indicated some columns. 'Until you get to here.' He pointed to the screen. 'See?'

John squinted to see what his attention was being drawn to.

'Recently, the monies in Daniel's accounts suddenly changed.' Ronnie Graham helped John to understand the figures in front of him. 'All pretty mundane stuff, small amounts here and there, in and out. Then, more recently, €1000 deposit, followed by outgoings of €284 to,' he scrolled across the page, 'Aer Lingus. Also, here,' again he indicated another expense, '€500 to some haulage company.'

The figures confirmed to John that Daniel had paid for his own flights and covered the cost of shipping his artwork to the States, but it didn't explain where the money to do so came from.

He asked his IT colleague, 'Any indication of where that €1,000 deposit came from?'

Ronnie re-examined the bank statement. 'No name or account number on the deposit.'

'What does that mean?'

'It suggests that it was probably a cash deposit.'

John scratched his head, trying to put the information together. Everything suggested that Daniel was New York-bound. He had flights organised. His paintings had been shipped there. His sister and the gallery owners were expecting him, yet all the evidence was that he hadn't travelled. Why? So where was he now? And where did he get €1,000 in cash?

His mobile buzzed. Looking down at the screen, he saw it was Jo.

'Well?' he asked without any formalities, frustrated as he was by the laptop's failure to disclose any new information.

'You were right. It was her the secretary saw Daniel with.' Jo hadn't seemed to pick up on the agitation in John's voice.

'So there was nothing going on then?'

'From what Ethan said it was purely business and he

believed her, so we've no reason to think otherwise. But you never know.'

'I think it's unlikely they were in sort of relationship – they'd only just met, after all. I'm actually here with the IT guy, who's just accessed Daniel's computer files, and everything I've seen, at least so far, between Daniel and Barbara Bradford is simply about the business of his paintings.'

'Yet another dead end then?' Jo asked.

'Looks like it,' he replied, trying once more to keep the frustration out of his voice.

'So it looks like fifty-fifty then?'

'Sorry, what?'

'Fifty-fifty. Your hunches. One right one wrong.'

'Clear off,' he replied, hanging up, unable, despite the setbacks, to suppress a small smile at Jo's observation.

chapter twenty-one

Niamh had got up early to make their breakfast. She had complained about not having a good night's sleep, mainly because of his restlessness. He knew she was right. He hadn't been able to get to sleep himself; he knew that he had tossed and turned and gotten up repeatedly to pace the floor or go to the toilet.

His mind had been in turmoil with regard to the missing boy. He knew that he was going to have to report his lack of progress to his boss, DCI Sean O'Brien, the man that John had little time for and whom he regarded as an over promoted pen-pusher.

But before doing so, at some time in the early morning as he lay back in bed trying his best to remain still and not disturb Niamh anymore, he really needed to go and see Daniel's father and brother once more. Just to be sure he hadn't missed anything or not picked up on something in his earlier interviews. John, at least, knew a little more now. Certainly more than either the ambassador or Daniel's brother Jake had admitted knowing.

He also wanted to see Sanders. There was the little matter of the money which still needed an explanation.

After a further short snooze as he got wearily out of bed, he nearly tripped. His leg for some reason actually felt even stiffer than it had before. But on the other hand, at least the feeling in his face now seemed to be slowly getting better. Dismissing the trip and subsequent limp as simply down to his lack of sleep, he made his way over to the chest of drawers. Opening the top drawer, he pulled out the letter from the hospital that he'd hidden under some T-shirts – mainly to prevent Niamh from examining it too closely and worrying.

The appointment with the neurologist was that morning. He wasn't going to miss it, even though he was distracted and his mind engulfed by the ongoing inquiry into Daniel's disappearance.

He got dressed slowly and made his way downstairs. The smell of a bacon being grilled lifted his spirits.

'You're up. At last.'

'What do you mean?' he asked.

Niamh was already fully dressed. She was wearing a knitted beige cardigan and a pair of cotton trousers. Although a simple outfit, John couldn't help admiring how good she looked. Even this early in the morning and especially after a disturbed night's sleep.

'You've got a busy day, haven't you?'

'Busy day?'

'Your appointment with the consultant, it's this morning, isn't it?'

Either she'd remembered the date from the very brief mention he'd made of it at the time of the tests or, perhaps more likely, she'd found the letter in its hidden place when putting some of his clothes away.

He had thought of going to the hospital by himself. If it was bad news he'd probably best hear it himself first before telling Niamh; if it was good news he'd have spared her the worry.

That wasn't going to happen now. It was obvious that she had every intention of sharing the consultation with him.

As he tucked into the bacon butty he looked at Niamh. It was clear that she had made a special effort and was trying to be supportive and suppress her own anxieties about the upcoming hospital appointment.

After breakfast, Niamh had insisted upon driving. He had enough on his mind, she had said, without worrying about early morning Dublin traffic and then, worse still, trying to find a parking space at the hospital.

In the end they found that there was in fact only a short queue to the car park at the private hospital – a definite advantage over its public health equivalents. Nevertheless, the queue was still only moving slowly, so Niamh insisted on dropping him off to make his own way to the outpatient department, stating that she would join him there as soon as she had got rid of the car.

Having checked in at the outpatient reception, the young woman behind the reception desk indicated Dr Moran's office and told him to take a seat outside it.

'The consultant will call you when he's ready for you,' she informed him.

As he waited patiently he spotted Niamh entering the building and approaching the receptionist. He waved over to her and she altered her path to come over beside him.

'Have you been in yet?' she asked.

'Not yet. I think he's running a bit late.' He looked at his watch. His appointment was five minutes ago.

He had no sooner raised his arm to gauge the time than the consulting room door opened and a face appeared at the door. John was embarrassed; he hoped the doctor hadn't noticed him looking at his watch.

If Dr Moran had, he chose to ignore it but politely confirmed John's identity and ushered him into his office.

Niamh got to her feet at the same time and started to move forward in tandem with her partner.

The consultant looked from one to the other and then, it appeared, questioningly at John.

'This is Niamh, my partner,' he quickly explained. 'Is it okay for her to come in with me?'

'Of course. As you wish.'

The window blinds in the room were drawn, but the office itself was modern, bright, with white walls upon which a single landscape print hung just above an examination couch on the far wall. The only other piece of furniture was a large wooden desk which appeared traditional and therefore incongruous with the rest of the room's appearance.

The consultant made his way back to the desk and then sat down, indicating to John and Niamh to join him there at one end of it.

The couple sat side by side. John felt Niamh's hand grip his.

Dr Moran formally introduced himself and then almost immediately started reading from his notes the letter that John's GP had forwarded to him.

The consultant, John noted, was probably in his early fifties, clean-shaven with a good head of hair, dark, but greying at the edges.

His shirt was of expensive material and hung open at the collar, sleeves rolled up. The modern doctor's uniform, John surmised, white coats being a thing of the past.

Having gone through the contents of the referral letter he put the notes down and asked John if it was a fair description of the problems he was having.

John confirmed the veracity of the GP's description of things, while noting that there was more paperwork in the folder that the letter was in.

'Before discussing things further, I'd like to—'

He didn't get to finish the sentence before John interrupted him: 'You mean the test results? You have got those, haven't you?' He felt Niamh punch him gently in the ribs.

He turned to glare at her, only to find her glaring back at him.

He realised she was just telling him to be patient, and that it was his own anxiety that had provoked his intervention.

'Sorry, just a bit nervous, that's all.'

'Don't worry,' replied the consultant, trying to be reassuring. 'Yes, I've got all the test results. I'll go through them with you in a moment. But first I want to examine you myself.'

'Of course, Doctor,' muttered John sheepishly.

He asked John to strip to his underpants, first asking whether he minded if Niamh stayed.

'I think she's seen it all before,' John replied, trying to lift his mood.

The neurologist then carried out many of the tests that the GP had subjected him to before. He was perhaps, though, a little more methodical in doing so and took his time when testing the power in John's limbs, not just the weak leg but the other and his arms as well.

As his own doctor had done he tapped John's reflexes, again both in the arms and his legs.

When the consultant made to scratch John's soles with the end of the patella hammer, he instinctively withdrew his foot, bending his leg up and away from the attempt to illicit the response that the GP had reported.

'What's wrong?' asked the startled consultant.

'Sorry, it's just that I've had that done before and it's pretty unpleasant.'

Dr Moran gave a small chuckle. 'I'm sorry. I know it is. But I'm afraid it has to be done.'

'Stop being a wuss,' Niamh added from the side-line.

With that Dr Moran gripped John's lower leg just above the ankle, pressing it down onto the couch, thus preventing him from pulling it away again, and carried out the scratching manoeuvre.

Then, much to John's displeasure, he did the same thing to the other foot.

'One last thing,' he said, helping John down from the couch.

'Yes?' John replied, with some trepidation given the preceding test.

'Can I see you walk? Up and down the office, please.'

As he did as he was bid, John tried to concentrate so as not to allow his stiff leg to drag, deliberately and consciously lifting it and moving it forward in as normal a walking pattern as he could achieve.

'Mmmm…' muttered the doctor to himself.

John took this to mean that he hadn't succeeded as well as he had hoped in disguising the limp.

'Finally, can you now walk heel to toe?' Dr Moran then demonstrated what he meant. Carefully placing one foot in front of the other, heel touching toe as he made his way across the office floor.

John laughed. 'Do you think I'm drunk?' he asked.

'Sorry?'

'I am a Guard, you know.'

'Ahhh. No, it's just a test of your balance, that's all,' the doctor reassured him.

John set off; he had seen this test carried out many times in his early career on the beat. He had little doubt he could perform walking heel to toe without difficulty.

As he tried he wobbled from side to side and eventually had to quickly place one foot out to the side to stop himself physically toppling over.

Dr Moran stepped forward and supported him by the arm. 'Okay, I've seen enough. Get dressed. Please.'

John was horrified by his inept performance in trying to walk the tightrope across the office floor. He replaced his shirt but again wobbled when he lifted one leg to slip the other into his trousers. He gripped the examination couch for support.

When he looked up all he saw was the worried expression on Niamh's face.

Fully clothed again, John sat back down at the desk as the consultant silently wrote copious notes into the folder in front of him.

Finally, Dr Moran looked up and engaged their attention. 'I have a diagnosis for you.' He spoke softly.

'Well, thank God for that,' uttered John without thinking. He felt Niamh's fist in his ribs again. 'So what is wrong with me, Doctor?'

'Let me just go through this with you. With you both.' He looked back and forth between John and Niamh.

John was worried again; he turned to Niamh and he could tell that she was worried too.

The consultant took a short pause to allow them both to settle. Then he started to speak. 'Mr McDaid, your story appears to be one of symptoms coming and going. Am I correct?'

'Coming and going? Well, to a degree, yes. My leg went funny – it seemed to get a bit better but for some reason just recently it's not as good as it was again. Then I got the numbness and pain in my face, but that has largely settled now. But that's all. Or at least all I can think of.'

Dr Moran consulted his notes again. 'Tell me, Mr McDaid, did you ever have a problem with one of your eyes?'

John thought for a moment. Niamh looked at him questioningly before she replied, 'I don't remember you ever complaining about your eyes, John.'

Her answer, though, seemed to awaken a memory. 'Actually. Yes, I did. It was quite a while ago, though.' He turned to Niamh. 'It was before we got together.'

The consultant continued. 'Tell me, what do you remember? In particular did it affect your vision at all?'

John got the impression that the doctor already knew the answer to his question before he even asked it. 'As I said, it was a number of years ago and it was only a temporary thing. I'd forgotten about it.'

'Okay, Mr McDaid, describe to me exactly what happened.'

'As far as I can recall, I was about eighteen,' he paused, 'so it must have only been a couple of years ago.' He laughed.

The consultant ignored the attempt at humour.

There was another dig in his ribs.

'Sorry, okay, I just remember a bad pain in my left eye and then my vision went.'

'All of your vision? Did you become completely blind in the eye?'

'No, come to think of it, it was a bit odd. It was only in the centre of my vision that I couldn't see – around the edges were fine.'

'But you say it came back?'

'It got gradually better over a couple of months and I've had no trouble since.'

'And did you see a doctor about it at the time?'

'I remember my mother being quite worried – I saw the GP and then I was sent to see an eye doctor at the hospital.'

'An ophthalmologist?'

'If you say so. He was an eye doctor to me.'

'So tell me, what did he think was the matter?'

'He said there was some inflammation in the nerve behind the eye and that it should settle down over a few weeks. He was dead right – it did. I was only to go back if it recurred. It never did.'

'Let me tell you what I think then, Mr and Mrs McDaid…' He caught Niamh's look. 'Sorry… Niamh… I am a bit old-fashioned, I'm afraid. I always presume couples are married.'

'Don't worry,' said Niamh, anxious to see what the consultant had to say.

'Your story about your loss of vision, albeit a number of years ago, fits with the findings of the visual evoked potentials test that we preformed.' Dr Moran noted John's puzzled look. 'The eye test. The one where you sat in front of a screen and we flashed lights at you.'

John nodded his understanding.

'That test measures how long it takes for the brain to register the flash of light.'

'That's why he had electrodes attached to his head?' Niamh asked.

'Exactly,' Dr Moran confirmed before continuing his explanation. 'If the response is slowed on one side, it usually indicates some damage to the visual pathway on that side, usually in the optic nerve.'

John and Niamh exchanged glances.

'Your test, Mr McDaid, showed a clinically significant slowing in the left optic nerve. That, in my opinion, fits exactly with what you've just told me about having been previously diagnosed with a bout of inflammation in your left optic nerve.'

'I don't really understand – what has what happened years ago got to do with what's happening now?'

'Let me explain.'

'Please do,' he said as he felt Niamh's grip tighten.

'Your story of your limp and then the facial nerve pain are also suggestive of bouts of inflammation elsewhere within in the nervous system.'

'So they'll get better just like his eye did?' asked Niamh hopefully.

John remained silent; he could see in the consultant's face that there was more to follow.

Dr Moran turned to Niamh. 'To a degree. Yes. They might.'

'Might get better?' Niamh had picked up on the word 'might'.

'Well, yes. But – and it is a big but – in my experience the more bouts of inflammation there are the more likely that some more permanent damage will be done.'

Niamh moved closer to John, sensing his growing concern at the doctor's words.

'Of greater importance,' the consultant continued, 'is to determine if there are other areas affected and to try to find out the cause of these disparate patches of inflammation.'

'So what do I need to do?'

'Actually, I don't think you need to do anything.' He reached behind him and lifted a large pink folder which had been resting against the far side of the desk. He started to extract, what looked to John and Niamh, an oversized X-ray from the folder.

'Here is your MRI,' he announced as he stood up to attach the scan to a viewing box. 'I think this tells us what the problem may be.'

John and Niamh stood up to be beside the consultant and regarded the scan in front of them.

'As you can see, an MRI is a very sensitive test. It takes pictures as though we have taken slices of your brain.'

John looked at the pictures in wonder; it did indeed appear to be images of the inside of his head at different levels – not that he actually knew what the inside of his head looked like.

'So what does this tell you, Dr Moran?' asked Niamh, who hadn't released John's hand and if anything continued to grip it even more firmly.

'Look here. And here.' He pointed to a series of small bright spots that seemed to be scattered at various levels and positions around the brain displayed before them.

'These,' he confirmed, 'are further patches of inflammation, similar, I suspect, to the one that previously attacked your left optic nerve.'

'But... But... there are loads of them,' stuttered John, looking intently at the pictures in front of him.

'There are, you're right. But not all have, or indeed will, cause you any symptoms. They are in areas of the brain which don't affect your day-to-day functioning.'

'But they will get better?' he asked hopefully.

'Indeed so. Most flare up quickly so the symptom – like your earlier eye problem, or indeed the most recent facial pain – will tend to improve albeit slowly. The nervous system can recover or take over the function of damaged parts, but in general, we are talking over weeks or months, not days.'

'My leg seems to have taken longer; if anything, I get the impression it's actually getting wore at times.'

'That can be the case, I'm afraid. The other electrical test you had, you remember?'

'How could I forget? It wasn't the most pleasant experience of my life.'

'That test measures the time that it takes for messages to travel up and down the spinal cord. Your test confirmed that there was indeed some damage within the spinal cord such that the messages are being disrupted, so that your leg will feel stiff and weak and your appreciation of some sensations may be impaired.'

'So again it's due to this inflammation, yes?'

'Yes, but when it attacks the spinal cord it is less likely to completely go away. It often leaves damage and scarring, so the symptoms are more long-lasting.'

'But why does it seem to vary? Some days it seems better than others?'

'I often hear that. It usually depends on other things, things outside the spinal cord itself.'

'Things outside the spinal cord? I don't understand.'

'For instance if you are tired, or you do too much walking, running or exercise, or even if the weather is very warm, then because some pathways are damaged, the ones that are trying to do their work for them get fatigued and so your symptoms get more pronounced.' Then he quickly added, 'That doesn't mean any more damage is happening or that you are causing any harm. Usually you'll find that if you rest, take it easy, things will get better again.'

John considered what had been said and realised that Dr Moran's words did ring true with his own experiences, particularly with regard to his leg problems.

'So what's causing these patches of inflammation?' It was Niamh who spoke, she had released John's hand and now leant forward around her partner to engage more closely with the consultant.

Dr Moran paused for thought and then, as if summoning up his courage, he answered her question. But he did so by answering it to John himself, not directly to Niamh. 'Given your story, my clinical findings when I examined you and now the results of the tests that we have just discussed, I'm afraid there really can be only one possible diagnosis.'

Before he could explain further, John heard Niamh take a sharp intake of breath; he could feel his own heart beating, convinced as he was by the consultant's tone of voice that the news was not going to be good.

He hardly heard the next part of the conversation and had to ask Dr Moran to repeat it.

'I'm afraid that all of what we have discussed all seems

to add up to a diagnosis of multiple sclerosis.'

John and Niamh didn't know how to respond. Of course they had heard of MS but had never given it a second thought. They simply sat motionless, staring blankly at one another.

After giving them a few minutes with their own thoughts, Dr Moran, probably well used to imparting unfavourable diagnoses as that which he had just delivered, started to try to explain in more detail why he had reached the diagnosis and, more importantly, the nature of the condition and what it might mean in the future for John and indeed Niamh.

John only caught pieces of the doctor's explanations. His mind was in turmoil; all he could see was a wheelchair and disability which was the sum total of his knowledge of this feared condition. He hoped Niamh was listening and could relate it to him later.

Dr Moran continued in the background. 'MS – or DS, as the Americans call it – refers to multiple, or disseminated, patches of inflammation, or sclerosis, throughout the nervous system. There are a number of types, but the most common one, the one you have described to me, is the relapsing, remitting type.'

John and Niamh just looked at him without speaking.

'That is, it comes and goes. There is a flare-up now, then it improves, but there may be another flare-up later.'

'How long between flare-ups?' asked Niamh, who was indeed trying to process the information more intently than John.

'Impossible to say, I'm afraid. In fact, just look John's own story. It was years ago that the optic nerve was attacked, then the leg and face come along closely together.'

'And we don't know what causes it?'

'Again, I'm afraid not. It is one of those diseases where there is still a lot we don't know about it, but we are getting better. The MRI, for example, means we can actually see the lesions for the first time.'

John seemed to wake up from his thoughts. 'Are there any other tests we need to do to make sure that you are right about this?'

Dr Moran didn't appear in any way perturbed by the challenge to his diagnosis, something John guessed that he was confronted with frequently when conveying bad news. 'We could do lumbar puncture,' he responded.

John and Niamh didn't know what a lumbar puncture was, so Dr Moran explained that it involved inserting a needle into the lower back between the vertebrae to sample some of the fluid that surrounds the spinal cord.

It didn't sound a very pleasant procedure to John and he was relieved when Dr Moran continued. 'I think we will hold off on that, though, at least at present. I think given everything we have so far, a lumbar puncture is not really going to add anything further.'

Again it was Niamh who spoke first. 'Given what you've said, Dr Moran, is there any treatment that John can get to cure this thing?'

'I'm afraid there is no cure for MS,' came the reply that Niamh had already expected.

'There are some things that we can do to help, but before getting into a discussion about which to try and when, let's try and put things into context first.'

'What do you mean, put into context?' John appeared fully engaged once more, recovering from the initial shock.

'Well, for example, what is your perception of MS?'

John and Niamh looked back and forth at each other, neither really wanting to answer the question in front of the other.

Sensing their reluctance to answer his question directly he asked a follow up question.

'Do you see it as leading to disability ending up in a wheelchair, perhaps in a nursing home totally dependent on others, for example?'

John and Niamh both nodded silently, each trying to avoid the other's gaze.

'Okay, well, here are the facts. Firstly, MS is a very variable disease. Yes, some people can be badly affected, but not all by any means. The true statistic is that only about twenty per cent of people with MS ever get near a wheelchair.'

Unable to disentangle the vision of himself in a wheelchair, John interrupted, 'But that's what we see.'

'Exactly, that's what you see.'

John was confused.

'If you have MS and you are in a wheelchair, it's obvious to others that you have a disability. But as most people have a flare-up now and again and are not disabled by them there is nothing to see; they tend to get on with things as normal and you wouldn't suspect that they have MS. In general most people don't tend to tell others except perhaps those closest to them that they have it. Hence the skewed perception.'

John could see the logic in what Dr Moran was saying, but he still harboured some inner fears.

'From what you've told me that your story actually began years ago with the eye problem and here you are years later with actually not that much to find. Yes, I can see that your legs are a bit weaker than they should be, but unless you overexert yourself no one, I think, would suspect that there was actually anything wrong. Your vision is fine and there's nothing to see in your face despite the feeling that you have.'

After taking a moment or two to rationalise what the doctor had said, Niamh went back to her original question. 'So what are the treatments you were mentioning?'

Dr Moran continued. 'As I said, I haven't got a cure for

MS, but that's not to say one won't come along – there have been major advances in the understanding of the disease in recent years – but we do have some treatments that can help the symptoms.'

'Like what?' Niamh interrupted.

John gave her a sideways glance but remained silent himself.

'There is a new drug, beta interferon, which only recently has been shown to reduce the number of relapses – that is what we call each flare-up, like your original eye problem and then the facial pain and numbness.'

'So how do we get that?' Niamh asked again.

'To be honest, I don't think you are bad enough to warrant it at the moment.' But then on reflection he added, 'That's actually a good thing.'

'What do you mean?' asked John.

'Beta interferon is reserved for people who have frequent relapses – more than three over two years is the usual requirement. You, happily, don't meet that criteria, and in people who have fewer relapses they don't really see the benefit of it.'

'I'm sorry, I don't fully understand?'

'Beta interferon is not a cure – as I said it reduces the number of attacks or relapses but by only about a third, so that if a patient only like yourself has an episode every what? You were eighteen when you had the optic neuritis and you're what?' He looked down at his notes. 'Thirty-six now?'

'Yes? Sorry, I still don't quite get you?'

'Okay, if beta interferon only reduces the risk of a flare-up by one third, as it does, if you have had only three attacks – your eye, your leg and your face – over a period of eighteen years, you would have to take the drug for another eighteen years to prevent just one attack.'

'But what if I have more attacks sooner?'

'Then I'll change my mind and we will start the drug.' The doctor picked up on John's continued worried expression. 'I promise,' he added quickly.

'So is there anything we can do now?' Niamh asked.

'Actually, yes, there is.'

That's a bit more like it, thought John, though he remained quiet.

'The attacks that you could see on the MRI scan, they are actually patches of inflammation. We have medicines which have been shown to reduce this inflammation and so reduce the symptoms of the inflammation itself.'

'What kind of medicines?' asked John.

'The most powerful anti-inflammatory drugs that we use in this situation are steroids.'

John had heard of steroids. 'Aren't they the drugs that athletes sometimes take?' he said, adding, 'Illegally.'

'Different kind of steroids. I've no intention of turning you into a muscle man. No, we tend to use a steroid called dexamethasone and we only give you a short course. Usually for about two to three weeks, starting with a high dose and tapering it down, quickly stopping it at the end of the course.'

'And if I agree, what can I expect?'

'I would hope that your facial symptoms would settle and your leg movement would improve a bit.'

'What if they came back?'

'If it got worse again later we could give you another course,' the doctor stated matter-of-factly.

John seemed content with the explanation, but Niamh asked, 'Are there any side effects?'

Dr Moran seemed to consider his reply for a few moments. Then: 'All drugs have side effects. Steroids are no exception, but as I am only going to prescribe a short, sharp course, I really wouldn't expect too much.'

'But what sort of things can go wrong?' Niamh persisted.

'Steroids can encourage the appetite. So,' he turned to John, 'you could gain weight.' But he added quickly, 'But as you are only going to be taking then for three weeks at most, I don't really think that should be a problem.'

'Anything else we should expect?' Niamh persisted.

'Again, steroids can increase your energy levels, give you a boost, make you feel too well. So just be aware of that, as when you stop them there can be a bit of a rebound.'

'Doesn't sound too bad,' John muttered, turning to Niamh.

Dr Moran reached for his prescription pad and wrote John's prescription before handing it to him. 'Come back and see me in a few days. You'll have had most of the course of steroids by that time and you can tell me how you are getting on.'

John and Niamh thanked the consultant and rose to leave.

Niamh turned back just before exiting and asked, 'He will be alright, won't he?'

Dr Moran nodded encouragingly before John pulled her out of the office. 'What did you ask him that for?' he said angrily.

'I am just worried about you, that's all.'

John recognised her concern and the two left hand in hand to find the car park.

Before they could retrieve the car, John's mobile buzzed in his pocket.

'Don't answer it,' pleaded Niamh. 'We have things to talk about.'

John looked at the screen. 'I have to, it's work,' he explained.

Niamh let go of his hand and walked on alone towards where they had parked the car.

John pressed the answer button and lifted the phone to his ear, watching Niamh walk on ahead of him.

'John McDaid. What can I do for you?'
'John, it's Jo.'
'What's up, Jo? I told you I was busy this morning.'
'They've found a body.'

chapter twenty-two

John stood beside his desk, flicking through some of the witness statements that had already been compiled. The inquiry had now taken a different turn. It was now a murder inquiry and the importance of it had escalated exponentially.

Not unsurprisingly, at least to John, DCI O'Brien, who was supposed to be in overall charge of the investigation, had opted out of conveying the bad news to the boy's family at the embassy, but then did insist on supporting the father through the formal identification process at the morgue. Thus giving the grieving ambassador the fullest of assurances that he personally would ensure that the circumstances of Daniel's death would be fully and thoroughly investigated.

The identification hadn't been a simple one, given the state of the body and the time it had lain undisturbed in the river. DNA samples had been taken and compared to those of Daniel's father and his brother, Jake. They had come back positive, confirming his identity. Jake had also confirmed that the stars and stripes shirt that the body had been found in was one of Daniel's favourite shirts and he often wore it to parties. He was also able to identify Daniel's phone which had been dredged from the river a little later in the day.

The phone was waterlogged and had been sent to the IT department to see if they could get it going and interrogate it.

'Keep DI Marshall up to speed,' had been O'Brien's last words before leaving the office that afternoon. John had little doubt that DI Marshall would be reporting any progress – or indeed, any lack of progress – directly back to the DCI behind John's back. The only saving grace was that DI Alan Marshall didn't display any real interest in aiding or abetting in any practical aspects of the investigation. He seemed content simply to remain at his desk within the office and request regular updates.

Jo stuck her head around the door. 'The pathologist has just rung. Thought you might be interested to have a chat with him about Daniel's PM.'

John had just witnessed Alan Marshall heading down to the café for a cup of tea before Jo had made her announcement. He quickly decided to take advantage of his absence, so, seizing Jo by the arm, he ushered out of the office as speedily as he could to pre-empt DI Marshall's return.

'What the…?' asked Jo, startled by his rapid escape.

'Don't ask. Let's just get down to the morgue. Follow me.'

The two of them made their way out of the detective's suite and down through the building to the car park and then drove to the morgue, which was part of the local major teaching hospital.

*

'Dr Sullivan. At your service,' greeted the pathologist. He was dressed in a theatre gown and hat, though no surgical mask – an unnecessary burden in his profession, unlikely as it was that he could to pass on any infection to the corpse.

Dr Sullivan was genial, ruddy-faced man, who, without the surgical garb, could have been mistaken for a local farmer.

He smiled at the two detectives, revealing a less than perfect row of teeth.

'I think I have some answers for you detectives,' he announced with his booming voice, before adding more quietly, 'Though probably not all.'

John and Jo looked at each other, neither quite grasping his meaning.

Noting their bemused expressions, he went on to elucidate. 'The PM was a bit tricky, obviously. Given the length of time to body had been in the water. However, a healthy male – late teens, I'd say.'

'Daniel was nineteen,' Jo confirmed.

'He had undoubtedly sustained a blow to the head, almost certainly before death.'

'A blow to the head?' John was interested.

'Yes, across the forehead there was a linear bruise – well, bleeding, not yet a bruise, indicating that it had occurred very shortly before death. Underneath there was a small, again linear, skull fracture.'

'Meaning what?' Jo asked.

'Meaning that the subject—'

'*Daniel*,' added Jo, not as able to demonstrate aloofness from the subject as proficiently as the pathologist.

The pathologist nodded his understanding. 'Daniel,' he continued, 'had suffered a blow to the head. One of considerable force, given the skull fracture. The lack of a formed bruise indicates to me that the blow was very shortly before death as any bleeding stops as soon as the heart stops.'

'Was that the cause of Daniel's death, the… the blow to the head?'

'No, undoubtedly not.'

'Why do you say that?' queried John. 'Given that you said it was a blow of "considerable force".'

'In my opinion, the cause of death was drowning.'

'Tell me why you came to that conclusion, Dr Sullivan?' Again it was John who pursued the point.

'Very simple. The lungs were full of water. They could only be filled with water if he was still breathing when he entered the water.'

'Okay. I accept that.'

'Also,' continued the pathologist, 'I have little doubt that *Daniel* drowned in the river that you found him in.'

'Why do you say that?'

'Within the water in the lungs there were bacteria, microbes, etc. We had a sample of the water from which he was fished out of and the make-up of the organisms is similar.'

'He couldn't just have been dumped there and these bacteria got in later?'

'Definitely not. No. To be so deep within the pulmonary tissue – sorry, lung tissue, they had to have been inhaled. In other words, when he was drowning, not afterwards.'

'So he drowned.'

'That's what I have concluded.'

'So what about this head injury? Did it happen before he fell in the water or afterwards?'

'That, Inspector, is why I said at the outset that I didn't have all the answers. It is impossible to tell exactly when that head injury did occur, just that he was alive when it happened and that it happened around the time that he drowned.'

'So he could have hit his head and fallen in the river, or he could have fallen in the water and banged his head on the way in, or even hit it on the riverbed?'

'I'm afraid that's the conundrum, Inspector.'

Jo had a thought. 'Is there anything else you can tell us about the injury – can you say, for example, what caused it?'

'Good question, young lady. Indeed. It was a linear injury –

a straight line, if you like. It was about six inches long, though that doesn't tell you much, given the curvature of the skull.' He put his hand up at the side his forehead to indicate that the area of contact only represented a portion of his palm, not the whole hand. 'However, of more importance, it was about an inch wide.'

'Meaning?'

'Well, it's impossible to be sure, but it looks to me as if he hit or was hit by a straight pipe or baton-like object – hard to say which but one that is about an inch in diameter.'

'Thanks, Doc. That gives us something to go on anyway.'

The two detectives turned to leave as the pathologist started to remove some of his protective clothing and gave them a short cursory wave.

'What do you make of that?' asked Jo.

'Was he pushed, or did he fall? That's the question, I guess.'

Jo indicated her agreement. As the two made their way back to the car John tried to decide just how much of the remaining uncertainties regarding the case he wanted to share with O'Brien, either through Alan Marshall or directly face to face.

chapter twenty-three

'We need to go and see the ambassador and his other son again,' John said, almost to himself.

Jo reached for her handbag and moved over beside him. 'Let's go,' she agreed.

*

As they stood on the steps waiting to be allowed into the embassy, Jo turned to John and asked, 'What are you going to say to him?'

'To be honest I don't really know, but there are a few issues I just need to clarify.'

Before Jo could interrogate him further, they were bade entry by a security guard and ushered into an anteroom.

'The ambassador will join you shortly,' the guard announced before turning to leave.

Before he could disappear out the door, John quickly asked, 'Could we speak to Jake?'

The guard looked nonplussed.

'The ambassador's son,' John clarified.

'I know who he is, Detective McDaid. But I will have to ask the ambassador first,' he stated before leaving.

The two waited a further five minutes in silence before Ambassador Wilson, accompanied by Jake, Daniel's younger brother, arrived.

'You wanted to see us?' The ambassador gestured for them to take a seat as he and Jake sat down across the ornate fireplace from them.

'Yes, sir,' started John. 'Firstly, can we convey our condolences?'

John noticed Daniel's younger brother's head drop and the anguish in his expression. He had clearly taken Daniel's death badly. The Ambassador remained stiff-lipped despite the family tragedy.

'Thank you, Inspector, Ms Roberts. So what have you got to report?' he asked unblinkingly.

John hesitated. 'Sorry, sir. You have got the wrong end of the stick, I'm afraid. At the moment we haven't got much to tell you. Actually, we just had a few questions we wanted answered.'

The ambassador's face hardened. 'What questions?'

'Do you know any reason why anybody would want to hurt Daniel?'

'Of course not.' The ambassador stared at them. 'He was a friendly, harmless boy.' He then seemed to take the question in and realised the meaning behind it.

'We were told Daniel drowned – an accident, by all accounts. Are you now telling me that you suspect foul play, that somebody else might be involved?'

'We just don't know, sir. We just want to examine every possibility,' John replied defensively. Then he continued. 'Could Daniel swim?'

Daniel's father exchanged looks with Jake and it was Jake who answered. 'We both had lessons when we were young –

Mum used to take us. Dad was always busy.' He stopped and looked up at his father as if to apologise.

His father nodded for him to continue.

'Daniel wasn't great. I don't honestly think he liked the water very much and when Mum died he just gave up the swimming lessons. He could get by, but he wasn't a strong swimmer by any means.' Jake reverted to his previous silent state once again.

'When he was found he was wearing a stars and stripes shirt,' John continued.

Jake lifted his head and exchanged looks with the two detectives.

'So given that he was wearing that shirt, do you think he was on his way to the party after all Jake?' Jo asked.

'He said he was, and if he was wearing that shirt I would say that he definitely was.' Jake looked adamant on that point.

The ambassador looked back and forth from his son to John seated opposite. 'Do you think that he was attacked and pushed into the river by somebody because he was wearing a stars and stripes shirt?' he asked incredulously. 'That it was some kind of terrorist attack? Aimed against me and my family?'

'We really don't know, sir,' was John's reply.

'But there was the head injury,' Jo butted in.

John shot her a warning look.

'What head injury? Nobody mentioned a head injury before.' The ambassador was on his feet, red-faced and almost shouting the question.

'Please calm down, sir.' John stared at Jo, warning her to remain silent. 'We are just exploring every possibility. It appears that Daniel had suffered a blow to the head in and around the time that he drowned. What we don't know is whether he hit his head when he fell into the river or whether it could have occurred before he entered the water.'

219

'You mean somebody might have hit him, causing him to fall?' The ambassador was on his feet again, this time pacing up and down as if trying to comprehend what he was being told.

Again John explained that they didn't know but assured the ambassador that they would get to the bottom of exactly what did happen to Daniel and that he would be the first to know.

Somewhat mollified, the ambassador sat down once again.

John decided to let Daniel's father cool down, so he turned to Jake. 'Jake, you said that Daniel never made it to the party and that possibly he was meeting somebody first.'

'Yes,' answered the teenager meekly.

'Do you know who he was meeting?'

'No,' came the curt reply as he tried to avoid John's gaze.

'Are you sure, Jake?'

'He's just said so, hasn't he?' butted in his father.

'But you went to the party, Jake?'

He nodded.

'You told us Cara was there.'

Again he nodded.

'How was she, Jake?'

The young man seemed to ponder the question for a few minutes as if deciding what to say. Finally he spoke. 'I didn't talk to her. She just sat in a corner by herself. She didn't really seem to talk to anyone – she looked upset.'

'Why do you think she was upset, Jake?' Jo spoke softly, trying to reassure the teenager that he wasn't betraying any confidences by telling his story.

'It was obvious, wasn't it?'

'Sorry, why, Jake?'

'Because my brother hadn't showed up, that's why. Cara knew he'd been invited and although he'd been acting funny recently I think she just wanted to see him. She was dead keen on him. And I had thought he was keen on her.' Jake lapsed into silence, once more feeling that he'd already said too much.

John wasn't letting go at this point but decided to take another tack. 'Jake,' he asked, 'did you know that Daniel was seen with another girl, that he'd been meeting up with her just before his accident?'

Jake looked troubled by the question; he glanced at his father, then reverted to staring silently down at the floor.

'Jake?' It was his father now who was encouraging him to tell all that he knew.

'Yes. I'd seen him meeting up with this American bird.'

'How did you know she was American, Jake?'

'One time when I saw them together I followed her back to her hotel and I heard her talk to the receptionist there.'

'Did she see you, Jake?'

'No,' he firmly stated. 'And anyway, she wouldn't have known me from Adam. Daniel never introduced me.'

It was the ambassador's turn to remain speechless, not quite knowing what revelation to expect next.

'Why did you follow her, Jake?'

Jake didn't answer for a few minutes. He was admitting that all this was a secret that he had kept to himself even after his brother had gone missing and he clearly felt guilty about it. 'I thought he was cheating on Cara. I liked Cara, I thought Daniel did too, but here he was seeing this other girl on the sly. I didn't think it was right, that's all.'

'Is this the girl?' asked Jo, holding out the photograph of Barbara Bradford.

Jake nodded.

The ambassador reached for the photograph and, taking it from Jo, he stared down at it. 'Who's this woman?' he asked. 'And what's she got to do with Daniel's death?'

'That's what we are trying to find out, sir. Again, when we know, you will.' John contemplated whether or not it was wise to push the subject of Daniel's planned escape to America and his possible defiance of his father's wishes to pursue an artistic career. That could wait.

Jake's father put his arm around his younger son's shoulders and pulled him towards him. 'I think maybe it's time you left, detectives.' The ambassador spoke with a certain firmness in his voice.

'May I ask just one other question before we go, sir?' asked John making up his mind, realising that they had probably already outstayed their welcome.

'What do you want to ask, Inspector?' replied the Ambassador, now somewhat tetchily.

'Did you know, sir?' John hesitated, knowing that his question might not go down entirely well. 'That Daniel had a sum of money and that it seems he was going to take off to the States?'

'Don't be ridiculous, Inspector.' The ambassador, who had sat down to comfort his son, was now on his feet again. 'Where would Daniel get money from, especially enough to get him over to America? That's a stupid suggestion. Now if you don't mind, I think Jake and I have had enough. I'll be having a word with Chief Inspector O'Brien about your insinuations – I'll see what he has to say about them.'

John and Jo got up to leave; looking back, John observed the ambassador once again holding his son, but he still managed to fix the pair with an angry stare.

chapter twenty-four

Back at the station, John rubbed his face. It had improved, but there was still some residual numbness in the cheek, though now only a small area, the size of a ten-pence piece, and the acute spasms of pain appeared to have eased. The steroids seemed to have kicked in, or at least he hoped that they had.

He nibbled on a doughnut which he had bought from the canteen before returning to his desk. The consultant had been right: his appetite had certainly increased since being on the medication.

Jo's phone rang. Watching her answer it and after only a few words into the receiver, she covered it with her hand and called over to John. 'It's Daniel's phone – they've managed to access it and download its contents onto a computer. Do you want to go over and see what they've got?'

'Absolutely,' John quickly confirmed, leaving the remains of the doughnut on his desk and moving over to join her. Then he had a thought: 'Ring Sanders at the embassy and ask him to join us.'

Jo looked at him. 'Why?'

'I think we need to keep his father in the loop, especially now that it's a murder case. Sanders can do that.'

Jo rang the embassy and quickly got put through to Tom Sanders, who agreed to come straight over.

John and Jo decided to wait for him, rather than having to go through the phone's contents twice.

It wasn't long before Tom Sanders was shown into the detective suite by the desk sergeant.

'Before we go up, Tom, can I ask you what you thought of the ambassador's suggestion of a possible terrorist link? Given who he was and the shirt, of course.'

The FBI gave the matter a few minutes' thought and then replied, 'Unlikely.'

'Why?' Jo asked.

'Daniel wouldn't have been a high-profile target, not for a murder at least. A kidnap, possibly, but a murder? No.'

'Could Daniel have tried to resist a kidnap and that got him killed?'

'Again, I say unlikely. Any terrorist group would have claimed responsibility by now and would more likely have claimed he was still alive and in their custody.' He paused as if thinking whether he should continue, but then decided to anyway. 'Not to put a finer point on it, but we have most of the terror groups, particularly those we consider a threat to the United States, under surveillance and my operatives are pretty sure that none of them were involved in this case.'

John wrinkled his nose at more covert US activity that was probably illegal, but then, he rationalised, also probably tolerated by our own secret service. So he held his tongue.

'Okay, let's go and see what we've got.' He pointed to the door.

'Have you guys already seen what's on Daniel's phone?' Tom Sanders asked.

'Not yet, we thought we'd wait for you,' John confirmed.

The FBI man indicated his appreciation.

*

Standing in the laboratory, the three huddled behind a white-coated operative who sat at a desk in front of a computer screen.

'What do you want to see first?' he asked.

'I guess the phone records,' replied John.

'I'll print them out – it'll be easier to examine them then.'

He was as good as his word and a printout quickly appeared from a nearby printer.

'How far do they go back?' queried Jo.

'About six months, as far as I can see. Do you know if he changed phones around that time?'

John looked at Sanders, who just shrugged his shoulders.

'It maybe that any before that have been automatically deleted anyway,' said the man seated at the desk.

'To be honest,' added John, 'anything before then is probably irrelevant to our investigation. Anything of any importance is most likely to be within a few days or a week or so, at most, before the time of his disappearance.'

'Or just after it,' offered Jo.

'Or just after it,' repeated John.

Examining the printout in turn, examining the timelines, nothing seemed to stand out to any of them.

John ran his finger down the list of numbers called. 'A few to the States, all the same number.'

Sanders googled the gallery in New York and confirmed that was their telephone number.

'That's Cara Williams' number, I'm pretty sure of it,' added Jo.

'I think you're right,' confirmed John, consulting his notebook.

They continued to scrutinise the long list of calls made but couldn't really see anything out of the ordinary.

'What about texts or social media?' asked Sanders.

The man in the white coat pressed a few buttons on the keyboard in front of him and once again the printer spewed out sheets of paper.

Again the trio looked over one another's shoulder to read the contents.

'Look,' exclaimed John. 'There, the last text message.' He pointed to the short message at the bottom of the second page.

'The last message. Sent, by the looks of it, on the evening of the party he was going to.'

Need to see you.
Something important to tell you.
Meet you there.

'That's Cara's number again,' pointed out Jo.

'Yes, it certainly is,' confirmed John.

'What was the something important, do you think?' asked Tom Sanders.

'Probably about his art exhibition and his pending trip to New York, I would guess,' John postulated.

'Almost certainly,' agreed Jo. 'Given the timeline.'

'If we're right though, it does suggest that he hadn't told Cara about it previously or at least not all of it.'

'We could be totally wrong. It could be about something entirely different, of course.'

'Absolutely.' John was pensive. 'But if so, what was the something important that he wanted to tell her? And could it have led to his death?'

The three lapsed into their own thoughts, trying to make sense of the message.

After several minutes had passed, the computer operative, getting impatient with his audience, turned away from his screen to ask, 'Is there anything else you want to see? Or are we done?'

'What else is there to see?' asked John.

'Well, I can track his movements using triangulation of the areas' telecommunications masts.'

'Do it,' ordered the FBI man. 'Let's see where he was on the evening in question.'

'It's not entirely accurate, and it relies on the phone being switched on,' explained the young man, again tapping away at the keyboard.

'Just do it,' ordered John, himself getting a bit impatient.

After a few minutes a map appeared on the computer screen onto which was superimposed a blue tracking line, marking the movements of the phone during Daniel's last day.

John pointed to the computer screen. 'That's the embassy – looks like he was there most of the day.'

'It does,' agreed the man at the screen. 'But then he leaves… and goes here and here.' He looked at John for support as to whether the pathway indicated was indeed Daniel's known movements.

John considered the blue pathway in front of him. 'And this is his timeline. This is where he went that evening.'

'Yes, I'm sure as I can be.' He added, 'Within the limitations of the technology that I said.'

Jo examined the route in detail. 'It looks like he left the embassy here. Then he made his way down this way.'

'He's going to that party,' interrupted John. 'That's the address down there.'

'He's certainly heading in that direction,' agreed Sanders.

'What's happened here?' asked Jo, pointing to the abrupt end of the indicated route taken.

'The phones been switched off?' offered the young man, re-examining the screen.

'Where is that? Where does it stop?' John asked quickly.

Jo leant into the screen. 'It looks like that bridge. The one just upstream from where the body was found.'

It was John's turn to stretch forward so he could more closely examine the area indicated. 'You're right, Jo. That is where it stops.' John straightened up and turned to Sanders. 'He didn't turn his phone off.'

Sanders looked puzzled. 'But your man just said?'

'I know what he said, but that's where the trail ends. Not because Daniel tuned his phone off, but because it stopped working when he hit the water.'

There was silence between them, before Jo concluded, 'So now at least we know that Daniel drowned not far from where he was found.'

'Yes, but what was he doing in the water in the first place?'

The young man reached to shut the computer down, but before doing so he felt it courteous to ask, 'Is there anything else you want to see, gentlemen?' before adding, 'And lady, of course.'

'Is there anything else to see?' asked John, impatient to get going.

'Well, you can look at his photographs if you want.'

'His photographs?'

'Well, at least those ones he kept on his phone. Though to be honest they're a bit boring. I checked them out earlier. A few selfies, a few landscapes, buildings around Dublin, that sort of thing.'

John and Tom Sanders were turning to leave, persuaded that examining the photographs would most likely be a waste of time.

Jo, however, hesitated. 'We really should have a look. What harm can it do?'

'Okay, roll them.' Reluctantly John bent down to examine the screen once more.

Slowly they scrolled through what seemed an endless stream of photographs. They were just as they had been told: mostly selfies, usually of himself with a landmark behind, or a selfie with Cara Williams in tow, a few family shots.

Just as they were about to leave the screen again, John spotted something. 'There. Go back.'

'The young man looked puzzled. 'Sorry, where?' He did as he was told, though, backing up a few pictures.

'What's that?' John pointed to the screen.

The young man bent closer. 'It's just a bunch of old caravans, that's all,' he said with some disdain, about to move on through the pictures once more.

'Don't touch anything. Leave it there.' John again pointed to the screen. He turned to Jo. 'Recognise those?'

Jo nodded. 'That's the Boswells' camp.'

'Why is he taking photos of it?' John asked.

'Remember he had some dispute with them?' Jo reminded him. 'Maybe he was gathering some evidence on them?'

John was still sceptical. 'Move on,' he asked the young man. 'Slowly,' he added.

The three bent closer to the computer screen once more as further pictures of the Boswells' camp unfolded.

'Pretty boring, if you ask me,' the computer operator felt compelled to state.

'Just keep going,' ordered Jo, interested once more.

'Stop,' John suddenly exclaimed. 'Who's that?' He was pointing at a man, smart-suited, clean-cut and probably in his mid-thirties – a subject who looked entirely out of place in vicinity of the Boswells' encampment.

Sanders leant further in, resting his hand on John's shoulder.

'That's Paddy Boswell with him,' indicated Jo.

They slowly scrolled through the next few pictures. There

were eight in all, all of the same scene, though the subjects changed positions.

Sanders remained silent as John and Jo speculated as to what was happening in the scenes depicted.

'It looks like Paddy Boswell's giving him something,' said John, squinting at the screen.

'It does,' agreed Jo.

The next picture seemed to be the reverse. 'Now he's giving something over to Paddy.'

'Can you zoom in? To see what's being exchanged.' John gripped the young man's shoulder as he spoke to emphasise his interest in the scene in front of him.

Again, with a few clicks of the mouse and a roll of its wheel the picture in front of them was magnified.

'Focus in there. On their hands,' commanded John.

As the requested area of focus enlarged in front of them, it became apparent that the stranger was handing a wad of notes over to Paddy Boswell.

'That's money. He's buying something from Paddy Boswell,' exclaimed Jo.

'Too right he is.' John turned to Sanders, who was staring at the screen but had remained silent throughout.

'Go back. Go back one picture. Let's see what it was that he was buying from Paddy,' ordered John, anxious to find out.

The scene in front of them changed. Now Paddy Boswell was again passing something over to the well-dressed stranger.

John and Jo squinted once more to try to make out the details. Even on John's request to magnify their hands it still remained unclear as to what was being passed across.

'It just looks like a small package of some sort,' muttered Jo.

'Mmmm… Yes, I can't be certain, but given Paddy Boswell's form, I'd bet my bottom dollar that that's drugs he's selling to that guy.'

Jo replied thoughtfully. 'So maybe Daniel was collecting evidence on the Boswells after all. To get his own back for being ripped off by them.'

'Definite possibility,' John said before turning back to Sanders, who had stepped a little way back from the screen and had still said nothing throughout the latter part of the picture show. 'What do you think, Tom?'

Tom Sanders remained engrossed in his own thoughts and didn't immediately make any effort to reply.

John repeated the question.

This time the FBI man seemed to rouse himself, at least partially. 'Yes, that's what it looks like, indeed it does,' he said almost absentmindedly.

John and Jo regarded their American colleague.

'What's wrong, Tom? You look like you've seen a ghost.'

Tom Sanders didn't immediately reply, but finally he spoke. 'I think I have.'

John looked puzzled; he looked over at Jo. She looked equally bewildered.

Nobody spoke for a few minutes, the two detectives allowing the FBI man a few minutes to gather his thoughts and then explain.

Finally he did so.

'I think I know that guy,' was all that he said.

chapter twenty-five

Tom Sanders sat slumped and silent in the backseat of the car.

John was driving both him and Jo over to the embassy once more. It had taken a while, but Sanders had finally told them whom the man in the video was. He had admitted that he recognised him because he was an employee in the US embassy.

It transpired that the subject in the pictures was an administrative clerk in the computer and IT division. Sanders had only met him briefly on a few occasions, but part of Sanders' role within the embassy was to screen employees to ensure there was no security risks. Benjamin Jackson, the subject in Daniel's phone, had not been flagged as a security risk, but Daniel's pictures of him seemingly buying drugs from an unscrupulous source suggested otherwise, and this was both an embarrassment and a concern to Tom Sanders.

Sanders was fully cognisant of the fact that any individual within the computer and IT department in the embassy had the potential to access many, if not all, documents generated from the embassy, sensitive, secret or otherwise.

Before leaving the Garda station Sanders had rung ahead,

asking his colleagues within the embassy to locate Benjamin Jackson, bring him to his office and keep him there until he himself arrived and could interview him. As an afterthought he also asked his colleagues to search Benjamin's workstation and his apartment within the embassy but didn't immediately specify what to look for.

When the colleague on the other end of the phone queried the FBI man's request, Sanders curtly told him, 'Just get on with it,' then hung up.

Arriving at the embassy Sanders brusquely ushered the two detectives through security, waving off any attempts to search or screen them.

They followed him as he made his way through the building towards his office.

Arriving, he threw the door open. Two large men wearing matching suits stood as if to attention behind a smaller, somewhat nervous young man, who turned around in his seat at the sound of Sanders' noisy arrival.

John immediately recognised the nervous young man as the person in Daniel's pictures.

Sanders rounded his desk and sat down, glaring silently staring at the increasingly anxious Benjamin Jackson.

John and Jo stood side by side at the back of the room. This was Sanders' shout and John was happy for him to conduct the interview, especially as he had no jurisdiction; technically this was United States territory and Benjamin Jackson was a US citizen.

Hardly diverting his gaze from Jackson, Sanders opened the top drawer of his desk and retrieved his laptop. Opening it and switching it on, he searched through his emails, still only fleetingly diverting his gaze from the young man seated in front of him.

Finally he found the email he was looking for; he

downloaded the attached copy of Daniel's picture diary that John had forwarded to him before leaving the station.

Still without saying anything, Sanders turned the laptop to face Benjamin Jackson and hit play.

As the scene unfolded, the young man paled but, John noted, he didn't seem surprised by the content. 'He's seen it before,' he whispered to Jo.

Jo nodded.

Sanders briefly looked up at the two detectives, his expression clearly a warning to them to keep quiet.

After several minutes to allow Benjamin Jackson to view the entire sequence of photographs before him, Sanders turned the screen back around and closed the laptop's lid. 'Well?' This was the first word he had spoken since entering the room and there was a definite malevolent edge to it.

Benjamin Jackson gave an involuntary shiver but remained silent, not quite knowing how to respond.

'So what have you got to say, Jackson?' continued Sanders, now obviously in full flow. 'Just tell us exactly what was going on in that sequence.'

Benjamin Jackson started to mouth something inaudible.

Tom Sanders just sat staring and waiting for a proper response to his question.

Eventually the younger man spoke; there was a nervous twitch in his voice. 'I was buying something from those people—'

'By those people, you mean the Boswells?'

Benjamin Jackson nodded and then bowed his head, trying to avoid the FBI man's face.

'And what exactly was it you were buying?' Sanders continued.

'I think that it's obvious,' Jackson replied.

'Just tell me, Benjamin, for the record.'

'Okay, okay, it was just some coke, that's all. It's a bit boring here and I just wanted something to give me a bit of a lift.'

'Have you used it all?'

'No, no. I've hardly touched it. I'm not an addict, you know. Just a snort now and again.'

'So where is it now?'

Benjamin Jackson looked around the room at the others there. He knew the game was up and he knew he had no option but to co-operate. 'It's in my bedside table, behind some books.'

Sanders nodded to one of his burly cohorts, indicating for him to go and fetch it, if those he'd earlier asked to search Jackson's room hadn't already found it.

Sanders sat back and waited.

Benjamin Jackson shuffled nervously in his seat.

A few minutes later the guard re-entered the room clutching a small, clear plastic bag containing a quantity of white powder. He held it up for the FBI man to see. Jackson had also turned around to witness the damning evidence arrive.

'Give that to Inspector McDaid, please.' Then, to John: 'You might want to have that analysed.'

John indicated his thanks, pulled a rubber glove from his pocket, put it on, so as not to contaminate the evidence further, took the small bag from the guard and placed it within another bag he held in his other hand.

'Inspector McDaid is from the Garda Siochana – he'll get that analysed and come back to me. You know that it is an offence to be in procession of an illegal substance?' Sanders was stating the obvious but obviously trying to intimidate the younger man. He went on. 'Not only is it a criminal offence but it is a potential security risk. You realise that? Altogether this is a very serious matter and will be treated as such.'

'I'm sorry,' was all Benjamin Jackson could mutter in response.

'Okay, Benjamin, let's just be open with one another.'

Benjamin nodded his agreement.

'You bought this stuff from Paddy Boswell and his clan knowing they were dodgy characters?'

Benjamin nodded again.

'Did they, or anybody else, try to blackmail you to leak any confidential material from this embassy?'

Benjamin leapt to his feet. 'No. No. Absolutely not. I wouldn't do anything like that,' he shouted directly at Sanders.

'Sit down, Benjamin,' Tom Sanders said firmly.

The young man, composing himself, sat meekly down.

'We will have to check up on this, you know that? If we find any evidence that you have passed any material to a third party, that is an offence against the state and will be treated as such.'

'You won't find anything, I promise. I wouldn't do that. You've got to believe me. Please, Mr Sanders,' he pleaded.

Sanders decided to try a different direction of enquiry. 'Have you seen those pictures before, Benjamin?'

John glanced over at Jo. Sanders was smart; he had obviously picked up on the same signs they had.

The young man again quickly glanced around the room and then sheepishly nodded.

'So tell me about it, Benjamin.'

After a few minutes' contemplation the younger man, now clearly broken, softly replied, 'Daniel Wilson. The ambassador's son,' he added, somewhat unnecessarily given the current circumstances. 'For some reason he was up at the Boswells' site – he arrived just after me. Obviously he recognised me and saw an opportunity, so it was him that took the photo.'

'We know that, Benjamin. But what exactly do you mean, "saw an opportunity"?'

Benjamin Jackson hesitated. Again he looked around the room and nervously shuffled his feet.

John formed the impression that he was probably thinking that if Sanders knew about the drugs and they knew that Daniel had taken the photos then they must know everything.

'He blackmailed me,' he stated bluntly.

John and Jo exchanged questioning looks.

'Explain,' continued Sanders, nonplussed by the response.

'He showed me the pictures,' Benjamin replied, almost staccato in his speech. 'He threatened to show them to his father. I knew that if he did, it was curtains for me. I'd lose my job, probably be shipped back to the States. God knows what else. So he blackmailed me.'

'What do you mean, blackmailed?' It was John who interrupted the interrogation. He already suspected he had guessed the answer to come.

Sanders shot him a look. 'Thank you, Inspector, but I think you'll find I'm in charge here. I am quite capable of conducting this inquiry, so please leave it to me.'

John shrunk back, chastened, recognising that Sanders was indeed correct in his assertion.

'Sorry about that, Benjamin, these Irish police, they don't always know their place.' He shifted his gaze briefly towards John once more.

Despite the reprimand John thought he detected just a hint of a smile at the corner of the FBI's man's lips.

'Go on, Benjamin,' he directed.

'He told me he needed money. That he would keep quiet about... about my indiscretion if I paid him off.'

'Your indiscretion?' Sanders laughed.

'Okay, you know what I mean.' Benjamin Jackson was regaining some of his control. 'He told me that he wanted to get away, go back home, he said – I guess he meant the States.

Anyway, he said that if I gave him the money, he'd leave and nobody need know about my indis…' He stopped, not wishing to be picked up again on his description of events.

Ignoring Sanders' earlier rebuttal, John stepped forward and confronted the young man. 'How much did he ask for, Benjamin?'

John could feel Sanders' eyes burning into his back as he stood between him and the interviewee.

'One thousand Euros,' he stuttered.

John looked up from Benjamin Jackson at Jo, who nodded and smiled, recognising the significance of the reply.

'And did you give it to him, Benjamin?'

Benjamin Jackson slowly nodded his affirmation.

John stepped back to allow Sanders his place once more.

Almost through gritted teeth, clearly annoyed at John's further interference, Sanders took control of the interview again. 'You know Daniel went missing?'

Benjamin Jackson nodded slowly, guessing what was coming next.

'And you know we just recently found his body?'

Benjamin Jackson stood up once more, shocked by the implication that was being laid out before him. 'You don't think I had anything to do with that?' he protested.

'I don't know what to think, Benjamin. Please sit down.'

The interview continued for a further hour, largely going over and over the ground already covered, but not uncovering anything more than what had been revealed. Benjamin Jackson had paid off Daniel, and that explained the money that Daniel had had to purchase the flight tickets and the remainder that was recovered from the holdall.

Benjamin Jackson continued, however, to protest his innocence and strongly denied anything to do with Daniel's subsequent death.

Finally, Sanders decided to give up. He turned to John. 'Anything you want to ask, Inspector?'

John couldn't think of anything, He thought that Sanders had actually been pretty thorough in his interrogation. He shook his head.

Sanders ordered the guards to take Jackson back to his room and told him to pack. He was being sent back to the States as soon as a flight could be arranged.

John protested, asking for Sanders to hold off, that there may be further enquiries and that Benjamin may need to be questioned again.

Sanders merely shook off John's protestations. 'This is an American matter. He says he didn't have anything to do with Daniel's death and I believe him. But don't think he's off the hook. Not by any means. My colleagues back home will arrest him and interview him again once he gets home.'

chapter twenty-six

Back at the station John and Jo were planning their next step. John had accepted his defeat in trying to prevent Benjamin Jackson's deportation. He also had to admit that he tended to believe that Benjamin Jackson was genuine in his claims of lack of involvement in Daniel's disappearance and subsequent death.

'I mean, if he went to the extent of paying Daniel off and he believed that Daniel was heading off to the States.'

'As it looks as if he was,' added Jo.

'Yes, I think from all that we've seen and heard so far he was definitely heading off.'

'So he would have been out of Jackson's hair.'

'Exactly, so why would he try and injure Daniel?'

John rested his head in his hands, his elbows on the desk, buried in thought.

After a few minutes he reached for a jotter and a pen and started to make a list of remaining suspects – suspects that may either be directly involved in Daniel's death or others that may still hold, even unwittingly, further information surrounding it.

He pointed to the name at the top of the list with his pen.

That name was Paddy Boswell.

He started to think things through and, at least partially to himself, he muttered, 'Daniel knew the Boswells – he had a gripe with them. We know now that he that he photographed Paddy Boswell selling drugs to Benjamin Jackson. We also know that Daniel had blackmailed Benjamin Jackson with the pictures.'

'So you're saying would Daniel have tried the same thing on Paddy Boswell?' Jo added.

'I don't really think Daniel would have been as foolhardy as to try that. He must have known what the Boswells were like. But even if he didn't, if Paddy had got wind of the fact that there were pictures of him selling drugs, I don't think he would take very kindly to it, do you?'

Jo shook her head. Everything John had said only reinforced her own opinion of Paddy Boswell.

'Do me a favour, Jo, check up if the lab has done an analysis on the powder we took from Benjamin Jackson, would you?' Then he added, 'I just got a hunch.'

Jo lifted her phone and dialled.

After a short conversation and then a few more minutes of silence the answer came through.

Jo nodded her head intermittently as the results were read through to her.

John fidgeted impatiently.

Finally she put the phone down. 'Looks like your hunch was right,' she confirmed, guessing John's thought process. 'The powder was indeed cocaine, but not only that, it was cut with an ethoxylate, the same one and in the same proportion as the coke we took from Paddy Boswell's caravan.'

'Right, let's get him in.' John rose from the desk but then hesitated. 'Let's order back-up first,' he added wisely.

*

Calling for back-up before attempting to arrest Paddy Boswell had been a prudent move. The rest of his clan had gathered around and tried to shield and prevent him being removed from the camp. In the end it was only by force of numbers that the desired outcome had been achieved.

John brushed the debris off the shoulder of his jacket as he entered the interview room, debris that had resulted from the scuffles in the arrest attempt. Paddy Boswell sat, arms folded in front of him, at a small table, a table which, along with three chairs, on one of which Paddy now sat, formed the only furniture in the bare, windowless room. A single Garda constable stood to attention at the door.

John and Jo pulled out a chair each and sat down opposite the suspect. For the next few minutes nothing was said.

Finally, it was Paddy Boswell that broke the silence. 'What exactly am I supposed to have done?'

It was John who took the lead. 'You remember that we confiscated some white powder from your caravan last time we spoke?'

Paddy Boswell nodded, giving nothing away.

'Well, we just got the analysis of the powder back, Paddy, and guess what?'

'Nothing to do with me,' he replied, holding his ground. 'Just because it was in my caravan doesn't mean it was mine.'

'You have to admit, Paddy, that it is pretty good circumstantial evidence, though. What do you say?' Jo followed John's lead perfectly.

Paddy Boswell said nothing, formulating his reply. 'Even if it were mine – and I'm not admitting to anything – it would just be for personal use. What's that, a fine? Why get your knickers in a twist over that, young lady?' He smiled contemptuously at Jo, revealing a row of badly kept teeth.

Jo turned to John, who smiled back at the perpetrator.

'What?' asked Paddy Boswell, clearly suspecting that there must be more to it.

'Well, Paddy, for a start we have evidence that you sold some cocaine to an American chap. Dealing that's a greater offence.'

'Evidence? What evidence?' He looked from one to the other.

Again John and Jo remained silent for a few minutes. Again it was John who spoke first. 'We had that American in the other day. Some white powder, again which turned out to be cocaine, was found in his room.'

'So what? Doesn't prove he got it from me.' He grinned, secure in his assumption.

John returned the smile and leant forward to confront the suspect more closely. 'Ah, but, Paddy, that's where you're wrong.'

Nervously now, Paddy again looked back and forth between them.

'See, Paddy, we've had both samples analysed. And guess what?'

Paddy Boswell's expression gave away the fact that he already knew the answer, but he said nothing.

So Jo reinforced his suspicion. 'The two samples were identical – both had been cut with an ethoxylate substance and, guess what again? In the exact same concentrations.'

'So what?' Paddy snarled.

'Meaning they came from the same batch,' she paused momentarily to let the information sink in, 'and that you sold some of it to our American friend.'

'You can't prove that. How do you know I sold it to him?'

'Well, there are the photos, of course,' Jo added, then left the statement to hang in the air.

Paddy Boswell wheeled around. 'What photos?' he almost shouted.

John took up the conversation again. 'The ones of you handing over the cocaine and him handing you money.'

'What? What? I don't believe you,' he stuttered. Then, after a moment's reflection: 'Where are these so-called pictures?'

Jo reached below the desk, retrieved a laptop from her bag and, placing it on the desk, she opened it and then spun it around so that the screen faced Paddy Boswell. She then pressed play.

The scene unfolded itself before his unblinking gaze.

Reaching the end of the sequence, Jo turned the computer back towards herself once more and the two detectives both looked towards the suspect. There was no need to say anything further.

'Where did you get those?' he asked, his voice trembling with emotion.

'You tell us, Paddy.'

'What do you mean? I've never seen those photographs before.' His voice was shaking in disbelief. 'I don't understand. Who took them?'

'Do you deny that that was you in the pictures?' John asked coolly.

'I think I want a lawyer. I'm not saying anything else till I get a lawyer.' With that he sat back determinedly, refusing any further interaction.

The two detectives rose to leave, and as they did so John turned to the constable still standing at the door. 'Charge him and take him down to the cells.'

The constable nodded his assent and stepped forward to guide Paddy Boswell down to the holding cells.

As the door of the interview room shut behind the departing prisoner and guard, John turned to Jo. 'What do you make of that?'

'I think he knows that we've got him banged to rights,' replied Jo.

'Yes, but what about the photos?'

'I don't think he'd seen them before. Do you, John?'

'No, I don't.' Then he added thoughtfully, 'And what's more, I got the definite impression that he didn't even know of their existence.'

'I have to say, he did look surprised when I mentioned them,' she agreed.

John sat back down at the table and simply stared at the now-empty seat in front of him.

After a few moments Jo sat down beside him. 'So where are we now?' she asked.

John didn't speak straightaway, still trying to formulate his thoughts. Then, as if coming to a decision, he replied, 'If he genuinely didn't know of the photos' existence, then he would have had no need to go after Daniel.'

'But Daniel was asking for his money back,' Jo interrupted.

'Yes, but given the Boswells' dodgy deals, I suspect he wasn't the first, and anyway, they would only have thought him a minor inconvenience. Certainly not enough to warrant killing him.'

Again, Jo could only agree with John's logic. 'So where does that leave us?'

'Back to the drawing board, I'm afraid.'

Jo went off to fetch them both a cup of coffee, leaving John with his thoughts.

Returning, the two sat imbibing the caffeine, possibly in the hope that it might stimulate some dormant thoughts.

'So we're left with a mugging?' Jo asked.

'Possibly, but they didn't seem to take anything – he still had his phone when he went into the water.'

'So it was just a terrible accident?'

John still looked troubled.

chapter twenty-seven

Arriving home that evening John felt tired, physically and intellectually drained. He'd rung Niamh earlier to see if she'd come over. As he opened the front door, he hoped that she had. He called her name expectantly, but as he did so he experienced a sudden stab of pain in his face radiating from his ear to his cheek. He, of course, recognised it immediately as the neuralgia he had suffered previously but had thought had calmed down. He rationalised that it was probably just because he was tired and would settle again once he got in and got his feet up.

Niamh appeared down the stairs and followed him into the living room. She knew better than to quiz him about his day; John was not in the habit of discussing his current investigations, even with his partner.

He slumped into an armchair and grabbed for the TV remote. Niamh stood beside him. 'You know that you're still limping?' she asked.

John hadn't been aware that he was limping; he had thought that the steroids had cured it or maybe he had just grown so used to it that he didn't notice it anymore.

'It's probably just because I'm so tired,' he explained. And he was tired, much more fatigued than was usual after a day's work, even a hard day like today.

'It's lucky you've got that appointment with the consultant tomorrow,' added Niamh.

'Tomorrow?' He gasped, sitting up suddenly and checking the date on his watch. 'I'd completely forgotten.'

'Well, you're going. You need to tell him that the problem hasn't gone away. See if he has any other tricks up his sleeve.'

'I can't, there's so much going on at the moment. I'll have to cancel.'

'Don't you dare.' Then, after a moment's thought: 'Anyway, you can't. It's too late, the office will be closed for the evening.'

Rising to his feet, he fetched his mobile from his jacket, which he had discarded before sitting down. 'Medics are open all hours.'

He looked up his contacts list and rang the number. After five rings it was answered by an automated voicemail. Frustrated, he slammed the phone down.

'Told you,' Niamh said somewhat smugly. Then, even more emphatically than before, she told him that he was attending the appointment come what may: 'And what's more, I'm going with you. Just to make sure you tell him everything.'

John acknowledged defeat and indicated his agreement. 'I'll have to ring Jo, though.'

'I'm sure she can cope for one day without you.'

John knew she was right. Jo was a perfectly capable young woman, much as he didn't want to admit so. Nobody was irreplaceable.

He dialled Jo's mobile number. She picked up immediately.

'What's up?' she asked. 'Another hunch?'

'Ha, ha, no, it's just that I have to be somewhere else tomorrow morning. I'll probably be in later, but can you manage on your own?'

There were a few seconds' silence on the other end of the phone; John realised he had probably said the wrong thing and undermined his colleague's abilities. 'Sorry, sorry, I didn't mean it that way. I just meant will you carry on with things till I get there?'

'What do you want me to do?' she asked at least partially mollified.

'I don't want to just accept that Daniel's death was just a freak accident. Not while there are stones left unturned.' He reached over and pulled the list he had made earlier from his jacket pocket, examining it, before continuing. 'Can you speak to Daniel's brother and his father again to make sure that we haven't missed anything?'

'You can't think they had anything to do with it, do you?'

'I don't think they would have intentionally set out to hurt him, no. But his father wasn't aware of Daniel's plans and, from what we've gleaned so far, he wouldn't have approved of them. But also, maybe, maybe, there's just something we've missed or that they've overlooked that's important.'

'I can do that, no problem,' Jo replied.

'See if you can talk to them separately. Jake, at least, is more likely to open up without his father hovering over him.'

He paused, thinking for a minute or so, and then added, before hanging up. 'Bring that guy Marshall with you – we've been avoiding him and he's bound to have griped back to O'Brien. It might keep him sweet to be involved for a while.'

Jo, somewhat reluctantly, he sensed, acceded to the request.

He laid the phone down on the arm of the chair and tried to decide if there was anything else he should do.

As he sat thinking he became conscious of Niamh now standing over him.

'What...?' he asked. 'I'm going, aren't I? I've just made arrangements for cover.'

Niamh continued to glare at him.

John shrugged his shoulders, mystified as to why she should be upset.

'You haven't told them. Have you?'

'Haven't told who? What?' he asked, genuinely uncertain as to what she was referring to.

'You know exactly what I mean.' She was angry.

John just sat with a gormless expression on his face.

'You haven't informed them at work. Have you? You haven't told them about your illness. Have you? Even though you know you can see for yourself that doing too much just makes you worse.'

With that she stormed off, slamming the living room door behind her.

John stayed seated; he made no attempt to follow her. He knew she was right. But he didn't want to admit it to himself. He hadn't told anybody at the station about his problem – in retrospect, he probably should have, and that was what Niamh was saying. He told himself he was only delaying telling the powers that be till he was certain of the diagnosis and its implications.

Subconsciously, though, he recognised that he just didn't want to admit his failings to his superiors. To do so might result in being side-lined to a desk job. Not a prospect he relished. John McDaid had always been a hands-on Garda officer. Always in the thick of things. He wasn't going to let a diagnosis of MS get in his way. At least not until he had to.

He sat watching the television until he started to nod off, only to wake up with a start each time his head started to drop. Finally, he admitted defeat, turned the television off and headed up the stairs after Niamh.

When he got to the bedroom, he opened the door cautiously so as not to wake Niamh. He tiptoed inside, making his way around the bed and then, as noiselessly as possible, undressed in the dark and slipped into bed.

The bed felt empty.

He switched on his bedside light. There was no sign of Niamh.

He got up and went back out onto the landing. The spare room door was slightly ajar and he could hear light breathing emanating from inside the room.

Niamh had debunked to the spare bed.

Not a good sign, he thought, as he made his way back to his own bedroom.

*

The next day, breakfast at home was consumed without much discussion, polite pleasantries were exchanged between the couple, but that was all. They left the house together still not talking and drove to the Blackrock clinic for John's follow-up appointment.

Parking at this time of the morning proved even easier than on their last visit. So they arrived early for the consultation. It was only as they sat in the waiting room that Niamh decided enough was enough and reached for his hand.

Feeling her grip his hand tightly, John realised that it was only her concern about his health that had made her angry. He had tried to dismiss it. But it wasn't something that could be just dismissed and he had, though reluctantly, had to recognise that.

He turned and smiled at her.

She in turn rested her head softly on his shoulder.

When John was called, both of them made their way into the consultant's office.

He greeted them kindly. 'So John, how has it been?'

'Not so bad, Doctor,' he replied, only to get a dig in the ribs from his partner.

Dr Moran picked up on the disagreement between the pair. In his experience it was not unusual for the patient, particularly a male patient, to try to belittle the problem, for their loved one to be somewhat more forthcoming. He repeated the question to Niamh.

'He's a bit better. The face doesn't seem to give him much bother now, but…' She glanced at John and took in his pained expression.

'But?' asked the consultant.

'But he's still limping.'

'Only when I'm tired,' John tried to say.

'John, you limp all the time – you just don't notice it. Yes, it gets worse when you're tired, but honestly, John, it is there all the time.' A tear rolled down her cheek; she brushed it away.

Dr Moran offered her a tissue from a box on the desk. He was readily prepared for upset patients and their even more upset relatives. 'Let me have a look at you, John. Climb up onto the couch.'

John did as he was told and the doctor repeated many of the tests he'd carried out before. After a few minutes he asked John to sit back down beside his partner.

The consultant moved round to his side of the desk, leaned forward and spoke softly. 'The good news is that the area of numbness in your face is much smaller and I suspect it and the neuralgia that accompanies it will continue to fade and, hopefully, disappear completely.'

'What about his leg, though?' asked Niamh, still clutching the tissue.

'To be honest, Niamh, you are right: there isn't much change there. But, and I do stress this, the steroids will continue to have an effect for some weeks to come.'

'Even though I've stopped them?' asked John.

'Yes. Though I have to admit that the spasticity in your legs—'

'Spasticity? What's that?' he interrupted the consultant's flow.

'Spasticity is stiffness, usually accompanied by weakness, both of which I can find examining your legs. That, John, is what is causing you to limp.' He let John take in what he had said before continuing. 'Spasticity such as yours often doesn't improve as much as we would like with steroids, but as I said, we still have time.'

'So what do you suggest?' asked Niamh. 'Is there anything else he can try?'

Dr Moran considered her request briefly before replying, 'I do have some other things we could try. Some medications can reduce the degree of the spasticity and others can slow any progression of the disease itself.'

'Well, we should we try those then' she almost pleaded, more tears welling up.

'My opinion at present is that we should hold off, wait and see, give the steroids a bit more time and then review the situation. Worst-case scenario we can recommend the use of a walking aid – a walking stick or a crutch, perhaps – something to help keep the weight off the leg and to help with any balance problems that might arise. But I'm sure it won't come to that.'

John was relieved, to a degree at least; he wasn't really somebody who liked taking medicine. Though he didn't like the discussion about a walking aid. Anyway, he decided to accept the medical opinion offered and was about to get up to go when Niamh spoke again about the issue that had troubled her earlier. 'John hasn't told anybody at work about his illness. Should he?'

John sat down again, his face betraying a look of annoyance at her question.

Dr Moran sat back in his chair and considered the question carefully for a few minutes before replying, 'I'm afraid there is no right answer to that, Niamh. On the one hand I would guess that John doesn't want to be looked upon differently from his colleagues and even to be discriminated against.'

Niamh looked troubled.

'Sorry, by discriminated against, I meant probably in a well-meaning way. In other words, his colleagues might try and protect him, or even overprotect him by shielding him from some situations or cases.'

John nodded; that was certainly his main fear.

'On the other hand,' he looked straight at John now, 'if you don't tell people and something happens to you—'

'What do you mean, if something happens?' Niamh interrupted, showing her concern.

'Ummm… Let me think. Okay, say you were chasing down a suspect and you tripped and fell, injuring yourself. Normally you would expect time off, compensation, etc. Yes?'

'That's true,' John agreed.

'But what if it then came to light that you'd seen me? That you knew you had a problem with your legs? It could be argued that you shouldn't have put yourself in that situation in the first place and the only reason you fell was because you have multiple sclerosis. So then not only would there be no recompense, but you would almost certainly be in trouble for not informing the authorities in the first place.'

'John, he's right, you know. You must tell them.'

Reluctantly John also agreed with the consultant's synopsis. 'So what do you advise?'

A few more minutes of thought then Dr Moran continued. 'I think the best thing is to have a word with your divisional medical department. You have a medical department, don't you?'

John nodded, even though it was not a department he had frequented previously, preferring to go to his own GP, and even then only sparingly.

'If you go to them, what you tell them, like coming to see me, is confidential. They will only communicate to your bosses what is essential, and even then only with your permission.'

'So I don't need to tell any of my direct line managers or work colleagues?' John sounded relieved.

'No, I don't think that's absolutely necessary, but you are free to tell anybody you trust, work with closely or you think should know.'

'Jo,' Niamh mouthed.

John wasn't so sure; he didn't know if he was ready yet to share this medical bombshell with her.

With no further questions to ask the consultation was at an end. So the couple got up and left the building, stopping only to make one further appointment with the receptionist.

Leaving the car park, John turned to Niamh, who had insisted on driving, and announced, 'Drop me at the station, will you? I need to catch up on what Jo's been up to.'

Niamh turned to him, aghast. 'You are joking, aren't you?'

But he wasn't joking and she had no alternative but to drive him to the Garda station and leave him there.

He waved solemnly after her as she drove off. He wasn't sure that she had looked back; she certainly didn't respond.

As he made his way through the station, he knew that he hadn't handled things with Niamh very well. He was somebody who tended to just take things in his stride and even ignore those that he didn't want to think about. Niamh wasn't like that. She took things to heart. She worried. She worried about him, especially now that there may actually be something to worry about. She needed time and she needed his support. Support, which by coming to work, was clearly lacking.

chapter twenty-eight

As he entered his section's office area with its open-plan design, made to accommodate rows of desks which were originally supposed to be 'hot-desked' but were now claimed by individual owners, he spotted DI Alan Marshall. He half stood, half sat, perched on the corner of Jo's desk. She herself was sitting in front of him. They were drinking coffee and were seemingly so engrossed in conversation that they didn't notice him arriving.

As he made his way to his own office area Jo looked up and waved. He glanced at Alan Marshall, whose back was still to him, raised an eyebrow and smiled.

Jo didn't respond but did make her excuses to her new colleague and sauntered over to join John at his desk. He noted Alan Marshall following her with his eyes as she did so before sloping off to the far end of the room.

'So how did you get on?' asked John, positioning himself carefully behind his desk, making sure that the stiffness in his leg, stiffness that he was now self-conscious of, was not apparent to his junior colleague.

'He's a sweetie, really, you should try and get on with him.'

'I didn't mean DI Marshall. I meant at the embassy,' he replied a little more tetchily than he meant to.

'Oh, sorry. Yes.' Her earlier enthusiasm now quashed, she sat down opposite him and filled him in on the outcome of their enquiries.

It appeared that they were lucky in their timings. When they arrived the ambassador was not in the building – he had some official meeting at the time – so they had requested to talk to Daniel's brother alone.

After some back-and-forth discussions they had finally been granted permission and were ushered into an anteroom for Jake to arrive a few minutes later.

He had been reticent, reluctant to talk at first, but with some persuasion he opened up.

John didn't really appreciate Jo's following fulsome description as to how adept Alan Marshall had been in getting Jake to relax and talk.

'So what did he say?' he asked abruptly.

Jo stopped momentarily, a little taken aback by his tone of voice.

'Sorry, just impatient to hear,' he explained.

'Not jealous?' She laughed.

'Just get on with it.' He benignly smiled back.

Jo Roberts then went on to explain that she took it that Daniel and Jake were quite close. He had known about Daniel's art ambitions, but as he talked about it, he was clearly nervous and kept looking over his shoulder as if his father might appear at any moment. After some persuasion he did admit, despite his earlier denials, that he had known of Daniel's plans to go to the States. He'd talked to Emily as well, but only after Daniel had disappeared. He'd actually rung her to speak to Daniel and try to persuade him to talk to their father and reassure him that everything was alright. But that was when Emily had told him he wasn't there. So he thought he'd just better keep quiet about it.

'Did he admit to anything else?' John had asked.

'He says that he might have mentioned to Cara that he saw Daniel with the other girl. He said that when he'd seen her at the party and she was so upset he wished he hadn't because Daniel hadn't shown up and he thought she might think he'd gone off with her. He said he didn't speak to her, though.'

'Did he say why he didn't speak to her?'

'I asked him that. He said he was a bit drunk. He and some friends had gone off for a few drinks before the party, so he was quite late getting there, and as I said, he was a bit the worse for wear. So he thought discretion was the better part of valour and he gave her a wide berth.'

'Probably a good decision. Anything else?'

'That's all we got from Jake. His dad arrived back and when he was told that we were there, he burst in and ordered us out. He seemed pretty annoyed.'

'So you didn't get to talk to him then?'

'Alan—'

'Oh, it's Alan now.'

Jo stopped and fixed him with a reproving stare. 'Yes, *John*. It's *Alan* now.'

'Sorry. Carry on,' uttered John reproachfully.

Jo hesitated a moment more before resuming her explanation. 'Alan tried his best, used all his charm to try to ameliorate the ambassador, but he wasn't having it. We were asked to leave and we did so. So we didn't get a chance to ask Daniel's father any questions.'

'Never mind. I suspect his father had told us all he knew the last time we spoke. From what you've said about Daniel's brother's demeanour and the fear of his father finding out, I suspect Daniel himself hadn't confided in him either.'

'So where do we go now?'

'Maybe we should have a chat with Cara again – she was the only other person that knew him well.'

'I'm not sure her father will be too pleased to see us again,' Jo stated needlessly.

'Can't be helped.' Then he had a thought. 'But perhaps we'll leave it till tomorrow.'

Jo looked at him quizzically.

'I've a few bridges to build,' was the only reply she received.

*

Having updated himself on the investigation John had thought the better of himself and headed home to face Niamh, who by now had decided to move in with him, at least temporarily.

The greeting he received was frosty to say the least. It was obvious that Niamh had not forgiven him for leaving her after the consultation with the neurologist.

'Surely you must have realised that we need to talk this through?' she complained.

'Of course I did, but I just wanted to get my head straight before we did. To be distracted for a while. I'm sorry, I really am.' He reached forward and embraced her.

She made no effort to push him away; rather, she accepted the embrace and snuggled down into it, resting her head on his shoulder. 'What are we going to do, John?' she asked softly. He could feel her cool tears running down his neck and under his collar.

'Look, we'll be okay. I promise. It's not so bad.'

She straightened up and pulled away from him. 'Not too bad!' she exclaimed. 'Not too bad! It's MS, for Christ's sake, not some common cold that you can just shrug off.'

'I've got a bit of a limp, that's all. You heard Dr Moran. It may still get better,' he defended himself.

She led him into the living room and made him sit down; she pulled a chair over towards him and sat down opposite him. 'I've been googling it,' she announced.

'Googling what?'

'Multiple sclerosis, of course. What do you think?'

'Ahhh, Dr Google, of course. Why don't you just leave it to the experts?'

'I needed to know. To know all about the condition, so I could ask the right questions next time we see him,' she asserted.

'So what did you find out?' he asked a little apprehensively.

'Mostly the same as the consultant had said—'

'I told you so,' he butted in.

Not to be deflected, she carried on. 'But a bit more besides.'

'Like what?' he asked, some scepticism in his voice.

'Well, there are different forms of the disease.'

'So?'

'Well, different types act in different ways and have different treatments.'

'I thought the neurologist said there was no treatment for the condition?'

'Will you shut up and listen!' She glared at him before continuing. 'What he said was that there is no cure – not yet, anyway – but there are treatments, treatments that can help some of the symptoms.'

'Like the steroids?'

'Exactly, and the painkiller drug you had for your face.'

'The gabapentin?'

'Yes. But more importantly there are others. Apparently, there is a fairly new drug called beta interferon, or something like that – the consultant talked about it, don't you remember? It can reduce your chances of having what's called a relapse.'

'A relapse?'

She glared at him to admonish him for interrupting her flow once again. But it was obvious to her that John hadn't really listened to, or at least taken in, all that had been explained to him by the neurologist at the consultation.

'A relapse is what they call it if it flares up – the article I read says that's what it does, it comes and goes, and this drug can help keep it at bay. From reading that, I think that was what Dr Moran was hinting at when he said he wanted to wait and see.'

'I'm sorry, I don't quite get it.' John was trying to follow her explanation, but he was struggling to keep up.

'I think he meant if it does flare up again, and from what I've read it actually might not, you can go into what's called a remission. That's where nothing actually happens.'

'So you're saying it might not get worse but if it did… what did you call it?'

'Relapse.'

'If it did relapse again he might prescribe that new drug for me.'

'He said that, didn't he?' She was getting increasingly annoyed by his failure to comprehend the facts surrounding his condition, or perhaps more likely his conscious dismissal of them.

He leant back in the chair. 'There, I told you it would be okay.'

Niamh jumped to her feet, exasperated. 'That's not what I said!' She stormed off to the kitchen.

John realised that it was not really anger that had prompted her response; it was concern. He got up and followed her.

Niamh was standing, hands on the edge of the sink, staring out the window at the small garden beyond. It was obvious to John that she wasn't really looking at anything, just staring blankly.

He leant on the worktop behind her. 'I'm sorry. I guess it's just because I don't really want to think about it.'

She wheeled around; there was only worry and concern in her demeanour now. 'I know, John, but you have to be realistic. We have to be realistic. You need to accept what you've got, take it seriously, monitor it and react accordingly. Most of all, John, you have to be careful.'

'Careful? What do you mean by careful?'

'One thing that came out time and time again when I searched it was the importance of rest. They all said that if you do too much you risk a relapse, a worsening of the condition.'

John was not a man who was prone to take things easy and she knew that; she knew she was going to have to try hard to get him to take heed of the warning.

'Look, John.' She persevered despite his obvious reluctance to accept what she was saying. 'You know I'm right.'

'How do know you're right?'

'Look at your leg, for Christ's sake.'

'Sorry?'

'What happened when you did too much.'

John didn't answer; he knew what was coming.

'Your leg got much worse. You were really limping. Am I right? Or am I right?'

John lowered his head in recognition of the veracity of her statement.

'So now will you listen to me?'

He nodded. 'I'm sorry – you're right.'

'John, if you don't take this thing seriously, you are going to end up needing crutches. You could even end up in a wheelchair.'

He remained silent and motionless. His only awareness of MS previously was of young people in wheelchairs. The thought frightened him – frightened him more than he would ever admit.

Niamh was right to spell things out to him. He reached forward and hugged her once again.

*

John suffered a sleepless night. His mind was in turmoil, the unsolved nature of the case turning over in his mind but being increasingly overwhelmed by the discussion with Niamh that evening and, more importantly, what the future might hold for him.

He suspected that Niamh was finding it a difficult night as well. He could feel her tossing and turning and sighing intermittently through the early hours.

He dropped off only a few hours before dawn and when he awoke he found that Niamh had got up before him. As he lay in bed simply staring aimlessly at the bedroom ceiling he could smell the aroma of cooked bacon and hear the clatter of dishes downstairs. Niamh was preparing breakfast for him. It was only recently that Niamh had started making breakfast for him. Previously, he would simply get up, dress, go downstairs and make himself a couple of pieces of toast and a cup of black coffee before consuming them alone, usually whilst watching the news on the TV or reading yesterday's newspaper. Before his illness Niamh was rarely up before him.

The noises and smell emanating from the kitchen were most probably as a result of the frank conversation they had had the evening before and Niamh's regret about it.

He dressed and went down to join her.

'Oh, you're up,' she said, surprised, when she saw him. 'I was about to bring you breakfast in bed.'

'I'm not an invalid, Niamh,' he said, before adding, 'At least not yet.' He regretted saying it almost immediately.

Niamh looked at him reprovingly. 'Don't joke about it, John.' She thrust a plate of bacon and eggs in front of him.

Nothing more was said between them. They both eat their breakfasts at either end of the breakfast bar, consumed in their own thoughts.

Finally, John pulled on his jacket, kissed her lightly on the forehead and made his way towards the front door.

'See you tonight,' he said to no one but himself.

There were still many bridges to be built.

chapter twenty-nine

Back at work that morning, Jo arrived just after him. Not bothering to take her coat off, she came over to him and asked, 'Will we go then?'

He didn't immediately understand what she was saying.

'To the Williams' – you said yesterday you wanted to talk to Cara again.'

'Sorry, yes. I did, didn't I? Bit distracted, that's all.'

'Something you want to talk about?' she asked kindly.

'No,' was his curt response. Despite what Niamh and the consultant had said, he wasn't yet ready to share his problem with anyone. Not even with Jo.

'Okay, let's go.' Then he looked at his watch. 'She may be at school, though.'

'She wasn't the last time we were there. She was sick or something, wasn't she? I remember she didn't look well.'

'Okay, let's go. We'll take our chances. Her father may not want to see us, but he sure as hell is not going allow us to interview her at St Columba's.'

On the way to the Williams' they discussed their tactics to try and deal with Cara's father and more particularly how to get Cara on her own without him breathing down their necks.

In the end they had to admit defeat, unable to come up with a workable plan of attack.

'We'll just have to wing it,' said John, more in hope than conviction.

In the end they didn't have to.

Cara wasn't in. She had recovered and had gone to school.

'She'll be back around five,' her father informed them as they stood on the doorstep, Cara's father blocking any attempt at entry.

'What do you want to see her for, anyway?' he asked irritably. 'You've already seen her. Surely she's been through enough?' He actually came over as being concerned about his daughter's welfare. Not an emotion John or Jo had witnessed from him before.

'We've been talking to Daniel's brother and some other people, and we just have a few questions we'd like to ask her,' John answered vaguely.

'You can come back later,' was the short reply. Cara's father then turned his back on them, starting to close the door and retreat inside.

'Just one more thing, Mr Williams,' said John quickly, inserting his foot between the door and frame in a time-honoured fashion to prevent the door from being slammed shut in their faces.

'What?' he asked, turning angrily around.

'Cara hurt her ankle playing hockey?' John asked.

'You already know that, Inspector.' He almost spat the final word.

'At the hospital they told her not to weight bear, not to stand on it? Is that correct?'

'Yes. So what? What's that got to do with anything?'

'At the hospital, did they give her a walking stick or a crutch or anything to help her keep the weight of the sore ankle?'

It was Jo's turn to look bemused.

'Yes. They gave her a crutch. Told her not to go out without it. She was in a lot of pain – it hurt her to put the foot on the ground. The crutch helped a lot. But so what?' His anger seemed to have been replaced by curiosity.

Jo stared questioningly at John, not really understanding where he was going.

Nonplussed, John continued. 'I don't suppose you still have the crutch, do you, Mr Williams?'

The father stood still but looked a little embarrassed, finally admitting that he did indeed still have it. 'It's upstairs, I think. We meant to take it back to the hospital – we just hadn't got around to it, that's all.'

'Not to worry, Mr Williams, I think loads of people don't return them. There must be thousands of them propping up something or other in people's houses.'

Before Cara's father could respond, John quickly asked, 'Could we have it, the crutch, Mr Williams? Would that be okay with you? We can always return it to the hospital for you.'

The older man could think of no reason for not handing it over and he certainly didn't want to get into an argument over possible stolen property. So he turned on his heel, saying, 'Wait there.' He slammed the door shut in their face.

Jo raised her arms as if saying, 'What's that about?'

A minute or two later, the door reopened and Cara's father, reaching through the narrow aperture he had allowed, thrust the grey aluminium standard hospital crutch towards the two detectives.

John pulled a plastic glove from his pocket and took the crutch from him.

'Is that all?'

'Thank you for your co-operation, Mr Williams,' John said with just a hint of sarcasm in his voice.

The door slammed shut in front of them.

'What was that all about?' asked Jo to John's back as he made his way back to the car and gently laid the crutch down in the boot.

'Send it to the lab and let me know if they find anything,' was all he said on the way back to the station.

*

John remained engrossed in his own thoughts, his head buried in his hands, elbows leaning on the desk, for the rest of the day.

Jo knew better than to disturb him.

After what seemed an eternity John signalled over to Jo, who, with nothing else to do, was busying herself with long-overdue paperwork.

He was bent over his computer screen. 'I think we might have missed something,' he said absentmindedly. He pointed to the screen.

'What?' Jo asked, looking at where he was pointing.

'There.' He pointed again. 'Daniel's last message.'

Need to see you
Something important to tell you.
Meet you there

She leaned further over his shoulder and stared intently at the screen. 'Sorry, I still don't understand. What are you getting at?'

He pointed at the last line.

Jo read it aloud. '*Meet you there*'. So what? 'He's arranging to meet her at the party.' Cara went to the party, Jake told us that and he told us that she was upset because Daniel didn't turn up.'

'Ah, yes. But Jake told us that he didn't get to the party

until late. He was out with his mates. So we don't actually know what time Cara got there. Or whether was she upset just because Daniel wasn't there or whether there was another reason. Jake never spoke to her, remember? So he didn't actually know why she was so upset.'

'But Daniel's arranging to meet her there. He says so. Right there,' protested Jo, pointing at the screen.

John turned to face her and, with a serious expression on his face, he took his time to once again point to the screen in front of them but this time just at the last word.

there

'"*See you there*".' He spoke directly at her. 'Don't you see?'

'See what?' Jo was mystified.

'There. We have presumed "there" meant the party. But what if it didn't? What if it meant somewhere else?'

'Somewhere else?' Jo still didn't follow.

'Somewhere that they had previously discussed meeting, maybe somewhere they always met. Cara's father didn't like Daniel, we know that, so maybe, just maybe, they had a place that they met up at routinely out of his way.'

Jo stood up. She scratched her chin. 'It's possible,' she admitted.

'Come on, it's more than possible. Why else was Daniel down by that river? What was he doing there?'

'You mean Daniel was there because he had intended to meet up with Cara there before the party?' Jo was beginning to understand John's line of thought.

John nodded. 'So my bet is Cara knows more than she's telling us.'

He checked his watch. 'Nearly five o'clock,' he announced, and signalled to Jo to follow him.

John didn't say anything more throughout the entire journey to the Williams' house.

On arrival and just as they were making their way up the garden path towards the house, Jo was sure she spotted the curtains twitch as Cara's father spied their approach.

'Hello, Mr Williams,' John greeted him on the doorstep. 'Here to see Cara as arranged.'

'There was no actual arrangement,' he replied grumpily, but reluctantly he let them in. 'Cara,' he called up the stairs, and a few minutes later she appeared, still limping but much less so than the last time they had visited.

'You look better, Cara,' commented Jo.

'Thanks, I'm feeling much better.'

John looked over at her father, who still hovered at the door to the living room in which they now all occupied.

'A cup of tea would be nice.' The request was made to Cara's father.

Jo realised immediately that John had formulated a tactic after all: distract the father, while at the same time imparting a feeling of ambience to the proceedings.

'Sit down, Cara,' John commanded, taking control.

Cara looked a little unnerved by the tone of the request.

Jo decided that that was probably John's intention.

They sat down opposite her and started talking before her father could intervene and disrupt proceedings.

'Cara,' John asked, 'the night Daniel disappeared...'

Cara Williams buried her face in her hands.

John continued. 'The night Daniel disappeared, did you see him?'

Cara nodded quietly without lifting her head.

'Before the party?' John asked.

Again Cara nodded without speaking.

'Where did you met him, Cara?' Then, after a short pause:

'Was it down by the river, Cara?'

Cara Williams visibly shook. She lifted her head from her hands and John saw that tears were streaming down her cheeks. The mascara that she wore ran in dark lines from her eyes.

'It was our place.'

'Your place?' Jo cut in.

'It was where we always met up. It was quiet and out of the way. Dad didn't like Daniel, so we couldn't come here, and at the embassy there was always people about – we could never have any privacy without someone butting in.'

'So you met up by the river?' Jo continued, trying to talk as reassuringly and supportively as she could. 'Tell us what happened when you got there, Cara.'

Cara lapsed into silence once more. But John could sense that she wanted to say more.

She was about to speak when her farther re-entered the room. He took one look at his daughter, quickly and purposefully set the tray he was carrying down, and came straight over to comfort her.

As he put his arm around her shoulders, he glared at Jo and John. 'What have you said? What have you done to upset her?' He almost shouted the questions at them, going red in the face as he did so. 'You know she hasn't been well – maybe you should leave. Now.' He stood up to emphasise the point.

It was Cara, still visibly upset, that spoke next. 'No, Dad. It's okay. They need to know.'

Her father looked her in the face and, with puzzlement in his voice, he asked, 'Know what, darling? Know what?' with concern tinged with his questioning demeanour.

'It's about Daniel.' She looked him in the eye.

'That waster. What about him?'

'I met him, Dad.'

'You met him. So what? You always were meeting up with him.'

Cara looked bewildered.

Her father continued, gripping her more tightly. 'You thought I didn't know, but I did. I worry about you, that's all. So I kept tabs on you.' Then he quickly added, 'Just to make sure you didn't get hurt, that's all.'

Cara pulled away from him. 'You followed me?'

Her father appeared shocked by the sudden reversal of roles. It was Cara who now expressed anger and her father who was cowed.

'Sometimes,' he said, quickly adding, 'Not often, just now and again.'

'Did you follow me that night?'

'What night?' Her father again looked mystified as to which night she was referring to.

'The night Daniel died, of course.'

John thought he could detect a hint of fear in her tone.

Her father lapsed into silence. He tried to put his arm around her once more, but she shook him off.

'I think we need to continue this conversation down at the station,' John asserted, rising to his feet and reaching into his pocket for his phone.

chapter thirty

John had arranged for another car to be brought so that father and daughter could travel separately to the station. Jo accompanied Cara, John, her father. He did not want to allow them any prospect of collusion before he had the chance to interview them.

On arrival the two detectives ushered father and daughter through the reception area and on towards the interview rooms. As they passed, the desk sergeant waved John over. Jo watched the two of them have a short discussion and the sergeant passing a small piece of paper to John, who scanned it, put it in his pocket and returned to lead the suspects into two separate interview rooms. While they waited for an appropriate adult to arrive to allow them to interview his daughter, the two detectives followed her father into the other room.

John read him his rights, explained that the interview was to be taped, switched on the recorder and started the interview.

'You didn't like Daniel,' was John's opening gambit.

'Not much, no.' The reply was short and surly.

'You said at the house that you sometimes followed Cara.'

'I was worried about her, that's all. Since we lost her mother she hasn't been the same. Always quiet and withdrawn. It's okay to worry about your offspring, you know.' He folded his arms defensively.

'Of course it is, Mr Williams. All I want to know is, did it go any further than just concern?'

'What are you implying, Inspector?'

'That night, the night that Daniel disappeared, did you follow Cara that night?'

'Do you think I hurt the lad? Is that what you're saying?' He unfolded his arms and gripped the table; his cheeks were ruddy.

'It's just a simple question, Mr Williams. Did you follow Cara to the party that night?'

'No, not that night.. . No. I knew she was meeting other friends that night so I thought she would be safe. But I don't like this line of questioning, Inspector and I'm not saying anything more till I see a solicitor.' He sat back and folded his arms across his chest once more.

John nodded his acquiescence, then spoke into the microphone, saying, 'Interview suspended,' before turning the tape off.

John and Jo left the room, asking a constable to call the duty solicitor.

John leant against the wall in the corridor between the two interview rooms. 'What did you make of that?' he asked his colleague.

'He's hiding something, that's for sure,' she replied.

John straightened before turning and heading into the other interview room.

The young Garda woman, who had been guarding the door, stood aside as they entered. John was pleased to see that the appropriate adult, a woman in her forties, had been assigned and now sat beside Cara Williams, trying to comfort her. Cara was still crying.

Sitting down, John indicated to Jo for her to lead the questioning.

'Cara,' she said in a conciliatory tone, 'you said you met Daniel the night of the party.'

She nodded, avoiding the young detective's gaze.

'Down by the river,' Jo continued.

Again Cara Williams nodded but remained silent.

'Do you want to tell us what happened when you met up, Cara?'

Cara slowly shook her head from side to side, the tears now streaming down her face. She rubbed her eyes to try to stem the flow.

Jo handed her a tissue, which the younger woman slowly and reluctantly accepted.

'Did your father hurt Daniel, Cara, is that it?'

Cara Williams looked up, suddenly shocked.

'Dad? No, he had nothing to do with it.' There was real force behind her voice this time.

John leant forward over the desk. 'So, Cara, tell us – what did happen when you met up with Daniel?' Then, to Jo's bemusement, he added, 'We know you couldn't walk very well with your bad ankle and you know we confiscated your crutch, Cara.'

There followed a few minutes of silence when nobody spoke, but in that time it was noticeable that Cara visibly shrunk back in her seat, almost as if she had lost the power to remain fully upright.

John, seizing the moment then, and almost theatrically, produced the piece of paper that the desk sergeant had handed to him minutes before.

Jo looked sideways at him, clearly wondering what was going on.

John took his time, reading the wording on the sheet silently to himself. Then he looked up quickly, startling Cara, who jumped. 'Cara, this is the lab report from their examination of your crutch.' He paused. 'Do you know what it says, Cara?'

Silently she shook her head.

'When they examined it they found traces of blood on the stem of the crutch, blood the same group as Daniel's.' Again he stopped for a moment, looking Cara directly in the eye.

Cara quivered.

'They also found Daniel's DNA in the same area.' He looked up again.

The young woman remained motionless, but all the colour had drained from her face.

'In addition,' he continued, 'the shape and diameter of the stem exactly match the shape and size of the injury to Daniel's head.' He looked up again. 'Have you anything to tell us, Cara?' His voice was quiet and controlled.

She wiped a tear from her eye and started to speak. 'He was just sitting there.'

'Sitting where, Cara?' Jo interrupted.

John shot her a glance. Her inexperience was showing; he had Cara where he wanted her and he sensed that she was about to open up and tell her side of the story. This, he determined, was a time for listening, not speaking.

Jo caught the look and retreated.

After a short pause Cara continued. 'He was sitting on the wall.' Noticing their exchange of looks, she explained, 'The wall on the bridge, the bridge over the river, the one you found him in.' She broke down again.

The two detectives remained silent. The other woman, who had, up to this point, sat quietly beside Cara, reached over to her and shot the detectives a warning look.

Cara, though, recovering her composure, shook her carer off and now, looking directly into her inquisitors' faces, she started to speak again.

'He was just sitting there, grinning from ear to ear. Wearing that stupid shirt he always liked, the stars and stripes one.' She paused for thought.

Jo and John remained silent.

'It was then that he told me.'

Again without speaking, it was John's facial expression that asked the question as to what Daniel had told her.

Cara looked back and forth between them before continuing. 'He told me he was heading back to America. That was all he said, and he was laughing as he said it.'

'And what happened next?' John encouraged her to continue.

'I just lost it, that's all. I saw red. He was leaving me after all this time.' Her face reddened and more tears followed the earlier ones. 'He was going back to America, and probably with that American bitch he'd being seeing.'

'You knew about her?'

'Jake had mentioned it. So yes. After he told me about her, I decided to see if it was true. I couldn't believe it of him at first, but I decided to keep an eye on him. I saw them for myself. They met up quite a lot – they were actually quite blatant about it. He didn't seem to care who saw them together. People knew that I was going out with him, knew that I loved him. I really did love him, but he just seemed to be rubbing my face in it.'

Jo seemed to be about to interrupt to explain the true nature of the meetings, but John shot her a glace and she immediately backed off.

'So when he started to laugh at me about going back to America, I struck out. I hit him.'

'With your crutch, Cara?' John asked.

'I had forgotten I was holding it. I just swung at him and it hit him on the head… and he fell, he fell back. Oh God, what have I done?' she wailed.

'Did he fall off the bridge into the river, Cara?'

She nodded silently.

They gave her a few minutes to compose herself and then John quietly asked her, 'What happened next, Cara?'

She took a few minutes to reply, clearly disturbed by the memories evoked. 'I looked over the wall, into the water, but there was no sign of him. He'd just disappeared. I stood there frozen to the spot for what seemed like ages, but there was no sign of him. I told myself that he'd swam off under the bridge and he was punishing me by hiding. I tried to convince myself.' She stopped talking again and once more buried her head in her hands before mumbling, almost to herself, 'But he hadn't, had he?'

'What did you do next, Cara?'

'I just stood there for ages – there was nobody around to help, so I just stood there looking over the wall, hoping and hoping that he would appear again. Then when he didn't I just walked around and around aimlessly. I didn't know what to do or where to go. I was frightened. Eventually I just went to that party – I honestly thought I could talk to somebody there, that somebody could help me, tell me Daniel was okay, that he'd just walk in as if nothing happened. But obviously he never did. So in the end I just sat in a corner and cried, especially when I saw Jake there. I just couldn't bring myself to talk to him.'

Jo couldn't hold back anymore. 'Daniel wasn't a strong swimmer, Cara. We think he got tangled up in the weeds on the riverbed, he couldn't pull himself free and that's why he drowned.'

'Oh God! Oh God! It's all my fault,' she wailed. 'What can I do?'

In a quiet and sympathetic voice, John spoke to her. 'You've done all you can, Cara, just by admitting what happened. It will give his family closure to know exactly the circumstances surrounding Daniel's death and I hope you'll feel better now it's off your chest.'

'Shall we bring your father in, Cara?' Jo asked.

Cara nodded slowly.

'Before we do, Cara, tell me, does your father know what happened?'

'I think he suspects that I had something to do with Daniel's accident,' she baulked at the word accident, 'that's why he's been so defensive about me, but no, I never told him.'

John regarded her. He thought she was telling the truth, not trying to shield her father.

They led Cara's father into the room. John could see that he was visibly shocked by his daughter's appearance. He seemed about to turn on the detectives, but before he could do so John explained everything that had been said within Cara's interview.

In the end all Cara's father could do was sit down beside his daughter, hold her tight in his arms and weep silently to himself.

John and Jo quietly left the room and then stopped and stood in the corridor outside.

'I'm going to have to charge her with manslaughter, you know,' John said.

Jo nodded. 'What about her father?' she asked.

'He didn't really know anything. He may, as Cara said, have suspected something, but he didn't actually know anything and was only trying to protect his daughter. I think we give him the benefit of the doubt. Do you agree?'

Jo nodded again.

'Let's go back in.' John turned to go back into the room.

'Before we do, shouldn't we tell Cara the truth? The truth about why Daniel was leaving.'

John thought about it. 'I don't know. Is it going to help that he wasn't actually leaving her, yet she killed him because she thought he was? Or is it going to help her realise that he did actually love her after all?'

'I don't know, John, I really don't, but I do think she deserves the truth.'

'Okay, let's do it.' He opened the door and let Jo go in ahead of him.

Father and daughter were hugging each other tightly. Cara openly wept. Her father was clearly struggling to contain his own emotions, for the sake of his daughter.

It was Jo who led this part of the interview. 'Cara, we have something to tell you. Something that may well upset you. But we think you need to hear it.'

Cara relinquished her hold on her father and sat upright.

It was her father who tried to intervene. 'Don't you think she's been through enough?' he said, venting his pent-up emotion in Jo's direction.

'We think it's important, Mr Williams,' John intervened.

The father relented and Jo carried on. 'Cara, we don't think that Daniel intended to move back to the States.'

'But… but, he said…' Cara stuttered.

'He said he was going to New York, but he didn't intend to stay there.'

'How do you know that?' she asked, reaching for her father's hand.

'Well, firstly, the air ticket he had bought was a return ticket.'

'That doesn't mean he was going to use it,' her father interrupted.

'No, Mr Williams, it doesn't, but do you know why he was going to New York?'

Father and daughter just looked blankly at her.

'You knew about his art?' It was a question aimed at Cara, who nodded, with a puzzled expression spreading over her face.

'We found out that he'd been offered an exhibition in New York. In fact, his paintings had already been shipped there. So he was simply following them out there to be at the gallery for the opening of the exhibition.'

'Is that why he was so happy?'

'I'm afraid so, Cara. You know that he was passionate about his art, so passionate, in fact, that he hid it from his father. So, when he was offered this opportunity it must have seemed like a once-in-a-lifetime chance to pursue his dream.'

Cara held her head in her hands and started to cry, visibly and loudly.

Her father reached for her again, but this time she shrugged him off. She looked up, and though clearly still grieving, she seemed to rally a little as she asked, 'But what about that girl he was seeing? What's she got to do with it?'

'Cara.' Jo spoke softly. 'She is from the gallery. They were meeting up and making the arrangements for the exhibition, that's all. There was nothing going on.' She repeated, 'Nothing.'

'Oh God, how could I have been so stupid?' she wailed, reaching for her father.

There seemed little else to ask, so the two detectives pushed their chairs back and rose to leave.

As they did so, something suddenly occurred to John. He turned around again and asked, 'Cara, do you have a tattoo?'

Both Cara's father and Jo looked taken aback by the question.

Cara looked up at the detective and hesitatingly admitted she had.

'Is it a flower, Cara?'

'Yes, it's a rose,' she responded.

'And is it on your shoulder? Your left shoulder?'

'How do you know that?'

Cara's father stood up angrily, about to intervene.

'Sit down, Mr Williams,' John commanded forcefully. 'Cara needs to hear this.'

Her father did as he was bid and sat down, though clearly not completely pacified.

'Cara, Daniel painted a portrait of you. Did you know that?'

'He said he did. But I thought he was joking.'

John hesitated, not completely sure whether to continue. But then, making up his mind, he said, 'He did, Cara. I've seen it. It is very good. It was on the wall hanging over his bed in the embassy.'

'You've seen it? But I thought he'd shipped all the paintings off to New York?'

'It seems, Cara, that that portrait was special to him. It was the only one he didn't want to sell. I think, Cara, that you were special to him as well.' Then he paused for Cara to take in all that he had said.

'I'm sorry, Cara,' were John's parting words as he and Jo exited the small room, leaving father and daughter to contemplate the enormity of what had just occurred.

chapter thirty-one

The weeks passed following Cara's confession. Despite the enormity of the crime, John had persuaded the court to allow her to be remanded on bail rather than immediately imprisoned. He had made the case that it was a crime of passion and that she was of no further risk.

The manslaughter charge, though, stood and had to be answered. Given the judicial backlog, though, the case was only likely to come to court sometime over the next few months. Both John and Jo hoped the judge and the jury would see the crime for what it was, and also take into account Cara's young age.

Discussing the case with his younger colleague, John was of the view that Cara would indeed face a custodial sentence. Though he hoped that at least part of it would be served in a young offender's institute rather than an adult prison.

John had also taken time to explain in detail the events surrounding Daniel's death to Daniel's family. They remained distressed by his untimely loss but also over time seemed to develop some understanding of the young woman's actions.

John had heard that later Jake had personally taken it upon himself to visit Cara and while there had given her the portrait

Daniel had painted of her, the act partially, John surmised, one of forgiveness but also possibly to salve his own conscience for misleading her about Daniel's behaviour.

The picture now hung above her own bed.

*

Sitting quietly at his desk immersed in paperwork, John became aware of Jo standing beside him.

'Look what I've got,' she announced.

John looked at what she was holding up. It was a recent copy of *The New York Times*.

'So?' he asked, not understanding what she was getting at.

'Here, look.' She pointed to an article on an inside page. 'One of Alan's friends is American and he gets the newspaper mailed to him. Alan thought we might be interested.'

John looked at her. 'Alan? As in Alan Marshall?'

'Yes. So what?'

'The guy that O'Brien sent to spy on us?'

'He wasn't spying. And anyway, we did such a good job he's gone back to HQ. So he won't be bothering you anymore.'

'Mmmm.' John considered things for a moment. 'But is he still bothering you, I wonder?'

'Oh, will you shut up and just look here.' She continued to point at the article in the newspaper.

John squinted to read it. Then he realised what it was about and took the paper from her.

It was a report of the opening of an art exhibition in the city. It was Daniel's exhibition. The article covered the details of the opening, reporting that Daniel's father and brother had both been present; there followed a story of the events surrounding the young artist's unfortunate and untimely death.

The report was fulsome in its praise of the artwork exhibited. It reported that many of the paintings had been quickly sold to dealers around the globe.

'Look at the prices these are fetching!' John exclaimed. 'I could buy a small car for that!'

'It's a fact that artists sometimes don't achieve fame till after their death,' Jo added.

'Too true,' replied John.

The discussion and the outcome of the investigation took away the pleasure of the report of the success of Daniel's exhibition, evoking a sombre mood to descend between them.

After several more minutes of trying to concentrate on the article in question, Jo, who had been sitting pensively spoke, interrupting his thoughts. 'There's one thing that's been bothering me. Something I just can't get my head around.'

'What's that?' he asked, looking up quizzically from the newspaper.

'How did you come to think that the hospital might have provided Cara with a crutch in the first place? The existence of that crutch proved to be the clincher in this case.'

'So' John asked.

'But how did you guess that the hospital might have given her a crutch to help her get around after her injury?'

John thought for a moment. 'It was just something somebody said to me once.'